The Narrow Fury

by

D. A. Joy

Domnall Publishing

Cover layout by Kyle Joy

Artwork by D.A.Joy

ISBN-10:0615975909
ISBN-13:978-0615975900

DEDICATION

To the boys, Al and Kyle

ACKNOWLEDGEMENTS

The following pictures are from www.history.navy.mil:

Chapter 1: Photo #: NH 91880-KN (Color) "The First Battle between 'Iron' Ships of War."

Chapter 2: Photo #: NH 63712 Lieutenant John L. Worden, USN, Commanding Officer of USS *Monitor*

Chapter 8: Photo #: NH 55524 USS *Cricket* (1863-1865, "Tinclad" # 6)

Chapter 9: Photo #: NH 55214 USS *Tuscumbia* (1863-1865)

Chapter 10: Photo #: NH 59004 "The Flotilla of Federal Gunboats for the Protection of the Ohio and Mississippi Rivers, Under the Command of Captain John Rodgers, U.S.N. -- From a Sketch by our Special Artist at Cairo, Illinois"

Chapter 11: Photo #: NH 73378 CSS *Arkansas* running through the Union fleet above Vicksburg, Mississippi, 15 July 1862

Chapter 15: Photo #: NH 54825 USS *Rattler* (1862-1864)

Chapter 16: Photo #: NH 54093 USS *Fawn* (1863-1865)

Chapter 18: Photo #: NH 58767 "The Fight at Corney's Bridge, Bayou Teche, Louisiana, and Destruction of the Rebel Gun-boat 'Cotton,', January 14, 1863."

Epilogue: Photo #: NH 76557-KN (Color), "Admiral Porter's Fleet Running the Rebel Blockade of the Mississippi at Vicksburg, April 16th 1863."

The following pictures are from www.en.wikipedia.org:

Chapter 3: http://en.wikipedia.org/wiki/ File:GideonWellesPortrait.jpg

i

Chapter 4: http://en.wikipedia.org/wiki/
File:Bombardment_and_capture_of_Island_Number_Ten_on_th
e_Mississippi_River,_April_7,_1862.jpg

Chapter 5: http://en.wikipedia.org/wiki/
File:Uss_Cairo_h61568.jpg

Chapter 6: http://en.wikipedia.org/wiki/
File:Battle_of_Memphis_I.png

Chapter 7: http://en.wikipedia.org/wiki/
File:Battle_of_Saint_Charles.jpg

Chapter 12: http://en.wikipedia.org/wiki/
File:USS_Queen_of_the_West_(1854)_watercolor.jpg

Chapter 13:http://en.wikipedia.org/wiki/File:USS_essex_1856.jpg

Chapter 14: http://en.wikipedia.org/wiki/
File:CairoIIIPerspectiveMap1885.jpg

Chapter 17: http://en.wikipedia.org/wiki/File:Admiral_Porter%
27s_Second_Dummy_Frightening_the_Rebels.jpg

Clash of ironclads

CHAPTER ONE

The train whistled again, the note clear and sharp over the clatter of wheels upon tracks. The car heaved slightly to the right as it rounded another curve, barely slowing on the slight grade. Becky started to slip away, but John Richards reached across and pulled her next to him. Even the pressure of his hand on her shoulder failed to rouse her from the deep sleep into which she had fallen. Gently, he laid her head back on his shoulder. He wanted to think of their coming marriage but could not. There was only the battle.

Two days. *God, had it only been two days?*

Richards was still stunned by the flurry of events. Dawn of March eleventh had yet to break as the train pounded westward from Baltimore. He wanted to forget the battle, tried desperately to forget the battle, but without success. Lorraine sat across from him, yet another reminder of the brief and bloody action. The destruction of the *COHOCTON*; the death of his friend and first lieutenant, René LaForge, and so many others.

He tried not to think of the *MERRIMACK*, the iron beast which destroyed his ship. He thought of his life in the navy. Carefree midshipmen days first at Annapolis, then aboard the *CONSTITUTION*. First he went to Japan on *SUSQUEHANA*, followed by anti-slavery patrol aboard *COHOCTON*. The last assignment was in the Mediterranean before the war began. These were days gone and past. His racing mind refused him rest and dwelled instead on the brief year he commanded the sloop.

Quiet days on the blockade contrasted sharply with the danger of the Port Royal expedition. His first meeting with John Worden in Pensacola counterpointed the disastrous cutting out attempt in which many of the crew perished. The harder he tried to ignore them, the faster the memories came until they ran full circle and returned him to Hampton Roads.

It might have been mere minutes before, the stark reality of the *COHOCTON* pounded to wreckage about him. The young powder boy, Potter, sitting on the deck, crying over a dead friend. The shapeless mass of flesh that had been LaForge. It was not worth it. *It could not be worth it.*

On his left, he discerned some of the passing landscape. The sky brightened to a dark gray as dawn asserted itself. To the east, a glowing band of sunlight defined the horizon. Sunrise: he might have appreciated its beauty on another day. If he were at sea, perhaps, or if not persecuted by his thoughts.

Court-martial. He dreaded the two words, but Fox held it as a possibility for him. It was perhaps even probable, given the testimony of Capt. Van Brunt, who commanded the forces against the *MERRIMACK*. He considered appealing to Welles for help, but shook his head. He was on his own, like so many times over the past year. He must stand on his own merits.

And Becky, what to do about her? She wanted to marry him as soon as possible. He could not possibly wed her with the cloud of a court-martial hanging over him. If things went badly and he lost his commission, he would never be able to face her again. But she was headstrong and he did not know how to convince her of the hopelessness of his position.

He yawned, surprised at how tired he was. Surprisingly, he fell asleep. It was short and light, but the lapse helped him considerably. He awoke with a start as Becky shook him.

"John, we are here." Short. Simple.

Washington.

He rubbed his eyes, trying to focus on the woman. She was disheveled after the night on the train. Her clothes, normally so neat, were wrinkled and twisted. Her hair was out of place. She did not fit the image he always carried of her in his mind. He stood, stretching and yawning as the train lurched to a stop. Bright sunlight flooded the car.

"Father will be waiting," assured Becky, turning to her friend and companion. She gently touched Lorraine, who awoke slowly. Even after a night's rest, the woman's eyes remained red and puffy from the tears.

They walked slowly, Becky close to Lorraine with her arm about the other woman's waist. Richards arranged for a Negro porter to move their baggage as Gideon Welles appeared. The Secretary of the Navy approached them briskly. Neither man spoke as they grasped hands firmly.

"I have a carriage for you out front, Rebecca," he said quickly to his daughter. "I am sure you will want to go to the house and freshen up."

Rebecca Welles brightened at the offer. "That will be lovely."

"Good," nodded her father. "You and Lorraine go ahead. John and I have a stop to make first." She opened her mouth to protest, but Welles would have none of it. "I have no time for arguments." Brusquely, he faced Richards. "John Worden was brought in yesterday from Hampton Roads. I thought you might like to speak to him."

Worden, the commander of the *MONITOR*. Richards had thought little of him, though knew he was wounded during the battle.

"Of course I want to see him!"

Sending the women off in Welles' carriage, the Secretary and the ship captain boarded a cab for the trip across the city. Welles was quiet and solemn while the cab lurched along. He spoke with foreboding.

"Things do not look good. Fox's telegram yesterday has the entire congress up in arms!" Richards nodded, unable to voice the turmoil he felt the past two days. "The other captains are supporting Van Brunt. They say you were ordered to avoid engagement with the *MERRIMACK*."

"They are..." Richards paused, searching for a word which would not set him directly against three captains. "...incorrect," he finished. "Van Brunt's orders were more general. I interpreted them to mean we were to prevent the *MERRIMACK* escaping into the Chesapeake. I felt it necessary to try and stop her."

"They may be *incorrect*," stressed Welles, "but it will be their word that is taken in a court of inquiry. The hearing will start on Friday."

Friday was only three days away. "They do not waste any time."

"You do not know the mood this country is in. Everyone - and I mean everyone - was mortified at the loss of the *CONGRESS* and *CUMBERLAND*. Then you lost *COHOCTON* after seeing their example." He paused and his tone softened. "John, they see the commanders of the other ships as being forced to engage. They look on you as throwing your ship away in a grab for fame. If the decision is to court-martial you, there is nothing I can do to help."

"Sir..." he started but choked, angered and at a loss for words. He fought down the feelings to continue. "Gideon," he said, using Welles' proper name for the first time he could remember, "I did what needed to be done. I have no delusions about the glory of war. I followed the orders I was given as I understood them."

"I know you did, John," reassured the Secretary. "But that is not what will be in the evidence. Commodore Stringham will head the board. With him, at least, you know you will be treated fairly."

Stringham was a friend, or at least as much of a friend as he could hope for in the situation. But the conversation ended when the cab stopped in front of the house in which Worden convalesced.

The two men were admitted into the house. The interior was dim, at odds with the bright sunlight outside. Worden's injuries were to his eyes and all windows were covered to prevent any possible further damage. The two visitors were led to a sitting room where Worden waited on a small couch, his legs outstretched on a stand before him. Most of the officer's face was covered with bandages. Richards spoke lightly.

"John?" He asked.

Worden's head straightened, cocked at the sound of the voice. "Richards?"

The commander knelt beside Worden and grasped his hand while placing his other firmly on his shoulder. "My god, man! How serious?"

Worden smiled slightly, the lips all but lost within the folds of his beard. "The surgeons say I will not be blinded, if that is what you mean. I took some powder and concrete in the face when the shell struck the pilothouse. I believe that is a defect Mr. Ericsson will have to correct on his next turret ship." His manner grew more serious. "But what is this I hear? The COHOCTON sunk?"

"True enough," returned Richards after a moment's hesitation. "The MONITOR withdrew when you were wounded. *MERRIMACK* headed for the mouth of the bay. I could not let her by." He stopped, again assailed by the memories. "It was not a long fight."

Worden reached for Richards, groping slightly before finding the man's arm. "I do not know what they are saying, but I think you did what was necessary. It is what I would have done."

The words were a salve to Richards' conscience. Someone, at least, comprehended his motives.

"There is talk of a court-martial, Lt. Worden," said Welles, still standing behind Richards.

Worden's head twisted at the new voice, undoubtedly recognizing the owner. "Court-martial? Ridiculous! John, if there is anything I can do, please let me know!"

Richards was grateful for the offer. The visit to Worden was doing him more good than he could possibly have imagined. "Thank you, my friend. I will do that."

There was a sudden commotion in the entry way. A tall, bearded man came into the room. There was no doubt of the newcomer's identity. Lincoln's eyes met Richards' for just a moment before he was at Worden's side.

"The nation owes you a debt of gratitude, lieutenant."

Instinctively, Worden knew who spoke the words. "Thank you, Mr. President. I can only say I did my duty."

"It was well done, sir, well done indeed," returned Lincoln solemnly. "If the men in my army were of the same sort as you, this rebellion would be finished by now."

Worden was deeply moved by the compliment. His voice choked when he answered. "Thank you, sir."

"Rest assured, lieutenant: or should I say captain?" Lincoln smiled at the small joke. "You will have a command waiting for you, as soon as you are able. We cannot afford to have men like you idle while the fate of the nation hangs in the balance." The president paused, letting the words settle before speaking again. "I am sorry I must leave so quickly, but there are other matters requiring my attention. Do me the honor of a visit when the surgeons release you."

"I shall be the one honored, sir," said Worden, sincerity clear in his voice.

Lincoln shook hands with Worden and stood to leave. But spotting Welles with Richards in one corner, he approached them first.

"Well, Gideon, who do we have here?" He eyed Richards more critically this time. There was kindness and sympathy in the face.

"May I present Commander John Richards, Mr. President," replied Welles formally. "He is to marry Rebecca."

Lincoln took Richards' hand briefly. "Ah yes, the lovely Rebecca." It was but a brief interlude. "You were the officer commanding *COHOCTON*," continued the president. The deep set eyes sought some sign of hesitancy from the naval officer.

"Yes, sir," returned Richards without flinching.

"I do not know what to make of your action, commander. On one hand, it was very brave. On the other, foolhardy!"

Richards sought for an answer. He could think of nothing that would not make him appear either a fool or a braggart. It was Worden who replied to the comment.

"Mr. President, if this man attacked the *MERRIMACK* against impossible odds, it was out of bravery and a conviction to preserve the nation."

Lincoln glanced first to the wounded man, before letting his gaze drift back to Richards. He nodded knowingly. "That is a very high recommendation, Captain Worden, and one I shall keep in mind!" He faced Welles. "Until later, Gideon." The president led his entourage from the house.

"It seems you have several friends in Washington,

John," said Welles slowly. "And it looks as if you have made another. His friendship may be what is necessary to save you."

Richards felt irritated at the notion of presidential intervention. "I hope my actions will stand on their own!" He tried to keep the bitterness from the words as he turned back to Worden. "I will be back later, John, if I may?"

"Please, and bring Rebecca. I could use a pleasant voice."

Breakfast the next morning was a somber affair. Welles maintained his place at the head of the table, Richards and Rebecca on either side. The naval officer poked at his food, unable to eat even the fresh bacon and eggs before him. For her part, Rebecca retained an air of concern.

"You must not let this get to you so," explained Welles. The navy holds hearings everyday. Few result in court-martial."

He pushed the half eaten food away. "That may be, but it is as you said yesterday." He tapped the previous night's edition of the Post lying on the table. "The country needs a scapegoat for Hampton Roads."

"Father," said Rebecca, her gaze fixed on her fiancé. "You are the Secretary of the Navy! Is there not something you can do?"

Welles shrugged a helpless gesture. "It is out of my hands, dear. The navy attends to internal disciplines. Unless I, or maybe Gustavus, can come up with something to prove John's lack of culpability, he is in the hands of the hearing board."

"But those captains!" Her voice rose in anger. "They are lying. They must be. How can they get away with it? They are just trying to lay the blame for their own mistakes on John!"

"That may well be, Rebecca," returned her father, the words harsh. "But neither I nor the board have seen proof of it. Until we do, I suggest you keep such comments to yourself!"

She was shocked at the reprimand and Richards stepped in before she could reply. "The navy is based on seniority and rank." The explanation seemed trite, even if true. "The word of three post captains will always be taken over that of a newly promoted commander."

"John..." He held up his hand to stop her.

"Becky, I understand what you are trying to do and I love you for it. I knew the risks when I attacked the *MERRIMACK*. I thought the action would be understood by the men who were there." It was a bitter thought, but he concluded it anyway. "Some, however, seem to place personal position and careers above loyalty. There's little to be done about it."

"John," said Welles as the man finished. "I will do what I can. You know that."

"And I appreciate it, Mr. Secretary. But if I must face a court-martial because of this, do not throw your career away to save mine. The country needs your help too badly."

Welles nodded, unable to reply.

"Father..." Becky got no further.

"The matter is closed, Rebecca. I will do what I can. John accepts this. Why cannot you?" He placed his napkin on the plate in front of him, and left the room.

Becky stared after him for a full minute before bringing her eyes back to Richards. He sat, dejected, staring at the article on the front page of the paper. She reached across and took his hand.

"I love you, John. No matter what happens."

He met her eyes. "I love you too, but this is everything to me."

"Everything?"

"I have no life without the navy!"

She took a deep breath. "I think we should set a date, John. You said we would the next time you were ashore."

He sighed. They had had the same conversation twice within the past two days.

"Everything has changed now, Becky. Until the board is finished..."

It was her turn to interrupt. "I do not give a damn about your board or your ships! You do not see it?" she pleaded. "This could be a blessing in disguise! It could get you out of the war - whole, alive! I cannot let it pass."

His brow furrowed. "Is that all this means to you? A chance to get me out of the war?" He pushed his chair away from the table. "My *life* is on the line! If the board finds unfavorably, you may have me out of the war, but I certainly will not be whole!" He started for the door but she grabbed his arm.

"Please, John, wait!" Her voice was controlled but tears welled up in her eyes. "The thought of losing you or having you hurt or crippled is unbearable. Please understand."

He stopped, his feelings for her welling up. He bent down and kissed her lightly. "I do understand, Becky. I really do, but you must understand also. If I lose my commission, we can never be married. It would be too hard on your father given his position and he has done too much for me to allow that to happen."

He did not wait for her answer. He picked his cap from the hall table and left the house.

The Navy Department had changed little since last seen the summer before. There was still the hustle and bustle of hurried activity; everyone with someplace to go, someone to see. Richards was not sure why he was even there. In two days, he would be called into the same building to sit before a hearing board of senior officers. It might be his end.

The endless activity of the building bothered him as he wandered the crowded halls. He came looking for something, a feeling of belonging. Instead, he found further isolation. The people in the halls were strangers to him. They were just faces in uniforms. For all of its activity, it was a lonely place.

Leaving the building, he walked towards the Potomac. At the navy yard, he found something he could understand. There lay ships of war. Of course, most of the navy's ships were engaged elsewhere. Two gunboats and a screw sloop lay at anchor, the furious activity about them meaningful and clear.

The sloop was new and not unlike his *COHOCTON*. Probably about the same rate, he concluded after a thorough examination. The gunboats were apparently employed along the river. One bore new planking in two places on her hull, the clean boards still awaiting a coat of paint. She had seen fighting, and quite recently. His heart beat a bit faster at the thought. When was the last time he was in action?

His lips turned up into a grim smile. *Sunday - three days before.* It returned in his memory. One day of fighting, one of utter destruction. It would not be lost, ever. But the men, the survivors who approached him after the fight, understood. They had said so. Maybe with their memory, he might survive a court-martial.

"Commander Richards!" The voice was old but strong and familiar. He faced Flag Officer Silas Stringham, surprised at the appearance of his old commander. Stringham appeared much healthier than the previous fall. When last they met, the craggy face was set and worn. The removal of the strain of command had eased his lot considerably. Now he approached at a brisk pace, smiling widely and hand outstretched.

"It is good to see you again, John!" he continued, taking

Richards' hand and shaking it roughly. "I see so few of the old school anymore. All Volunteer this and Acting that! It's impossible to keep track."

Richards found himself smiling in spite of himself. The old commodore had lost none of his warmth and humor in gaining another stripe on his sleeve. "It is a pleasure, sir." The feeling was not allowed to last.

"I saw you down at the Navy Department, but you did not here when I called to you. Someone thought they saw you head in this direction."

He started walking slowly along the pier, pointing to the damaged gunboat. "We lose good men everyday. She came in just yesterday, her captain killed in a skirmish. She will be back along the river tomorrow, keeping it open for traffic." Richards nodded and Stringham continued with barely a pause. "Last summer, I told you to accept the fact you will lose men. Now I am to head the hearing on the loss of your ship." He waved off a comment. "I know, son. I know. I have plenty of faith in your ability. Unfortunately, Van Brunt and Marston have friends in Washington. Besides, the loss of the CUMBERLAND and CONGRESS must also be accounted for."

"Do we blame the loss of ships on junior officers now?"

Stringham stopped short. "That is uncalled for, commander! If you come into the hearing with such an attitude, I will toss you out on your ear!" His words were sharp, but he finished on a friendlier note. "You know what I mean. Captains have their political base, their careers to protect. They see a way of hiding behind you. There was little choice on Saturday. On Sunday, the decision was made by you and you alone."

Richards let out a long sigh, angry with himself for letting the depression of the moment color his thoughts and words. "I know, sir. Perhaps it is the hardest part to bear. I thought it was necessary. Given those circumstances, I would do it again."

Stringham accepted it. "I have no doubt, but it is facts that will count, not your statement of intention. As long as Van Brunt stands by his orders and is supported by the other captains, your situation is none too good.

"What a waste." Stringham shook his head sadly. "We are not satisfied with fighting the rebels, but we also have to destroy some of our own. I will do what I can to see it does not happen to you, John. At the very least, I can assure you of a fair and open hearing."

"When I heard who was in charge," returned Richards, "I never doubted it for a minute, sir."

"We will do what we can, boy. I know you - it will be a fight. And no more of this self pity. It is unbecoming a naval officer."

Richards chuckled. "As you say, sir."

"I do say." The face was warm and kindly. "I will see you Friday morning."

"Aye aye, sir."

Captain John Worden of the *MONITOR*

CHAPTER TWO

The Hearing Board opened with due formality on Friday morning. Richards sat in a straight back chair, holding himself stiffly upright under the gaze of the board members as the statements from the frigate officers were read into the record. Van Brunt's was the most damning: a document intended to keep its author clear of any misconduct in the affair. Richards felt his blood grow hot as the words echoed through the room.

....nor was there any intent of allowing any of the wooden warships to engage the ironclad frigate MERRIMACK. The events of eighth instant proved this could only result in the destruction of a vessel assigned to such an endeavor.
Signed,
Captain Henry Van Brunt,

USS MINNESOTA,
Officer Commanding,
Hampton Roads

Commander Hess set the paper onto the table before him. "That concludes Captain Van Brunt's statement. He clearly communicates his intentions from the night before the loss of the *COHOCTON*. It is equally clear Commander Richards' actions were, at best, a grave error in judgment. It is even questionable they were not a deliberate attempt to grab some sort of glory or recognition by being engaged against the *MERRIMACK*."

Richards sighed, an action impossible to stifle. A group of men who were not present saw fit to pass judgment on his actions. But there was also doubt creeping into his mind. It appeared all the frigate captains understood they were not to attack the ironclad. Perhaps he *had* misunderstood the orders. And if that were so, then why had he attacked? Was there any reason to account for the loss of the ship, the loss of LaForge and the others?

Hess sat down with a flourish, confident he had placed several nails into Richards' professional coffin. Stringham's gaze shifted from him to the junior officer sitting in front of the panel.

"I hardly feel we are in a position to judge Captain Richards' actions without hearing from him, commander," he said, the merest stress on the difference in titles. "I can say from personal experience with the officer in question he has always displayed coolness under fire and good judgment on professional matters. But he sits here before us! Please tell us your side, commander."

Of five officers arrayed before him, only Stringham showed any sign of sympathy. The others were like Van Brunt - more interested in keeping clear of the affair than having their names associated with the losses. He cleared his throat and related his experience.

"March eighth was a hard day. We witnessed the loss of the CONGRESS and CUMBERLAND. All the frigates were run aground in their attempt to reach the scene of the fighting." The words came in quiet even tones, but his mind was elsewhere, caught up in the flurry of smoke and shell and the destruction of the ships.

"The tide dropped and the MERRIMACK withdrew. The tables showed the tide would be early the next day, and we had no doubt she would reappear. There was no hope for any of the squadron unless withdrew, but with the MINNESOTA grounded, that was not possible."

"You say all the frigates were aground?" asked Stringham.

"Aye, sir. You are all familiar with the waters in the roads. The ROANOKE and ST. LAWRENCE were towed by tugs. The MINNESOTA was under her own power. They ran aground on a shoal, the same one that saved them, in fact. The MERRIMACK apparently draws even more water than they do."

"Go on, commander," prompted Hess.

"The MONITOR arrived late in the evening. Both ROANOKE and ST. LAWRENCE were got off earlier, but the MINNESOTA was still hard aground and the tide was falling. The only hope was to get her moving the next morning, but there appeared little chance of it. Captain Van Brunt called us to the MINNESOTA to discuss the next day's action."

Richards was all too aware of his position. He could not call the three captains liars. To do so, even if his words were accepted, would destroy his career as surely as any court-martial. He must walk a careful line to state his position with no hint of slander.

"We arrived by the light of the CONGRESS - the entire area was lit by the flames. Van Brunt was worried about the MINNESOTA; she was the obvious first target the next morning. But he was also worried about containing the MERRIMACK. He felt if we could keep her in the roads, then only the ships on blockade were threatened. If she were allowed loose, the whole coast, even Washington itself, might fall prey to her. He was adamant about it."

"You say you were all there," asked Stringham. "All the ship's captains?"

"Aye, sir. Myself, Lieutenant Worden, Captains Marsten and Purvience."

"Continue, captain."

"As we surmised, MERRIMACK appeared the next morning with the tide. Worden took the MONITOR in and the fight was a stand off. It went on for close to four hours..."

"We are aware of all this," snapped Hess. "How did you lose the COHOCTON?"

Richards swallowed, the memory coming back. "There was a shell hit forward on the MONITOR. I saw it explode. Worden was wounded, though I could not know it then. The ironclad drew off into shallow water, away from the MERRIMACK. The rebel turned east. She was not heading for the MINNESOTA. It appeared she was making for the deep channel into the Chesapeake."

He took a deep breath. "The engines on ROANOKE were disabled; ST. LAWRENCE a sailing frigate; MINNESOTA aground. The COHOCTON was the only ship capable of engaging the MERRIMACK. My first and I had discussed a plan of action. We hoped to use our superior speed and maneuverability to shell the ship, and then board and storm." He swallowed hard.

"Their first broadside caught us." It seemed the hell of COHOCTON's deck erupted about him as the memories came back. "Two guns were damaged, some rigging disabled, but we were still operating under steam. We reversed course and fired again." The sound and confusion played through his mind: the smell of powder; the shriek of splinters in the air. "A mast came down; the boiler was hit. The MERRIMACK was ready to finish us when the

MONITOR reappeared and drove her off."

Richards returned to the present, unwilling to relive the sight of *COHOCTON*'s gun deck. "The ship grounded and we received help from the other ships." He took another deep breath. "I attacked because *MONITOR* appeared damaged. It seemed *MERRIMACK* was heading for the bay and Captain Van Brunt had made it clear she was not to escape. My ship was the only one in position and condition to engage her. We did our duty." His last words were the hardest of all. "In the same situation, I fear it would be necessary to do it again."

"Captain," started Hess, his words pointed. "How do you explain that none of the other officers present felt it their duty to engage the ironclad?"

Richards locked eyes with the senior officer, proud he did not flinch. "As I stated, mine was the only fully mobile ship remaining in the squadron. I am sure any of them would have done the same, had they been able."

"Or had they thought it necessary," said Hess. "They all believed Worden and the *MONITOR* had the situation in hand and saw no need to sacrifice their ships as you did."

"I did not sacrifice *COHOCTON*!" stated Richards loudly, leaning forward. "Captain Van Brunt ordered us to prevent the *MERRIMACK* from escaping. She was about to do just that!"

Hess spoke again, his words cold with menace. "You appear to me as one of these hot blooded young officers who are trying to make a name for themselves in this war, Commander Richards. It is equally apparent you threw your command away in just such an attempt...." He was interrupted by the bang of Stringham's gavel.

"Commander Hess, this is a hearing board, not a witch hunt. You may express your personal opinions on this matter to this board when it is in closed session. I will not allow you to slander this officer at a preliminary hearing! Is that clear?"

"Yes, sir." The tone was unconvinced.

"Do you have any more to add, captain?" asked Stringham.

Richards shook his head. "Only what I have stated, sir. I felt it was both necessary and within my orders to engage the *MERRIMACK*. There were no other options at the time."

"Thank you, captain." Stringham pulled out his watch and checked the time. "Well, gentlemen, it grows late. I suggest the hearing board meet tomorrow in closed session and plan to reconvene Monday morning with a decision. Is there any discussion?"

The other officers accepted Stringham's direction. The old man banged the gavel and Richards stood while the board members filed out. He had an enemy in Hess, for whatever reason. It remained to be seen how much Stringham could sway the members to his point of view. The next two days would be the longest in his life.

"This place feels like a tomb." Welles' his deep voice shattered the silence at the dinner table. "Things may not be going well, but they have not hung you yet, John."

Richards snorted, pushing the still loaded plate away from him. "Can there be any doubt? I am beginning to wonder if I did not misunderstand the orders that night! What if I was wrong?"

"Enough of that!" scolded Rebecca. Her hand took his, but there was little comfort in the action. "We know you did what was necessary. We stand with you, regardless of the outcome of the hearing."

Richards managed a weak smile. "Thank you, Becky." He squeezed her hand slightly. "I know you mean well."

"Son," said Welles, his words grave, "everyone has to make decisions in their lives. Like it or not, they do not always work out for the best. Either way, you have to live with the results. If you do not...well you just cannot go on living."

There was truth in those words. It was the same as the cutting out expedition. There were a hundred different decisions that could be made - yet there was only one to live with. Richards pushed himself from the table.

"I would prefer they meet tomorrow and we have it finished. Then at least, I would be past this damnable waiting."

"If you were afloat, you would have heard by now," smiled Welles. "Ashore, the hierarchy does things more slowly."

"All the same, I think I shall retire early," said Richards. "This will be a long two days."

Richards started for the stairs, but got no further than the parlor. Rebecca grabbed his arm to stop him.

"John, I would like to talk with you for a while," she said, steering him for the couch. He allowed himself to be led, sitting next to the woman but kept at a proper distance by the wide hoops in her skirt. "We need to talk about us."

"Yes?" The single word carried little in the way of emotion.

"I want to set a date for the wedding," said Rebecca firmly. "I have let you avoid it long enough."

"How can I do that?" he asked. "If I am court-martialed, we cannot be married!"

"Poppycock!" she snorted. "I love you and statements by all the naval courts in the world will not change that! I will not take 'no' for an answer, John Richards."

Richards smiled. It was, for a change, one of true humor. He loved this girl, as much for this spirit as anything else. "If I am acquitted, you can pick the date," he replied. "Beyond that, I make no promises."

"Then I will just have to see you acquitted," she

answered. There was little doubt in her voice she would try to accomplish just that.

"Now, Becky, I have had a long day. I would never have thought just sitting in a room could be so tiring. Good night." He kissed her cheek and went to his room.

He removed his clothes slowly, thinking about the day's events. Everything seemed precast, his destiny and the ruination of his career a firm fact awaiting the word of the majority of the board. For over a year, he faced dangers at every turn: rebel shells, mutinous crewmen and nature herself. Yet nothing was inevitable; he was in control of his life and future. Now that feeling was gone. Other people were in charge, and there was nothing he could do to influence the decision. In recognizing the fatalism in his outlook, he still saw no chance for his career.

If he were not a naval officer, what would he be? He looked at the chest sitting in the corner of the room. He approached it slowly, almost cautiously. His family heritage lay in the chest. He opened it, looking at the neatly folded ensigns within. He pulled out one, the one which belonged to his father. The flag was torn and stained, the darker marks of dried blood standing out on the red stripes. He withdrew his own, the flag flown by the COHOCTON at Hampton Roads. The same powder burns and dried blood marked it, but none of it was his.

For over eighty years, the Richards were part of the navy. The navy was more than that to the family. What would his uncle Andrew say when he heard the news? Would he accept it calmly, as he had when his resigned rather than take up arms against fellow countrymen? Or would he feel rage at seeing their name sullied in such a manner?

Near the bottom of the trunk lay a yellow flag. It was all Richards needed, for he had seen it many times in his childhood. It bore a rattlesnake and the words 'Do Not Tread

Upon Me'. Words of independence and defiance. He needed defiance now, the defiance that drove his great-grandfather to break with his English heritage and cast his fate with a new country.

The thought brought new life to his thoughts. This was his country and there were men trying to destroy it. He needed to be involved in its salvation, no matter what the cost. He had to find a way to make the board understand, to let him back into the thick of the action where he could do his country some good.

He replaced the flags and closed the lid. The old sea chest was his heritage and so was the navy. It was the navy his great-grandfather fought to build and he could never do anything to harm it. If the results of the board were negative, he would resign and save both the family and the navy the embarrassment of a court-martial.

He rose and finished removing his clothes, laying the uniform carefully across the stand. He climbed between the covers of the bed, reaching over and turning down the kerosene lamp. His mind continued in turmoil, his eyes open and struggling to adjust to the darkness of the room.

The house was unlike a ship. Afloat, there were always the sounds of the ship and the sea, even at anchor. There should be the wash of water about him; the clatter of block and tackle as the deck heaved to the swells. The hull should be humming with the wind in the rigging or throbbing to the beat of the engine. There should be the creak of the boards working against one another, not the still solidity of the house. There was no sound of the watch moving about on the deck above or the hushed whispers of a helmsmen coming through the skylight. It was not a life he would easily adjust to.

His eyes were drawn towards the door by a quiet squeak in the darkness. A misty form stood there, a light blur against a deeper darkness.

"Who is there?" he whispered, surprised at the

apparition.

"It's me."

Rebecca moved closer, her form changing shades as her nightclothes dropped to the floor about her feet. She stepped over them, though Richards could make out little more than her shape as she raised the covers to move the warmth of her body next to his.

"Have you gone mad?" he demanded, struggling to keep his voice low. He felt the press of her flesh against him. "Your father..."

She pressed a finger to his lips. "Father had a late call to the White House. He will be gone for a few hours," she said. She pressed her lips to his, the pressure of her breasts against his chest welcome despite the danger of the moment. "I will be gone by the time he returns. I just needed to be with you."

He touched her, caressing her breast, her side, her thigh. As much as it was wrong, he wanted her and needed her. He took her with a passion he found surprising, yet wondering how he could give her up if the board found against him. He regretted it when she left, for the bed without her was like it had been earlier, lonely without the sounds of the sea.

Saturday was interminable, a day without beginning or seeming end. Richards survived it by strength of will alone. Sunday proved no better. By mid-afternoon, he forced himself from his room and onto the street, walking briskly in an effort to make the time move faster. He was unused to the unlimited space afforded for walking ashore and continued for a long while before turning back towards the Welles residence.

COHOCTON was an open wound. He missed LaForge, Sims and Healy. They were more than shipmates: they were friends. The year together in war had brought them close to one another, and it was the pain of their loss which affected him over the wood and metal and canvas of the vessel. His resolution was obvious. Next time would be different. Next time, there would not be the loss of any friends. He would have no friends on his next ship.

As he approached the house, a female figure walked in his direction. He recognized her as she drew closer: Lorraine, LaForge's French bride. Something like panic gripped him when he realized he would have to speak with her. It was something he had both consciously and unconsciously avoided since the loss of the COHOCTON. But her eyes met his, still rimmed in red.

"Good afternoon, capitaine." Her voice remained heavily accented, despite the last year in the states.

"Good afternoon, Lorraine." He stopped when she did, facing each other.

"I like walking in Washington," she said slowly, eyeing the wide street. "Especially in thee spring. Eet is very beautiful."

"It is not something I am used to," he replied. He stood aside to let her proceed, and then stayed in step next to her. "I am very sorry about René," he continued. "If there was anything I could do to change it..." His words failed him.

Her hand came up to her mouth and it appeared she was about to start crying. Instead, she lowered it and looked to him. "I know you mean that, capitaine. You were a good friend for René. He loved you very much."

Richards was surprised. He had never thought of their friendship in that fashion, but the words were true.

"I shall miss him." The comment carried a depth of emotion.

"Yes, capitaine. We all shall."

Richards smiled and held out his arm. She took it lightly. "John, please."

"Very well, Jean."

They walked in silence, looking at trees just preparing to bloom in the new spring. The afternoon passed much easier while spending the time with her.

Richards sat in his best uniform, holding his back straight. Whatever awaited him, he was ready to face it. The board filed into the room, all particularly solemn except Stringham. He wondered at the expression upon the senior officer's face.

"Admiral Stringham," started Hess, ready immediately to push his opinions forward. "I am ready to state the majority opinion of the board."

Richards' hopes fell. With Hess fighting for the privilege to make the announcement, there could be little doubt as to the outcome.

"One moment, please, commander," returned Stringham. "I have a comment to make first.

"We have heard the statements of the senior officers of the squadron and the testimony of Commander Richards. On this basis, we were ready to render a judgment. However, it has come to my attention there is another witness to be heard from."

There was silence in the room. Richards had not thought of such a thing. Obviously, the prosecutor had not considered the possibility either.

"Another witness?" queried Hess, surprised. He blinked, as though he did not quite comprehend the senior officer.

"Yes, there is an officer in Washington who was present at the captain's call on the night of the eighth. His testimony must be heard."

Richards was perplexed at the turn of events. Who could this other officer be and what would he have to say?

"By all means," concurred Hess. "Let this officer come

forward!" It was all too clear the commander considered this the final blow to the young captain.

Stringham looked to the back of the room where an aide waited at the doors. "Help the witness in, lieutenant." A younger man turned around, holding the door open. When he returned, he was leading a naval captain with a bandaged face.

"Gentlemen, I would like to present Captain John Worden, commander of the *MONITOR*."

Richards was stunned by the officer's appearance, as were the other members of the board. If Stringham had announced the Archangel Gabriel, the results would have been much the same. The new witness added a melodramatic flair to the hearing, exactly what the commodore hoped to achieve.

"Thank you for coming, captain," said Stringham as Worden slowly lowered himself into a chair. "I appreciate your leaving the doctor's care to attend."

Worden's bandaged head turned at the sound of the voice. "Of course, commodore. I am only interested in seeing justice done."

The wounded hero presented a stirring figure as he sat, answering the questions posed by the board. His uniform appeared a size too large, emphasizing his coming from a sick bed. At the same time, the new gold braid glinted brightly on his sleeves, hammering home his recent promotion. Worden answered each question carefully but frankly, the board members hanging on his every word.

Hess began his questions hesitantly, but with confidence. "How would you characterize Captain Van Brunt on the night of the eighth, Captain Worden?"

"Worried, even panicked. The day had gone badly."

"What were his orders for the captains of the wooden ships?"

"To let me and the *MONITOR* handle the *MERRIMACK* in the morning."

"And if you failed?" Stringham prompted.

"Then the other ships must do their best to keep the *MERRIMACK* from escaping and threatening the capital," replied Worden unflinchingly.

"When you withdrew from the action," asked Hess, "did you intend to return to the engagement?"

Worden smiled the action incongruous with the bandaged face. "My intentions were a little muddled at the time, commander. When I regained my senses sufficiently, I ordered my first to re-engage *MERRIMACK*."

"And it was during this time *COHOCTON* was sunk?"

"So I am told."

"But if Captain Van Brunt was so adamant about preventing the escape of the ironclad, how do you explain the inaction of the frigates at this point?"

Worden shrugged. "I cannot. My only surmise is they were unable to act because of lack of engines. *COHOCTON*, on the other hand, had shown herself to be a fully maneuverable vessel run by a man with the will to place her where necessary."

"So you condone the loss of the ship?" asked Hess pointedly.

"Condone the loss?" questioned Worden. "Only John Richards can answer whether the loss was necessary - and he has given you his reasons. I can only state it helped to know he was standing by to come to our support during the battle. I can think of no other I would rather have had there."

Hess opened his mouth, but only a slight fluttering sound emerged. After a moment, he lapsed into an embarrassed silence.

"Any further questions?" asked Stringham. He did not wait for a reply. "Captain Worden, thank you for leaving your sick bed. You have been an inestimable aid here this morning."

"My pleasure, sir." Worden stood and was led from the room by the aide. He groped out for Richards as he passed. Richards took his hand thankfully. "Good luck, John," said Worden softly.

"Thank you."

The discussion amongst the board members was none too silent as Worden left. Obviously in a quandary, they were trying to decide what to do. They could not convict Richards without casting aspersions on the hero of Hampton Roads. Neither could they dismiss the words of three post captains without calling them before a board for somewhat the reverse of the charges they had attached to Richards. But Stringham took control, guiding them to the decision he wanted.

"It is the decision of this board," announced Stringham as the discussion died away, "that Commander John Richards disobeyed the orders given on the night of the eighth instant and this disobedience resulted in the loss of his command. However, Commander Richards reacted to a changing situation which did not allow time to request direction from the senior officer afloat. His actions were for the best motives, were dictated by the situation in which he found himself, and were for the good of the ships in his squadron as well as the country.

"This board rules Commander Richards' actions were justified under the circumstances and were in the best traditions of the United States Navy. No blame is attached for the loss of COHOCTON and the board trusts they will see Commander Richards reassigned to active command as soon as possible. This hearing is adjourned."

Commander Hess spared him only one acrid glare before standing to leave. Richards was so shocked at the sudden train of events he could only stand in silence as the Board members filed past and voiced their congratulations.

Stringham was last, taking him by the arm to lead him from the room.

"You see, my boy," said the old man, smiling broadly, "everything works out for the best."

As they emerged, Richards saw Worden at a side bench, the aide still close at hand. Stringham called out to the newly promoted officer as they approached.

"A fine bit of histrionics, captain. The bandages were a good touch."

Worden stood as Richards took his hand to shake it. "The doctor did order that I wear them for another week. I take it my testimony turned the trick."

"I thank you for it," said Richards.

"Tut-tut," replied Worden. "Cannot let those old fogies who would just stand by and see your career ruined get the upper hand."

"None the less..." Richards started.

"This is the end of it, John," said Stringham, his voice firm. "The same for you, Captain Worden. Those men did not take the same action you felt was required. Who is to say at this point who was right and who was wrong? As it turns out, *MERRIMACK* is contained and that is the important thing."

Richards nodded, grateful for his deliverance. "Thank you again, John," he said to Worden, laying a hand on the man's shoulder.

"Come by and see me," said Worden. "And bring your fiancé. Next week when these bandages come off, it will be a pleasure to *see* you both!"

Rebecca appeared in the hall, her bright smile showing she had already heard the results. She wrapped her arm around Richards'.

"It appears we will have the wedding after all, John," she said. "But come, the carriage is waiting." She looked to

Worden. "Perhaps we could give you a ride home, Captain?"

She placed her other hand on Worden's arm. He reached up and patted it.

"I would be most grateful, Miss Welles," replied Worden gallantly. "And I dare say you are the best of the guides I had this week!"

Secretary of the Navy, Gideon Welles

CHAPTER THREE

Richards awoke with a start. For a moment, it was the deck of the COHOCTON, shells and splinters flying about him. In reality, it was a dark hotel room and a soft bed. Becky, her naked skin glowing softly in the pre-dawn light, was next to him. He lay back slowly, placing his arm around his new bride.

"Good morning," she whispered, lips pressing against his neck.

She wasted no time with the marriage plans once the verdict cleared his record. April of 1862 was barely begun and he was now her husband and had to consider a wife in his life's decisions. He slipped an arm about her waist and brought her closer. She broke the stillness, slow and dreamy as she awoke.

"Do we have to return to Washington so soon?" Hands ran across his body, the pleasant sensation forcing his heart to beat faster. It was not unlike his feelings that day on the COHOCTON. He kissed her, replying slowly, moving down her neck.

"I am a naval officer and there is the war." His breath quickened as he finished. "There is work to be done."

Her hands pressed his lips to her breast, her back arching at their touch. "But not today." Her words came in a rush.

He wanted to answer, to deny her plans. Instead, he remained silent, his passion taking control to drive him into her. Her body welcomed him without question, wrapping him in warmth and security. It did not occur he need not be driven from it.

Rebecca said hardly a word on their afternoon trip from New York. Scenery rushed by, brushed with green from the growing spring. He sat by the window, his attention outside, conscious of the silent woman. An explanation was unnecessary, but Becky did not always agree with his ideals. He cleared his throat uncomfortably.

"I am sorry we could not stay longer."

She grunted, an uncharacteristic sound. "I must still compete against your damned war."

He disliked the reference to his war but ignored it. "I have a part to play in this and I mean to do it."

"Or what?" She paused, searching his eyes. "You are still worried about the ship, are you not?"

He looked back out the window, shocked she could see into him so clearly. "Should I not be? Those men died because of me."

"Your dying in return will not change that. The court-martial agreed you were not at fault; you did what was needed."

"The bloody court-martial was not on the deck of COHOCTON!" He regretted the outburst immediately. "I am sorry, my dear," he said, forcing his voice to be soothing. "I think about it all the time. I constantly question my decision and wonder if there were not some other way."

She lay her head on his shoulder. Her hand rested on his knee, reawaking some of their earlier passion.

"If you were half the butcher you imagine yourself to be, I would not be sitting here now. Father offered you an appointment in Washington. Will you take it?"

"I am a sailor, Rebecca." As before, his words were harsher than he would have liked. "I belong on a ship."

"Well, we do not always get what we want, commander," she returned. There was deep resolve in her words, too.

Welles had his way and John Richards found himself behind a desk in the Navy Department. The job was not trivial. He was in charge of what was becoming known as intelligence, sifting the reports from the fighting fronts for information on their enemy's strengths and intents.

Whereas other offices had charts available, his contained a map on one wall. Dispatches from the front landed on his desk to be merged into a larger picture of what the so-called Confederate States were planning. Tossing another report to his desk, he rose and stepped to the map.

The eastern seaboard was well contained, but marks on the map indicated southern ironclads under construction. Of particular note was the Hatteras area, where Pamlico sound with it multitude of inlets and easy availability to lumber made an ideal location for ship construction.

The Gulf coastline was quiescent, hardly a rumble heard once New Orleans was taken. Mobile and Corpus

Christi were still points to reckon with and it proved difficult to get word on those areas. In the meantime, Farragut drove his forces north, up the Mississippi. Even a thousand miles from the scene, it was obvious such a move would split the rebellious states in two parts. To aid it, a gunboat fleet battled its way south to join with Farragut.

Richards paced, the shipboard habit asserting itself in the confines of the office. Every action report he read was another trickle of longing added to his growing flood of intent to leave Washington. Somewhere, somehow, he must leave the city and get back afloat. At the moment, the Mississippi was where the action was occurring. If the reports about rebel efforts on the Yazoo River held any truth, it would soon be more so. On his cluttered desk sat a third request for transfer in as many weeks at the job. He could not fight the depressing thought it would be rejected as quickly as the others. His thoughts were interrupted by a knock on the door.

"What is it?" he yelled, angry at the intrusion. Becky entered, closely followed by Lorraine.

"That is hardly the way to greet your wife whose come to take you for some lunch." She spoke pleasantly, her face all smiles.

He fought to control his irritation. She was so complacent when she got her way.

Yes, Rebecca," he said, hardly apologetic. "I lost track of the time." He smiled to Lorraine, aware of his dreadful manners. "Good day, Mrs. LaForge. How are you feeling?"

"Better this morning, capitaine. Thenk you." She smiled back, her face still carrying lines of internal pain.

He took his cap from the desk and held out his arm for Rebecca. "And where shall we dine today, my dear?" Her reply was forestalled by another knock. "Now what?" he demanded, pulling open the door. A young ensign cowered in the doorway.

"Par...pardon me, sir," the man stuttered. "The admiral wanted the report on the Mississippi fortifications..." The voice trailed off, weak and unsure.

Richards took a deep breath in an attempt to calm himself. "I will bring them up directly, ensign," he said, stepping back to his desk. "Pardon me for a few minutes." He spoke to Becky as he took the sheaf of papers from beneath another pile. "I will deliver these and return straightaway."

"That is fine, John." Rebecca sat in one of the office chairs. Lorraine took the seat beside her, but the other woman's eyes followed Richards from the room. "And what are you thinking, Lorraine?" she asked.

"It will not work, Rebecca," said the French woman.

Rebecca's eyes flashed with anger at the comment, but her voice was cool. "And what is that?"

"Keeping the capitaine here." Lorraine reached over and took Becky's hand. "I know you love him. I loved my Renè, but I had to let him go."

Rebecca Richards straightened her back. "I have no intention of letting him run off to be killed. I will have my father keep him here for the rest of this damned war!"

Lorraine shook her head sadly. "Do not you see, Becky? You are hurting him just as badly by doing that."

Richards cornered Welles after dinner when they retired for a cigar in the library. Though a man of Puritanical habits, Welles allowed himself this one luxury.

"When will I get another command?" His tone was more a demand than a question.

Welles eyed him carefully. "Do you think I hand out commands to junior officers?" asked the secretary.

"You know what I mean, Gideon." Richards stood and commenced his nervous pacing, trying to expend his pent up energy. "I have spent my whole life training as a naval officer, not to sit behind a desk!"

Welles' head shook sadly as he rose slowly from his chair. "You place me in a difficult position, son." He walked to the window, staring into the darkness. "My daughter is determined to save you from yourself. What am I to do?"

"If you will not give me a ship, please tell me how you expect me to live with myself!" demanded Richards.

Welles stood in silence, his eyes contemplating the small yard outside the house. There was little to be seen in the night. "Perhaps there is a way to give you both what you want," he said at length, turning to face Richards. "Do you believe in compromise, John?"

Richards grew wary. "In what way?"

"I trust you and your opinions. Things are moving at a fast pace along the Mississippi. I need an observer to report to the department independently of those running the battles." He held up his hand to forestall Richards' reply. "This will not entail a command position. You will be attached to Commodore Foote's staff.

Richards considered his options. It was not what he wanted, but it would be away from the desk and away from Washington.

"At least I will be near the action." There were times when it did not do to argue. "I will take the posting, Mr. Secretary, for I shall go mad if I spend another week in the department."

Welles smiled sadly. "I knew you would, John. You will find your orders awaiting you in the morning." The secretary withdrew his watch. "I will talk to Becky first, if you do not mind," he said, gazing at the time. "And I best do it quickly, before she retires for the evening."

Richards went up to the room, knowing Rebecca's reaction to the news, wondering what he would say to allay her fears. Lorraine was at the door to her room.

"Good evening, capitaine." She smiled.

"Please call me John", he instructed again. Richards was still concerned for the wife of his friend and how well she was handling his death. "How are you feeling?"

Her eyes darted nervously and glanced away. "How did you know?"

"Know?" he returned, perplexed.

"Nobody knows!" She swung to face him, her hands across her stomach. "You guessed I am with child!"

He was stunned by the announcement. Lorraine and Renè spent their last night together a week before his death. It was not even eight weeks previous.

"I did not know, Lorraine." He tried to make his words soothing. "There is no need to keep it a secret."

"But I have no husband!" she cried. "How will I take care of the baby?"

"Becky and I will see you are provided for."

He opened his mouth to speak again, but the sound of shouting drifted up from the library. Becky's voice argued with another person who remained unheard. Welles, at least, was controlling his temper.

"So." The corners of Lorraine's mouth turned up in a small smile, her previous concerns momentarily forgotten. "Mr. Welles is releasing you."

Richards nodded as the sound of the library door slamming echoed up the stairwell. "Yes, I have. You had best be gone," he said, opening the door for her. "I think Rebecca and I shall have a small discussion."

"Thenk you, capitaine, for your words." Lorraine brushed her lips against his cheek as she passed and stepped quickly to her room.

He continued to hold the door to their room for Becky to enter. She stepped loudly to the center of the floor fuming, her foot banging an angry tattoo on the hardwood as she spun to face him.

"How dare you use my father against me!" she said, her voice low but angry. "I thought we were agreed..."

He cut off the comment.

"You agreed!" he said, letting his anger match hers. "You plan out my life without any concern for what I want to do. You do not want a husband, you want a lapdog!"

Her eyes were hard, the anger uncontained. "You need the war so badly? Badly enough to lose me?"

"I am going to the Mississippi," he responded. "I was hoping you would come west, to Cairo. We would have some time together."

"I will not support you in this, John," she seethed.

"I will not be commanding a ship," he offered, trying to allay her fears. "I will be a staff officer."

"I know. *An observer.* That is what father called it. But I know you, John. You will find away around the restriction."

"And if I do?"

"You will do something stupid! You will get killed, or worse," she replied.

"Men have died to preserve our country! Who am I to protect my life?"

"There are many ways to help," she said. She came close, and there were tears running down her cheeks. "The work you are doing now is important. It can make a bigger difference that being aboard some river boat!" He remained silent. "Your going to the river will not bring back René!" she shouted.

Her words were true, though he refused to admit it to himself. Her fears brought a thought to his mind. Was he going back to the war because of COHOCTON? Because he owed those dead men a debt? He ignored the thought.

"I am going."

She slapped him, the force stunning as his face turned to the blow. He brought a hand up to the stinging cheek. She went to the bureau, throwing the doors open.

"Lorraine!" she shouted, her voice ringing in the room.

"What are you doing?" he demanded.

"I will not take this! If you do not want to stay with me, that is fine. I have a home, a safe one. I will go back to Hartford."

He sighed. "So it ends like this?" he asked.

She faced him, her hands on her hips. "And why not? It is me or the war, John. You made your choice." She fairly spat the last words at him.

The door to the room opened hesitantly, and Lorraine cautiously peered around the corner. "Rebecca?" came the soft voice. Everyone in the house heard the discussion.

"I am packing to go home, Lorraine. Tonight! I need your help!"

Lorraine entered, taking the armload of clothing which Becky tossed at her.

"Where is that valise?" demanded Becky.

"Downstairs..." Lorraine got no further.

"I will get it, Lorraine. Fold those!" The door slammed with a loud crash behind her as she stormed out.

Lorraine stood, tears and a new pain in her eyes. "Capitaine?" she asked.

Richards looked at her softly. "Do what she wants, Lorraine. If this does not work out..." He let out another deep breath. "Well, maybe it was just never right."

The Western Flotilla

CHAPTER FOUR

The Mississippi River broadened as the small supply steamer hissed its way south. Richards walked along the upper deck, surrounded at times by the smoke from the stacks set well forward on the small superstructure. Even that irritation was refreshing to the officer who had grown so tired of waiting in the city of Washington. Three days after he arrived, a supply steamer was sent to the fleet with ammunition and he took the opportunity to take up his new position.

The trip to Cairo was quickly arranged after he obtained his orders. Rebecca stormed off to Hartford with Lorraine in tow within a day as she promised. He found little time to consider the future of his marriage as events rushed forward. He boarded the train west, thinking more of the fighting along the Mississippi than of his wife.

He spent a few brief days in Cairo and inspected the Naval Yard there that was like no other in the Union. Few ships were constructed from the keel up: most were steamboats were converted into warships by a genius river man named Eads. Besides the type of work progressing, the nature was also different. There was only a very small shore establishment in Illinois, the bulk of the machinery and tooling was aboard ships anchored in the confines of the yard. The place was filled with makeshift warships in all stages of completion packed together in the small anchorage and a terrific sense of urgency.

The LITTLE BELT was a common river boat with only a small army field gun on the main deck for protection. He spent most of his time examining the river banks as they slid by on either beam, slowly pacing between the stacks at the fore of the superstructure and the small pilothouse at the rear.

"'Mornin', cap'n," said a deep voice. The riverboat's pilot, Ezra Thorn, appeared at his side. He was a large man in perpetually dirty clothes. He sliced a piece of chewing tobacco from a plug and placed it firmly into one bulging cheek. On previous occasions, he had offered Richards a quid but did not do so now.

"Good morning, captain," returned Richards, stopping his pacing momentarily. They were only two days out from Cairo, but the regular naval officer had his fill of the small, cramped boat and its dirty men and conditions. Richards tried to maintain civility with the "acting volunteer ensign", as Thorn was rated.

"We should be reachin' the flotilla today sometime," continued Thorn casually. "They's south of number ten, that's cert'n. 'pends how far they's moved since my last trip." Thorn spit over the side, the splash lost astern of the slowly moving boat. "We's makin' good time, you know," he pointed out, as if in answer to Richards' unspoken impatience. "The LIL' BELT can only make about seven on her own, but we's got the current with us." He spat again, wiping his darkened lips on his sleeve. "Be glad you ain't goin' upstream with us. Bit more to port!" he shouted over his shoulder towards the pilothouse, the change breaking into the one sided conversation.

The supply boat entered another of the many twists and turns in the river bed. Thorn's order brought it closer to the outside of the great bend.

"Yeh, cap'n," said Thorn, reverting to his slow drawl. "The channel's a might tricky through here at times. 'Specially when she's arridin' deep like this."

The LITTLE BELT probably drew all of three to four feet light, and no more than six or seven at full draught mused Richards. "Tell me, Captain," he said, pointing towards the interior of the bend. "Why do not we hold closer to the inside of the curve? The river seems swift enough for a deep channel there."

"Well, thas' true, sir," replied the river man with a chuckle. "But there's a snag stuck in there at the moment and all our good snag boats are bein' turned to gunboats back at Cairo. Lost a supply ship just about here las' month findin' out about it. The whole bottom of her just ripped right away. There!" emphasized Thorn as they rounded the bend, a chubby finger stabbing off to starboard.

Richards nodded his understanding, angry with himself for not accepting that this man, no matter how crude, was capable of doing his job. The tops of two smokestacks stuck out from the surface of the water there, small wakes trailing behind them downstream. It was as far as the stricken ship had gotten before sinking.

Thorn spat again. "Nex' thing you'll be tellin' me how to stoke the damn fire," he said, turning to the pilothouse.

"My apologies," said Richards. "You will forgive me for being anxious to get to the fleet."

"Fleet!" snorted the river man. "You can have your blood and gore, cap'n. I am happy makin' a profit deliverin' the means."

Richards sensed the sound at first, but strained to make

it clearer. It was a deep note, barely audible above the noises of the ship.

"Your estimate appears accurate, Mr. Thorn," he said, his heart beating faster in his chest at the sound. "That is cannon fire in the distance!"

The sound grew louder as the ship plowed its way south. Soon, the periodic explosions could be felt as a physical slap when they crossed the ship. True, it was cannon fire, but Richards could not place the type of gun involved. Two or three pieces were firing at irregular intervals, for they had grown close enough to sense a slight difference in the direction of the sounds. It seemed an interminable wait and his impatience grew as he expected to sight the squadron at each bend in the river. At last, they rounded the final bend separating them and the ships came into view, anchored near the west bank of the river.

The Western Flotilla was a river force and Richards knew the ships which composed it. He had often read and reported on their activities over the past six weeks. None-the-less, his first view of the squadron was a disappointment. Instead of neat, smartly turned naval vessels, they were just a made over group of river boats.

At a rough guess, twenty-five to thirty powered ships were present, with much of the space between occupied by lighters and barges. It was difficult to sort out transports from tugs from gunboats, as all had the same rough, grimy appearance. A few ships did stand out in the motley group.

Four low, iron black vessels lay slightly apart from the rest. Little smoke drifted from their stacks as they sat quietly, a few figures visible on their upper deck. Richards recognized them as distinct from the others, for these were the ironclads built for the flotilla. Unlike the gunboats, they were purpose built ships. Lower and longer, their gun ports were covered by heavy shutters of iron. These were open at the moment, admitting air into their interiors. The snouts of the guns could barely be made out in the shadows.

Further down the river, another group of boats were anchored on the opposite bank. A flash of light followed closely by a blast from one showed who was doing the firing on this day. The vessels were odd, slab-side affairs and only the upper rim of their single gun was visible above the side. These then were mortar rafts, reasoned Richards, for he had never seen their like before. Anchored with them were another one or two tugs, each of the boats apparently responsible for towing several of the little gun platforms. The realization of the nature of the firing also explained why he had been unable to identify the type of guns. The flat explosion of a mortar, with the large round merely sitting on top of its powder charge, did not match the sharper roar of a normal naval cannon.

Two more ironclads caught his eye. They sat downstream, near the mortar rafts. Guard boats, he quickly deduced, but one with only minimal steam, judging from the smoke issuing from their thin stacks.

"Over there, cap'n," spoke Thorn, pointing at the ironclads. "Thas' where you are headed. Thas' the *BENTON*."

Their ship slid past the anchored flotilla before turning north. Fighting against the current, the supply boat lost way. Richards expected to anchor some distance from the flag, but instead Thorn steered straight for the ship with the command flag at the fore. Fighting against the current, Richards had time to inspect the *BENTON*, for she was considerably different from a sea going ship.

The vessel was long and wide. The bulk of her was made up by a gun box, extending almost completely from bow to stern. For all her length, only five guns were mounted on the side visible, though another four ports were open forward. An enclosed pilothouse sat atop the citadel, just taller than a man in height. Two tall stacks were sighted roughly a third the way back from the bow, and a rounded construction projected above the gun box well aft. It was obviously the enclosure for the ship's wheel.

The armor, all dark grey, was sloped, and no entrances

presented themselves. Instead, ladders were provided on all the sides, with entrance and egress through the roof of the gun box. The only other notable feature of the vessel was the three light masts, one each at fore, mid and aft. Too light to carry sail, they functioned solely for signaling and displaying the vessels colors. And other than the pennant at the fore of this ironclad, there was little to separate it from the others grouped nearby. There were funnel bands to distinguish the ships, but he wondered if they would be of much use once the shot started to fly.

Slowly (and skillfully, Richards grudgingly admitted) the *LITTLE BELT* eased toward the ironclad. Thorn reached over and pulled the port engine repeater. With a quick double ring, he pulled it back.

To his initial surprise, Richards watched as the port half of the stern wheel slowed and stopped, then reversed direction. As a result, the transport's turn tightened.

"I am a fool," said the commander to the ship's captain. "I saw the twin engines and boilers and it did not even occur to me there were two separate wheels."

Thorn spat over the side. "Learn somthin' new every day."

He quickly rang the left engine again, changing its direction as they drew parallel with the river fleet's flagship. Men worked quickly on both ships tossing rope coils between the vessels before they bumped together The two were lashed together as lines were tossed to the flagship.

"Well, cap'n," said Thorn, moving past the pilothouse and to the steps, "are ya' comin'?"

He followed Thorn up the side of the vessel. There was only a small party to greet them, for while of command rank, he did not command a vessel in the fleet. A young man, smartly turned, extended a hand to him as he reached the vessel's upper deck.

"Lt. Wesley," he said quickly in introduction. "We were

not expecting any officers for the fleet."

Richards saluted the stern and returned the handshake. "I am from Washington," he replied.

"Then you want to see the commodore," said Wesley. He did not wait for a reply, but headed for an open hatchway. "Leave your gear," the lieutenant shot over a shoulder. "I will have one of the men collect it for you."

Richards did as he was told, following the man at a quick pace. After the brightness of the sun, the interior of the ship was a dim place and he was forced to slow his pace while his eyes adjusted. To his surprise, all the gun ports were filled, a somewhat unusual condition for a warship. The officer's quarters and wardroom were amidships, between the stacks and the wheel box. Wesley led him to one room, knocking quietly on the door. A soft voice spoke from within.

"Enter."

Wesley opened the door slightly and stuck his head inside. "An officer from Washington, commodore." He stepped back to allow Richards to enter.

Richards examined Flag Officer Andrew Foote in the brief moment as he stepped into the cabin. The flotilla's commander lay propped in his bed, a set of crutches against one wall. While the room was dim, a shaft of bright light entered through a small skylight above. Apparently to protect against this intrusion, the man wore a set of dark green goggles.

"Commander John Richards, sir," he ventured, producing his written orders. "Detached from the Navy Department."

"Richards, huh?" he questioned, carefully opening the orders. "I have heard that name..." Realization came to the officer slowly. "You were commanding *COHOCTON*, were you not?"

"Aye, sir." Richards regarded the older man. He was gray headed and slimly built, his chin covered by a short beard. One leg was elevated, the foot heavily bandaged.

"A bad business that." He paused, his eyes scanning the pages. He set the official papers down and opened the letter from Gideon Welles.

"Son-in-law, are you?" asked Foote, setting the paper down.

"I do not expect any special..."

"Nor shall you get it," interrupted Foote. "Still, Gideon is an old friend. I shall try to keep you out of trouble. But I do not need a spy from the Navy Department," said Foote brusquely, returning the orders. "I have been hobbling around the deck of this ship for the past two months since Ft. Donelson. Damned wound will not heal. I have requested to be relieved, Mr. Richards." He tapped one of the lenses on his goggles. "It is even affecting my eyesight."

Foote let a sigh of frustration escape. "Well, you are here and there is no purpose in sending you back. You can watch over our shoulders while we get about this war."

"I will try keep clear, sir," returned Richards.

"Damn right," replied Foote. The conversation was broken by the slap of another mortar shot. "Right now, we are bombarding what the rebels call Ft. Pillow. It is built on an island around the next bend there. It is filled with naval thirty-two's."

Richards nodded knowingly. "More of the legacy from Gosport, I am sure."

"Undoubtedly. We will wear them down for a few days before running the batteries at night. Once a couple of our gunboats and some troops are between them and their source of supplies, they leave the guns quick enough. We have done this before."

"I read your report on Island Number Ten."

"Humph!" grunted Foote in rough appreciation. "At least the department sent us someone who knows what is going on! I will have my flag lieutenant help you get settled."

Quarters on the *BENTON* were tight, even when compared to sea-going vessels. There was the sound of water gurgling past the hull and small movements of the boat. But still, it was not a proper warship as far as Richards was concerned. Warships belonged on the ocean, not penned up in any damned river. And as he lay on his bunk, he missed the purposeful rocking of the ship's hull as it met the oncoming waves.

He breathed a sigh of relief as he was struck by the pressure of another mortar round. The sound of battle, the first he had heard since March. The prospect of seeing action welled up in him. If reports were true, this fleet would be very busy over the next year, forcing their way south towards the Gulf. It would be a change from the constant tour of blockade off the east coast, and maybe a more exciting change. And if his father-in-law and the navy department thought he would remain a simple observer, they were badly mistaken.

He pushed himself from the bunk and headed into the ship. There would be plenty of time for rest. Now he wanted to examine his new surroundings.

The interior of the ship was large, but deceiving. A large armament of cannon was fitted to the vessel, facing out all ways and occupying the exterior deck housing. The interior of the main deck, which on a normal warship would have been left open by this armament arrangement, was instead occupied by the upper portions of the boilers and the engines as well as the wheel box. True, additional bulwarks were built to protect the machinery, but Richards worried about such an arrangement if and when it became time to engage in combat.

This was the result of the ship's design requirements. She belonged on the river, as the large paddle wheel declared. Her slight draught did not allow for any such thing as "below decks." True, there was a lower deck filled with coal and supplies, but by and far the bulk was above the waterline, open to whatever deviltry the rebels might throw at her.

On the upper deck, Richards was able to examine the fleet more closely. The *BENTON* and her sisters were, to his mind, the best looking vessels present. They presented a clean, war-like appearance compared to the other makeshift conversions surrounding him. He thought of the previous summer and capturing the gunboat outside Georgetown. More, he remembered the battles fought against vessels like these and their extreme vulnerability to gunfire. He began to doubt his decision to come west. Would he really want to command such a little tinderbox?

The thought had hardly formed when it was dismissed. He yearned for action, more than he could ever recall having the feeling. The desire was so strong, it was all he could do to keep from going down to offer Foote his services immediately. Yes, he would command one of the little gunboats if given the chance. He would take anything that floated and carried guns and he would see she got into action!

There was little time to ruminate on how to achieve his goal of getting a command afloat. Foote, the steadfast commander of the fleet, was visibly slowing due to his injury. In spite of his best efforts, the pain of his wound was proving too much for his constitution. It was only a few days after Richards when Captain Charles Davis arrived to assume the position of second in command to the ailing Foote. And Foote, knowing how quickly his health was failing, lost no time in turning over the command. He announced his intention to depart on the same vessel which had brought his replacement.

The ship was bustling with activity as the commodore's belongings were gathered. Richards found himself pushed aside, hardly able to find a place where he could keep out of the way of more purposeful activity. Finally, he went to the upper deck, where he encountered a familiar face. Henry Walke stood before him, a commander's twin fouled anchors on his shoulder boards. He recalled Walke was commanding one of the ironclads.

"Captain Walke," he said evenly. "I have not seen you since Pensacola." Richards took the firm hand and shook it.

"Bitter days, those," replied Walke. He lowered his voice. "I heard about the COHOCTON. A tough bit of luck."

Richards nodded, unwilling to discuss the painful memories. "It was," he returned. "But how did you get out here?"

Walke shrugged. "They needed experienced men. Too many old friends were to be found along the coast in different uniforms. This was a safer place to uphold the honor of my country's flag."

Henry Walke. Richards remembered the days of vacillation outside Pensacola, when Walke could not decide on a course of action for their ships to take. The result was the loss of the naval yard and the near loss of Ft. Pickens. In fact, it was he and Lt. Henry Erben who had been the driving force behind the actions to quell rebels attempts at federal property.

"Which ship are you commanding, sir?" Richards could not put those times behind him. Too much anger returned at their memory.

"CARONDOLET." He pointed to one of the ironclads that lay close by. "We are doing quite well with her. Looks as if these rebels will not stand and fight if you have got a bit of iron between you and their shells."

"The CARONDOLET was the first to run Island Number 10." Richards had read the report, but did not remember Walke being mentioned in it.

"I have always tried to place her in the forefront of the fighting," commented Walke. He pointed to another of the ironclads. "The one with the yellow bands on her stack is the *ST. LOUIS*. Henry Erben has command of her. "

Richards smiled at the thought of him and Erben destroying the powder store at Ft. McRee in Pensacola.

"It will be good to see Henry again."

Walke switched subjects, focusing on the younger officer. "But what brings you out? I remember you as a firebrand lieutenant, hardly the temperament to want a gunboat command."

Richards grinned, for the comment was most likely true. "I am to keep an eye on things for the Navy Department, commander. Make sure you are not using too much shot and powder, you know."

Walke laughed. He was not fooled by such a transparent excuse. "Are things so slow for you on the coast?"

"This is where the action is at the moment," replied Richards, frankly. "I think I will do what I can to see my share."

Walke considered the other man for a moment. "I do believe you will, John."

"May we borrow Commander Richards for a moment?" The voice belonged to Wesley. He gestured to where Foote and Davis stood on the upper deck near the pilothouse.

"Of course," said Richards. "Captain Walke and I were just recalling some time spent together down at Pensacola."

"Yes, I have heard about the Pensacola," sniffed Wesley as he led Richards to the commodore. Obviously, the lieutenant had heard enough stories about times at Pensacola.

The two men saluted the older officers as they came to the pilot house.

"Richards," said Foote brusquely, "I would like you to meet Captain Davis, who will be replacing me."

"Captain," said Richards.

"Commander." Davis was tall and thin, his eyes bulging slightly in their sockets. His face was framed by a long mustache and equally long side whiskers.

"Commander Richards was sent here from Washington to keep an eye on things," explained Foote. "As if we needed more officers from out east in the way."

"I am sure the commander will do his job well," commented Davis. "Richards," he mused. "I recall you during the Port Royal expedition."

"Of course, sir. We met briefly when you were Admiral DuPont's Flag Captain."

"You handled your ship very well on that occasion."

Richards maintained his composure over the brief discussion of COHOCTON. "Thank you, sir."

"You may get a chance to see more ironclads, commander," explained Foote. "These damned rebels have several building along the river."

"I was planning to talk to you about my position, commodore," he said to Foote. "I would not be adverse to accepting a command."

Foote snorted. "We have damned few of those to hand out. But that shall be Captain Davis' problem, commander."

"Yes, sir."

Foote hobbled forward of the pilothouse. Most of the crew was gathered on the small, open bow of the river vessel. Though the man's voice was weak, there was perfect silence as he spoke his parting words. The emotion of the moment was palpable, even to one who had been present so briefly. Old gunners, men in the navy for over thirty years, displayed visible tears at the parting of their commodore.

When too choked to continue, Foote bade them farewell and headed for the side. Several of the hands rushed to help him to the transport that was to carry him away. The decks of all the other vessels were lined as the old gentlemen settled aboard the vessel and it began to move slowly north. It was not until the ship disappeared beyond a bend that action returned to the union fleet.

"Mr. Richards." He turned to the sound of Davis's voice. "Since you are here as an observer, I would suggest you observe."

"Sir?" he asked.

"The CINCINNATI and MOUND CITY are being sent down tonight to relieve the guard boats with the mortar fleet. I would like you to accompany one of them."

"Which one?"

Davis shrugged. "You are the observer, Mr. Richards. Take your pick."

"Which is to be the forward vessel, commodore?"

"The CINCINNATI, I believe."

"Then I shall go with her."

Davis smiled. "I cannot say I am surprised."

USS Cairo, one of the Pook Turtles

CHAPTER FIVE

Richards awoke early and reread his notes to this point. The report was properly formal.

Sirs:

I have the honor to report...

He tossed his pen down on the mostly empty page. He had the honor to report nothing. For four days, he observed the operations of the river forces. His requirements were to report "periodically" to Washington but there was little to write about. The mortar boats maintained their position around Plum Point, firing their shells at irregular intervals towards the rebel fort on the far side of the bend. On rare occasions, one or more of the rebel gunboats were sighted, but they declined anything more active than a few challenging shots and a retreat downstream to the protection of the fort.

There was an unfinished letter sitting next to the report.

He realized he was exaggerating to call it *unfinished*. There was little more than the greeting on his letter to Rebecca and he had as much difficulty finding the words to send her as he did for the Navy Department. He sighed. Picking up his pen, he dipped it in the ink and pulled the report closer.

The previous night, he had transferred quickly to *CINCINNATI* and rode with her the three miles downstream to the guard position. The *MOUND CITY* stopped about halfway between them and the balance of the fleet. These two boats were nearly identical, and slightly smaller than the flagship. Both mounted only four guns per side, with three fore and aft. He found himself sharing a cramped cabin with a junior lieutenant who held the night watch and there was only one bunk between them.

Now he sat in the wardroom, staring at the blank page. A commotion suddenly rose about him, followed by a call to quarters. A face appeared briefly in the door: that of his sometime roommate.

"Looks like the rebels are coming upstream, John!" announced the young man quickly. "Best get out on deck if you want to see this action for yourself!"

Richards did not need any more prodding than those words. He ran for the pilothouse, making for the upper deck through the confusion and noise of the ship being prepared for action. The gun deck of the ship was a mass of crewmen running about, readying their guns for action. Richards almost collided with a young powder boy rushing towards his station. But he ignored the lad as he proceeded up the stairs.

There was a blast from a mortar. With the boat less than a mile on the other side of the river, the concussion from each shot seemed to lift his feet from the deck. They were not engaging the rebel gunboats. Mortars were used to fire at fixed targets. It was just their next shot at the fort and happened to coincide with the appearance of the rebels.

"We just spotted them," explained Stembel, the ship's captain, as he came alongside the man. The ship's captain held a telescope and scanned downstream. Beyond the boat, the air was filled with haze and only dim shapes could be discerned in the direction the rebels must approach.

"How many?" asked Richards, unable to count them in the poor visibility.

Stembel shrugged. "They have somewhere between eight and ten boats we are aware of. They are also building ironclads farther south. They might have one of them finished and travelling in company."

Richards felt an involuntary shudder pass through him. *An ironclad.* He was unimpressed by the strength of the federal iron ships. They were, in fact, not fully clad. The bow glacis was covered, and an area abreast the machine room on each side. Beyond that, they carried only the standard protection of a wooden warship: a foot or more of oak. The *MERRIMACK* would deal with such a boat quite easily. If the other rebel armored ships were of the same caliber, they would present a threat to the entire union force.

"I trust that has not happened." He glanced up the river where the rest of the fleet lay. "Why aren't they moving out?"

"Damn!" cursed Stembel. "Probably have as little steam up as we do!" He shouted to a midshipman assigned to signals. "Get those bastards moving up there! Fire a gun to get their attention if you have to!"

But that action was already too late for the shape of the rebel boats hardened in the dim morning light. Four were firing quickly, though with only a couple guns per boat, and bore down upon the *CINCINNATI.* Four more forged ahead, past the point where the ironclad lay anchored. Swinging around with the current, they aimed straight for the *MOUND CITY.*

"They mean to ram!" shouted Richards.

"Cast off!" yelled Stembel, moving to one side. A crewman was working on the anchor cable. "Damn it man, cut that cable! We can fish up the anchor later!" The order was followed by the thud of an axe on the deck.

"Bring her hard port," he instructed, not paying much attention to the helmsman. "Engineer, full steam when you have it!"

There was a tinny reply from below as they swung ponderously into the river, the wheel thrashing slowly under the low pressure of the boiler. The helmsman pointed the bow halfway up stream, counteracting the current enough that the ship made its way straight west across the river.

The bravery of the men manning the Confederate ships could not be in doubt for they charged straight for the ironclads, ignoring the storm of shot and shell issuing from their sides.

Richards had only a brief glance of a large ship bearing down upon them. There was a shower of splinters and cotton bales from the bow of the enemy ram as the first of their shots struck it, but it was too late to deter the rebel. They were struck full in the side by one ram, and another blow was just as quickly delivered to the stern. Almost immediately, the yankee ship began to list. As the ram backed away, a gaping hole was evident in the side of the ironclad. Water rushed in to drag the vessel beneath the river. But even as the river tried to claim the union ship, there was an explosion of steam from the first ram, and she drifted helplessly down river.

Stembel nearly collided with Richards as he turned back to his helmsman. He appeared surprised at the presence of the other officer. In his excitement, he shouted at the other man, though they were but a pace apart.

"Go below and help on the gun deck! It is fight or swim today!" He paid no more attention to Richards as he turned to the helmsman. "Head her for shore! Smartly, now."

The gun deck was a welter of confusion, some crews standing by their weapons, others leaderless as their officer lay bleeding on the deck, cut down by a minne ball.

"Man your positions," shouted Richards, oblivious to the layer of water already covering the deck. Through the damaged side of the ship, he sighted another rebel as it approached.

"Quickly now!" He grabbed a man who stood in a stupor and pushed him next to the gun. "Sponge and load!"

Whether due to the force of his personality or simply hours of training, the gun crew stood fast and performed the motions of loading the weapon. Richards threw himself on the lines and helped haul the gun back to the gun port. Already, their antagonist was close aboard.

"Hold!" he ordered, as the lieutenant in charge of the gun deck prepared to signal the guns to fire. There was a moment's stillness before they were struck, this time abaft the wheelhouse. The gunboat healed heavily at the blow and more water rushed in. Then the ram lay directly abeam, the muzzles of the gunboat barely a foot clear of her side.

"Now!"

"Fire!" shouted the lieutenant.

The four guns exploded as one. The side of the enemy ship collapsed under the weight of iron. There was a blast of steam, felt even within the confines of the ironclad. Their late antagonist was destroyed, drifting and turning as she went south with the current.

The other union ships were now moving, but much too slowly to help the ships under attack. MOUND CITY was struck twice, the ship listing but still moving. By now, the BENTON approached the guard boats, followed closely by another of the makeshift union warships.

"Keep firing!" shouted Stembel, his words heard the length of the gun deck. Already, the men were in water to their calves. But the discipline of their service kept them at their posts. Still, the ship's firing died away as their powder became wet and unusable.

The flagship's guns fired into the rebels. Their gunnery

was passable, for at least two of the rebel ships suffered hits from the first broadside. But the flagship was not spared return fire. Still, Richards had more immediate concerns.

With the guns disabled, he organized crewmen to start getting the wounded assembled. He thought about ordering them to take to the boats, but there was only rope and boards hanging from the davits on the port side. The ship continued to list, and he feared she might not turn over. Even as the thought crossed his mind, the ship grounded.

Leaving the gun deck in charge of the ship's lieutenants, he returned to the pilothouse. Stembel lay on the deck, a crewman standing over him with a bandage pressed to his face.

"What happened?" demanded Richards.

"He is shot in the mouth!" replied the crewman, his voice hysterical. Stembel struggled against the poor efforts of the crewman to help, his words muffled in the bandage and blood. Richards bent and helped get the wounded officer to his feet.

"Get him down to the surgeon!" he ordered, guiding them to the companion. He watched them leave, then inspected the fleet.

The union ships milled about, oblivious to Davis's signals attempting to reestablish control. The second rammed ironclad lay north of them, mostly awash but also lying on the bottom. Damaged union vessels were moving slowly towards the shore and several were having problems controlling the ungainly vessels in the swifter current at the center of the river.

"Thank you for your help." It was the first officer, his pants wet to the waist and his arm wrapped in a blood soaked bandage. He went from the pilothouse to examine the damage done to his ship. Richards followed to the gun deck.

"She will not be battle worthy for a while," he observed.

Water and light moved freely through the gaping hole in the ship's side.

"No, she will not." A deep sound escaped his throat. "I suppose we shall not need an observer from Washington, either. Once things are organized, I will see about sending you back to the *BENTON*."

Richards nodded in agreement. It had been a short tour of detached duty.

"Damn," said Davis when Richards regained the upper deck of the *BENTON*. The commodore looked at the observer, his face pleading. "We had most of them in our grasp!" he complained, shaking a fist. "It is everything the rebels have afloat between us and Vicksburg!"

"Aye, sir."

"Damn!" repeated the commodore. "Look at that!" he said, gesturing to port. A gunboat limped past their beam, a blackened smear where a shell exploded at the pilothouse. A letter 'N' hung loosely between her stacks. The commodore shook his head angrily at the sight. "We shall have to do better than this!" He paused, realizing where Richards had come from. "How are things aboard the *CINCINNATI*?"

Richards shrugged, gazing down stream at the two waterlogged ironclads. "They are *hors de combat*, I am afraid. Stembel is wounded, but I have not heard how seriously. The casualties were not too severe, fortunately."

He could only guess at the thoughts passing through the senior officer's mind. In command less than twenty-four hours, and already he had lost two of six iron ships. It was a poor start.

"I can imagine what they will say in Washington when I report this," continued Davis. He eyed Richards carefully. "It would be improper to ask for advance disclosure of the contents of your message, I am sure."

"I am a line officer, commodore. I can assure you I will present the facts as simply and truthfully as I can. But as I said the other night, I would prefer a command afloat. I have been in two battles with these damned rebels in the last three months, and had a ship sunk both times! I would relish the opportunity to return the favor!"

Davis rubbed his chin, considering the prospect. "I will look into the matter, Richards," he said at length. "But any man willing to lay his ship alongside the MERRIMACK has more mettle than just displayed by these river men!"

Two days after the action, most of the visible effects of the battle were gone. Only two reminders lay on the Arkansas shore where the ironclads sank. Already, the salvage parties swarmed about the grounded MOUND CITY and were preparing to pump her out to refloat the vessel. Divers were repairing underwater damage on the CINCINNATI and awaited a salvage vessel from Cairo to complete their efforts.

The dull crash of mortars still pummeled the BENTON. To Richards, little had changed since the brief fight. He watched the progress of the bombardment from the upper deck, savoring the few minutes of action he'd been granted. Davis had redeployed his vessels, keeping some nearer the mortar rafts with steam up at all times. But the action was too late, for the rebel's River Defense Fleet showed no wish to put in another appearance.

"Boring work, is it not?"

Richards looked to his left, then bolted upright. He had not expected the flag officer to seek him out. "Yes, sir," he agreed quickly. "Along the coast, we would go in and have a direct shoot at the fort."

Davis grinned slightly, then leaned on the rail in imitation of Richards' posture. "Aye, that we could, Mr. Richards. But we do not have fifty gun frigates with us here. And with these underpowered beasts unable to work against the current over most of the river..." He paused, letting the comment lie as self evident, then changed the subject.

"Flag Officer Foote was unwilling to give you a ship, commander. Do you know why?"

The younger man shrugged. "I am supercargo in his eyes, sir. He did not want a spy from Washington behind him all the time."

"Partially true," Davis agreed. "I think there is more to it than that, however."

"Such as?"

"*COHOCTON*, for one." He did not allow Richards to comment. "He has the right to question an officer who lost a ship under such circumstances. I think there is also a question of rank, Mr. Richards."

"Rank?"

"I do not believe that is a problem," continued the older man. "Commodore Foote felt you outranked too many of the other officers within the squadron. My flag captain is only a lieutenant commander."

Richards found himself adjusting to the term. Throughout his entire career, it was always 'lieutenant commanding'. Now in the first year of this war, it had suddenly changed. But these thoughts had little to do with the subject under discussion. "I am a sailor, commodore, and a naval officer. If the best place I can serve is in a gunboat, I will take the posting!"

"I found a letter from the Secretary of Navy in your papers, Mr. Richards. He had a special interest in your non-combatant status."

Richards smiled drily. "Not as much him as his daughter, Captain Davis. She is my wife."

"I see." Davis looked at the river, at the ships gathered under his command. He was a thin man, his whiskers and bulging eyes presenting more the appearance of a mole or a squirrel than a flag officer. But he was a man of decision. "I cannot afford to waste an experienced officer, regardless of his marital relations," he said. "And Gideon Welles is not an old school chum as he is to Commodore Foote."

He pointed into the fleet, the gunboat with the identifying letter 'N'. "The MACHINEEL was damaged in the battle, her commanding officer killed. She is small, underpowered - like the rest of this fleet. You may take her if your wish, and I will not have a spy from Washington at my back."

Richards held his gaze locked with Davis. There was no need to consider his reply.

"When do I report aboard?"

No side party greeted him as the boat drew alongside the gunboat. Instead, there was only an older man in an ill fitting, partial uniform. He extended his hand to Richards and helped him across the small gap to the deck of the warship.

"Acting Volunteer Ensign Luther Crook at your service, sir," said the man, the energy in his voice belying the age in his face. "How may we be of assistance?"

"Commander John Richards," he returned. Obviously, this man had no idea of his reasons for being on the ship. They became clearer as one of the sailors deposited Richard's kit on the deck next to him. "If you could muster the crew, Mr. Crook," said Richards, eyeing the bag meaningfully.

The regular officer inspected his new command as the ensign disappeared to assemble the crewmen. The MACHINEEL was a dirty little ship and Richards fairly winced at the grime left on his hand after gripping one of the railings. She was a fairly common riverboat, slab-sided and stern wheeled. The 'N' suspended between her stacks proclaimed her identity to other friendly vessels. Smoke drifted slowly from only one of the stacks.

After the COHOCTON, she was a tiny and cramped

vessel. Her forward bow was open and the space occupied by a large rifle, possibly even a hundred pounder, on a pivot mount. A glance into the enclosed deck showed four other, smaller weapons mounted on standard carriages two to a side. A last gun, an army field weapon, presented itself as Richards reached the upper deck. It was the only spot with enough open space to assemble his crew.

Bales of cotton lined both sides of the main deck and the upper deck as well. Richards had seen the practice on other gunboats, wondering if it was effective as surrogate armor as everyone seemed to think. He had only a brief moment to notice how little of the damaged pilothouse was repaired before his crew began to appear.

The number of crewmen aboard matched his expectations. Seven gun crews, firemen and an engineer. From the reports, it was clear Crook served as pilot, his profession before the war. Seven boys to carry powder, ten soldiers as marines. One hundred, ten souls in all, less a captain. Now, one hundred, eleven.

There was little order or respect as the men gathered. When Richards realized they must all be present, he reached into his pocket and withdrew the orders. He opened them carefully, eyeing those before him in turn before reading.

"Pursuant to orders received this morning, Commander John Richards hereby takes command of the steam gunboat *USS MACHINEEL*. Acting Ensign Luther Crook and all other ratings will retain their current postings. Signed Flag Officer Charles Davis, Commanding U.S. Naval Forces, Western Waters."

There was little visible effect on the crew. Richards folded and replaced the paper before continuing. "I have little experience on the river, and I hope you shall all help me learn," he said, the words sounding hollow even to himself. "In the meantime, there is much for you to learn about the way we do things in the navy. I shall help you learn them." He faced Crook. "Section heads and officers to meet in my quarters in fifteen minutes, Mr. Crook." He headed for the steps, realizing he did not even know where his quarters were.

It took most of the stipulated time to find his quarters and unpack his modest belongings. The room was large, for river boats were not nearly as concerned with conserving space as were true men of war. Compared to the ironclads, which were converted from snag boats, the vessels made over from river steamers were much more spacious. He waited by a modest side port while the officers and ratings filed in and took up the chairs.

Crook was fairly typical of his new crew. The half uniform was common. When all were present, Richards had Crook make the introductions.

"Second Officer, Ensign Colburn Keeler."

The man was young, too young to be a seasoned river man. Perhaps he was only an adventurer seeking excitement in this war. He hardly needed a shave.

"What was your job before the war, Mr. Keeler?" enquired Richards.

"Trainee pilot, sir. I was workin' here aboard the ol' MACHINEEL, cap'n." The face was honest and open. Perhaps Richards had been wrong in his opinion.

"You will find several of us worked the MACHINEEL 'fore the war, sir," said Crook.

"Did you all volunteer together?"

Crook snorted. "You might put it that way, cap'n. It was either fight to re-open the river when the navy bought the ship, go ashore unemployed, or join the army. I knows the river." He stepped to the next man in line. "Engineer Jeremy Anson."

The man, dirty and unshaven, was covered by the grime associated with his profession in any coal burning ship. "Cap'n," he said, his voice neutral. He barely raised his hand to his cap, and remained slouched in his chair as he spoke the single word.

"Our gunners," continued Crook. "Chief Gunner Carsten Lewis, Acting Masters Oliver Sowden, Sheridan Shepard, Will Dossel, Allen Schoening and Dick McMahon."

The first three men were cast from similar molds. All were heavy built and unshaven. Sowden possessed fair hair and dark eyes, whereas the other two were dark haired with blue eyes. Dossell was a painfully thin man, to tall to serve aboard a regular steamer. Schoening and McMahon were youngsters, probably fresh from an army training school. Their attitude was lackluster.

Richards stepped back, sitting on the edge of the small desk. These were the men he was to lead into battle. They were a sharp contrast to a normal federal warship.

"Who functions as ship's carpenter?" he asked at length.

Shepard straightened slightly at the request. "Me, cap'n."

"I want the repairs to the pilothouse completed," he continued. "By tomorrow."

"Well, sir," drawled Shepard, "I's do not know..."

"Tomorrow, Mr. Shepard," reiterated Richards. "Or I shall have a carpenter who can follow orders."

Shepard's eyes widened at the cut, but he made no further protest. "I will need some men..."

"Draw them from the gun crews, Mr. Shepard. The *MACHINEEL* might not be much in my experience, but we will see she makes a difference on the river." *We will.* The young commander almost sniffed at the thought. These river men were less than enthusiastic for their job.

"Normal regimen is to be up at sunrise and wash down the deck, Mr. Crook. As first officer, it is your duty to oversee that function."

"We haven't worried much about such things, cap'n."

The voice was direct, pensive. "We have been more worried about staying alive."

Richards cleared his throat. "That did not do the previous captain much good, ensign. The best way to stay alive in a war is to fight better than the enemy. I intend to stay alive." He looked to each man in turn. "Is that clear?"

They all nodded in assent.

"I shall provide a schedule of activity. In general, we will address maintenance in the fore noon, gun drills in the dog watches. This afternoon, I will conduct an inspection. All hands to stand by their posts." He held up a hand as Shepard opened his mouth. "Your work crew excepted."

Now there was more expectation in the faces. They were no longer uninterested in this new man in their midst. But the gazes definitely contained overtones of dislike. Not a good beginning, concluded Richards.

The bow gun was the most important piece of ordnance on the small vessel. A 110 pounder Parrot Rifle, it had the largest field of fire. It also occupied the most exposed position. Richards wrote further in his small notebook, a growing list of things to address and change aboard the ship. The bow was strengthened to withstand the weight of the gun. He wondered that the additional framing would not also help the ship as a ram. MACHINEEL was not much of command, but at least it was a command.

"Let us continue aft, Mr. Crook," said Richards.

The interior of the superstructure was warm and stale. Too many of the portholes were covered; more scratches on the sheet. The four interior weapons were thirty-two pounders, all mounted in the forward area. The restraining cables were slack and worn. The pencil moved again.

They walked aft, Crook leading Richards slightly as they inspected the makeshift warship. The crews quarters were above and around the engine compartment. If the ship was dirty, this particular area was filthy. Richards shook his head.

"After scrubbing the decks tomorrow, get the men working in here."

"The men are happy with it like this," ventured Crook.

"Aboard a ship in continual contact with the shore, you must be aware of sickness, ensign." Richards wrinkled his nose at the odor. "This sort of place breeds illness."

The tour continued, room by room, from bow aft, top to bottom. If Richards thought little of the vessel when he came aboard, he thought even less when he finished. They would spend weeks making *MACHINEEL* presentable.

At length, he relented in the darkening evening, releasing the men to a late dinner. For him, he returned to his room to set the plan for their transformation into an effective warship. It would not be easy.

He worked on in the gloom, finally lighting a lamp on his desk. A meal was served, and he ate quickly, returning to his labors with hardly a notice of the food served. He became aware the ship had gone to sleep about him and a glance at his watch was confirmed by the chiming of bells on some nearby vessel. *Midnight.* He stacked his papers, preparing to quit for the night. A knock sounded on his door.

"Enter," he said, turning the lamp up to brighten more of the room. The door opened and Crook entered from the exterior shadows. "Good evening, Mr. Crook." Crook stepped over to the desk, ignoring Richards' motion for him to take a seat.

"I think we need to talk some, cap'n," said Crook. There was a smell of whiskey on his breath, a rarity in Foote's tea-totaler fleet.

"If you think so. Be seated."

Crook pulled a chair roughly to the desk and sat heavily into it. "This ain't no warship, Richards, an' it will do you no good to play like she were."

He considered the comments briefly. "If she is not a warship, the navy department has certainly made a mistake, Mr. Crook."

Crook waved a hand, angered at the reply "That ain't what I means an' you knows it. These are river men mostly. By and large, they's the crew we had before this damn war got started. We ain't in this for the glory or the killin'. We's in it to make a livin' 'til we can get back to movin' cargo."

Richards nodded. "I understand you, Mr. Crook. I, being a regular officer, will not give your men consideration for their position."

"Exactly." Crook mellowed. He felt he had gained a concession.

The young commander took a deep breath. He had seen this discussion coming all afternoon in the state of the ship and the attitude of its crew and officers. Crook's appearance saved him the effort of going to the first officer.

"Mr. Crook, we are a warship and we are in the middle of a war. If you or your men think otherwise, you will have to change your thinking." He raised his voice as Crook opened his mouth. "And we will function as a warship, if I have to replace you and every man aboard her. Is that clear?"

Crook stood, leaning over the desk. "Aye, aye, sir!" He spat the words in anger.

Richards stood and stared the first officer straight in the eyes. "Perhaps your captain might still be alive if he had given more thought to that fact!"

"The same might be said of COHOCTON, captain! By your leave, sir!"

Crook turned and left the room. Richards stared at the door, long after it had closed. Even on the Mississippi, COHOCTON haunted him. He reached over and turned down the desk lamp as he slowly sank into his chair.

Not a good beginning indeed.

The Battle of Memphis

CHAPTER SIX

There was the bang of another mortar and Richards pulled his watch out. A half hour exactly. He even took the time to muse that the sound had replaced the ships' bells within the squadron. The crash of the artillery only momentarily drowned the sound of the holystones upon the decking. An inspection inboard gave Richards the gratifying sight of the crew at work on their new morning ritual.

Outboard, an ironclad sat close to Plum Point just upstream from the engaged mortar raft. Smoke rose from its stacks to indicate steam was up and she was ready to react to the presence of the Confederate rams. Further down and in sight only occasionally, a wooden gunboat plied the river, eyes trained even farther down its course. Davis would be sure there was no repeat of the events of the 10th instant.

MACHINEEL changed considerably in the two weeks since he came aboard. The decks, while not spotless, were at least presentable. The crews quarters were spotless, however, and their minor health complaints disappeared with the grime. The ship was halfway painted with gray siding and white upper works used as a standard in the flotilla. While not changing the nature of his vessel, it gave her a more professional appearance.

And other changes were completed, also. The worn cables on the guns were replaced and properly taunt. Ammunition lockers were correctly secured and arranged. Even the engine room had suffered with his presence, requiring a separation of their coal and wood bunkers, with other inflammables carefully stored below the waterline. He had obtained additional cotton bales and chains to provide more protection to the boilers.

The look of his crew improved to the point even the commodore commented upon it. The men were in proper uniforms and, if not clean shaven, at least neatly kept. While there was continued grumbling at the changes and, in particular, the work, the crew expressed a new found pride in their ship and their service. The few regular navy men aboard welcomed the improvement and were vocal in their support of the new commander. Shepard, after the initial reluctance, was the most vocal of his supporters. Quite a change for only eleven days effort.

Crook walked aft and touched his cap, another sign of the transformation aboard the gunboat. "Cap'n," he said, voice carefully neutral.

"Good morning, Mr. Crook."

"Work parties are told off to complete the painting. I think we should be through 'fore lunch."

Richards nodded. He brought out his pipe and carefully tapped some tobacco into it. He held the pouch up towards Crook but the officer declined the offer.

"You managed to cut another thirty seconds from the time to clear for action yesterday," commented Richards, striking a match and bringing it to the bowl. "Thirty more and it will be down to acceptable standards."

Crook shook his head sadly. "I do not see what the hell

difference a half minute makes one way or the other."

Richards sighed. For an officer on a warship, Crook was hopeless. "You will when those seconds tell the difference between you getting the first shot into them, or the other way around."

"Oh, the men are comin' 'round to your way of thinkin'. I can see it in 'em already."

Richards struck another match and relit the pipe. "I have been thinking, Luther. There are plenty of transports attached to the fleet. I could request you be assigned to one of them if you would be more comfortable there."

Crook snorted. "*MACHINEEL's* my ship, Richards. I have been on her since she first tasted water. I don't have another home."

"I need a fighting officer, ensign, not someone protecting his home."

The volunteer officer's reply started with a nasty grin. "But ain't that what this whole war's about, Captain?"

Later, Richards went across to the *BENTON* for officers call. There could be little doubt as to the reason for the summons. The previous day, they were joined by six more ships. On their first approach, he had mistaken them for mere transports. A closer inspection showed they were the union counterparts to the rebel ram fleet.

The vessels were all of medium size. Forward, the area built up to withstand the impact of a collision was sheathed in iron. No gun ports or guns were obvious on the newcomers. Nor did they display the colors properly for a naval vessel. The word in the fleet was they were Army boats, built and maintained at the direction of the War Department.

This trip also gave him his first chance to inspect his small command from afar since joining her. He was pleased with what he saw. The ugly damage caused by the shell explosion which killed her former commander had disappeared. Instead of dirty sides and peeling paint, the ship was now dark grey and white. No longer were crewmen pointlessly lolling about the decks. Their activities were directed and purposeful.

BENTON was also a ship in transition. Foote, for all his popularity with the men and successes over the past year, was not a well man and his command suffered from it. It was another instance of the war taking its toll: the Navy Department left him in command well after the officer himself realized he was no longer fit for the post. Davis was healthy, but as inexperienced at river fighting as Richards. Never-the-less, the new commodore brought with him an infusion of energy badly needed by the flotilla.

"Commander Richards," greeted Phelps as the former entered the wardroom. Samuel Phelps was a mere lieutenant commander, but was captain of the *BENTON*. By position, he was also flag captain of the entire flotilla.

"Captain," he replied, touching his cap.

"The commodore asked to see you privately as soon as you arrived, John." He pointed towards the rear of the room.

"Thanks, Sam."

That was another difference Richards noted. As an *observer* from the Navy Department, he had always been held at arm's length by the other officers. Since taking command of the gunboat, he was welcomed back into their fraternity.

Richards proceeded aft, passing greetings with some of the other captains. He saw Henry Erben to one side, and had a chance to exchange a quick nod of recognition with his old friend. The presence of several men in army uniforms confirmed the rumors about the new ships. Davis turned his owlish features upon him as he approached.

"Commodore," greeted Richards.

"Commander," returned the senior. "You have done a

fine job with the *MACHINEEL*, at least from what I can see from here." It was an open, friendly comment.

"Aye. They just needed an introduction to the real navy."

"Good. Tomorrow morning, you will be posted down at the point. Give you a chance to work them up under steam."

"Thank you, sir."

Davis nodded and gave him a wink. "We may be deep water men, but I think we can learn the ways of these river rats. But that is not why I called you over here. I have news I thought you might be interested in. On the 10th, we took Gosport."

Richards heart seemed to stop momentarily. Gosport - the *MERRIMACK*'s home. "And the ironclad, sir?" he asked, his voice low.

"Escaped up the James River, but it was only a temporary respite, my boy. The next day, the rebels blew her up or she would surely have been captured."

Richards felt unsteady. Thoughts of the iron ship still plagued him, and now she was destroyed. The fact the work was done at the rebel's own hands detracted only slightly form the overwhelming occurrence. The retribution for the battle at Hampton Roads was delivered. Davis touched his arm.

"Steady, lad. There is more. While you here out there getting your feet wet aboard *CINCINNATI*, we also took the navy yard at Pensacola." He smiled at Richards' discomposure. "You see, I am also familiar with your jaunt south. Now have a seat, and we will get this underway so we can all get back to work."

Davis did not waste many words. With a quick introduction, he brought forward the *colonel* commanding the army rams. This man, named Ellet, in turn introduced the commanders of the remainder of the vessels. They were easy to remember as the commander of each shared the name of Ellet with their leader. One was a boy of no more than eighteen or nineteen.

Once this process was completed, it was time for the main purpose of the gathering. Davis gathered his officers about a chart on the table, and reviewed their current situation.

"Commencing tomorrow, two mortars will be pounding Pillow on a continual basis," he said, tapping the chart at the location of the fort. "General Halleck is moving through Arkansas, trying to reach Corinth, south of the fort. Once that is completed, the fort's supplies will be cut off."

Charles Ellet nodded, eyeing the chart carefully. "Why do we not just run past the fort, as you have in the past?" he asked.

"We have always had army support to take positions downriver of the fort. That has not been the case so far. Also, we have not had to face a well organized defense afloat," continued Davis. Walke added to this thought.

"Commodore Foote would certainly have thought twice of sending *CARONDOLET* past Island Number Ten if a squadron of eight rams was known to be waiting below."

"How long do you plan to sit here?" asked another of the Ellets.

Davis shrugged. "The *MOUND CITY* is to return within a day or two, with the *CINCINNATI* close behind. That will bring the ironclads back to full strength." He looked at Colonel Ellet over his glasses. "Your force adds considerably to our fleet, but you are under separate command. I plan to wait for the ironclads. Meantime, Colonel Fitch and I have been making plans for taking the fort."

Ellet smiled, an action barely noticeable beneath his luxuriant beard. "We may be under separate command, Commodore, but I have no doubt we can *cooperate* on this venture. When you are ready, my rams will be more than pleased to run the batteries, if only to get at those rebels boats."

"Thank you for the offer, colonel," returned Davis. He straightened and spoke to all his officers. "Regardless, we must remember our goal is to press south. Captain Farragut and his ships are moving north. When we join them, we will have split this 'confederacy' in two. It is nothing less than that which we hope to achieve."

He reached down and rolled up the chart. "But you are correct on your other point, colonel. The next time we encounter them, we must clear these rebel rams from the river. If not, we shall always find them standing between us and the Gulf Squadron."

More details were hammered out before the officers were released. Most made their way to the upper deck, glad to be clear of the stuffy cabin and into the fresh evening air. A voice called to him as he emerged on deck.

"John!" It was Henry Erben stepping forward. "John Richards! What the devil are you doing here, man?"

Erben laughed, an easy going mannerism Richards remembered from the time spent together at Pensacola. "Same as you now, I am sure," he returned. "Davis gave me MACHINEEL. I hear you have ST. LOUIS.""

"Yes," replied his friend. "An unmanageable iron beast in these close waters."

"But still, a top command on the river. What have you been doing?"

Erben chuckled. "A shoot here or there. Supporting the army, guarding transports." He let out a sigh. "I hate these damned, close waters. If it were not for the pilots, we would not have gotten ten miles below Cairo."

Richards nodded in agreement. "It is like trusting a ship to the master's mate. Unfortunately, it is a completely different style of ship handling in these currents."

There was a murmur of greetings aft of them. The thin form of Walke strode onto the deck, nodding greetings and exchanging comments with the other ship captains.

"I did not expect to see him held in such prominence," said Richards. "After Pensacola, I mean."

Erben lowered his voice. "You will discover he's well thought of on the river, John. It will not do to make such a comment too loudly!"

"I have read the reports. It hardly seems the same man from last year."

Erben shrugged. "Once the die was cast, the old man knew where his duty lay. He has been a tiger ever since."

There was a shout from the main deck.

"*ST. LOUIS!*"

Erben smiled and grabbed Richards' hand. "Best not to keep the lads waiting. We will speak again!"

The lieutenant was off quickly towards the stern. Richards had seen his rank, but had not let it register until that moment. A lieutenant commanding for sure, but still only a lieutenant with all the action on the river? It seemed odd his friend had not been promoted at some point in the last fifteen months.

MACHINEEL moved to its new position overnight. The next morning was bright and clear, and the ship cruised slowly back and forth across the river, just in sight of the enemy fort. Richards held his post in the pilothouse, though removing his wool uniform coat in the growing heat. Crook appeared, his shirt open to the waist, a large gut apparent and covered by an dirty undershirt.

"Is it always this damnably hot on the river?" asked Richards, mopping the back of his neck.

Crook wiped his forehead with the back of a forearm. "'Tis only May, cap'n," he answered. "It will not get hot until July." He chuckled at his little joke.

The air about the ship was still and heavy. Richards swatted at a mosquito on his hand and waved to shoo a swarm of gnats from his face. The slow speed of the vessel added little to freshen the air on the upper deck.

It was a new type of ship movement for Richards. While in constant motion, the vessel still fought the current of the river. Thus, the bow always pointed upstream to counteract the flow. Neither could a course be set and the bow held at a set angle. The force of the river's current changed as they moved back and forth. The helmsman constantly moved the wheel to adjust to this variation and keep the ship on a straight line.

A mortar fired, followed immediately by the other. Involuntarily, Richards looked up and caught just a glimpse of one of the shells as it slowed near the top of its trajectory. Following the line of flight, it plunged towards the earthworks constructed by the rebels. There was a heavy explosion behind the wall, a column of dirt and debris hurled back into the sky to show the effects of the bomb.

"Ship moving south of the point," commented Crook.

Richards immediately brought up his telescope and trained it on the just visible column of gray smoke. All thoughts of heat and insects disappeared.

"Time to see how well your training is paying off, Mr. Crook. Beat to quarters, please."

The comment was certainly more formal than either the occasion or the surroundings called for. The *MACHINEEL* carried neither drum nor bugle, so the call to quarters was simply echoed by the men after the first shout. Another order sent a set of flags up the mast to inform the rest of the squadron of the approaching vessel. They would know soon enough what was coming, for the rebels announced their presence by opening fire from the fort.

MACHINEEL cruised well over two miles from the rebel battery, and the shots fell short by several hundred yards. The rebel ram appeared abreast the fortification, circling in the river to stay clear of the fort's fire.

"Just one of them." He swept the area downstream carefully, alert for smoke from accompanying vessels. There was none to be seen.

"We're a bit too far for them rebel guns." Crook also examined this new comer.

"Mr. Keeler," said Richards, addressing his signals officer, "make to flag - 'One Vessel in Sight'."

"Yes, captain."

"And when they acknowledge, make 'Request Permission to Attack'!"

Crook lowered his glass and glared at the naval officer. "Are you mad? They have seven more boats waiting."

"Not with steam up, or we would see them," shot back Richards. The rebel guns fired again, this time joined by one from the ram. As before, the shells fell short.

"It would be foolhardy," continued Crook. "The fort has at least twenty guns, and it is located right at the bend in the river! Those waters are tricky."

"I would not know about that, Mr. Crook," said the commander. Behind him, Keeler was busy bending on the flags for the second signal.

"I would," the river man returned. "This is nothing more than a trap!"

The halyards squeaked as the new flags were raised. In his mind, Richards calculated how he might take the rebel vessel. Turn south and run with the current. Fire bow and starboard guns. Swing back into the current, firing with the bow and port batteries. A couple of good hits would disable their opponent. It would be tricky to take the prize in tow and return the rebel to the fleet, as they would be under the guns of Fort Pillow most of the time.

"Signal from the flag, captain," said Keeler, interrupting the brief reverie. "Denied."

Richards looked up sharply. He was about to order

another signal in protest, but it was already too late. The ram turned with the current and headed downstream, unwilling to await his convenience. Even the fort ceased firing.

"Damn," he said. "There goes our chance."

Crook snorted. Words were not needed to convey his opinion.

Richards formed a rebuke, but thought better of it. "Very well, Mr. Crook. Secure from general quarters. I shall be in my cabin if you sight another." He did not wait for an answer. He left the pilothouse quickly and went below.

A week after the taunting appearance of the rebel ram, the union fleet moved south. Word was received of the capture of Corinth. In spite of Ellet's promise of coordination between army and navy ships, he quickly ordered two of his rams past the fort without informing Davis.. They did not receive any fire for their effort. A landing party sent ashore found the works abandoned.

They were still two hundred miles north of Memphis, the next major rebel city on the river and they could not know how many forts lay between them and the city. With the ships steaming in column, Davis led his fleet south.

Richards was glad to be on the move. With the exception of the attack on the ninth, the wait at Ft. Pillow was as boring as blockade duty. At least with the ships heading south, there was the prospect of action, for the rebel River Defense Fleet lay somewhere before them.

Every branch and fork of the river held the prospect of ambush. But the two gunboats which forged ahead as scouts did not sight any of the rebel rams. On leaving Pillow, in fact, the fleet covered a hundred miles the first day. The next day, Davis brought the fleet to a halt just upstream of the city. But it was a smaller fleet, as gunboats were assigned to protect the lagging transports or sent off on other investigations. Only a half dozen of the boats, accompanied by a like number of rams, were at the anchorage. *MACHINEEL* was one of those.

Her captain walked the deck in the sweltering heat of the evening. Though the sun disappeared an hour before, the heat clung to the gunboat as though she were afire. Smoke drifted lazily from one stack, the fires banked for the evening. It climbed slowly into the air, as oppressed by the heat and humidity as if it were living.

He ran his hand along the barrel of the field gun, wondering what the morning would bring. So far, the rebels had failed to make a stand. A fort had been passed earlier in the day, the works rapidly abandoned at their approach. Still, it was clear the rebels would not let go of Memphis without a struggle.

"Evenin', cap'n." The voice belonged to Shepard, his dark form barely visible on the deck.

"Mr. Shepard," returned Richards. He usually found the mate at this work, and they exchanged words on a nightly basis. Though he was ship's carpenter, during a battle, Shepard commanded the field piece. Richards' resolve to remain uninvolved with his crew was forgotten during the discussion.

The part-time gunner walked over to the field piece and knelt to examine the lashings. "I figure things will get a might hot in the morning," he said, obviously not referring to the weather. "Thought I would check her out before turning in."

Richards lit his pipe and took a slow draw. "It is likely," he agreed, blowing the smoke out slowly. "Are you ready?"

Shepard smiled, white teeth glinting. "We still owe them for that tussle up at Pillow, cap'n." He stood, his hands resting on the oversized wheel of the carriage. "I guess we will get a chance to repay them."

"That we shall, Mr. Shepard. I have no doubt on that score."

*   *   *   *   *

The predictions of the night before came to pass very rapidly in the morning. The *MONARCH*, flag of the rams, was near the *BENTON*. Davis and Ellet were visible on the decks of their ships, speaking across the short distance between them. *MACHINEEL* was anchored too far away to discern the subject of discussion, but the two commanders were not allowed to finish their talk. The rebel rams were sighted, coming up the river towards the union gunboat flotilla.

For all the wondering at the prowess of the army boats, they showed no hesitation. They all moved out immediately, two forging ahead faster than the rest.

"Full steam!" shouted Richards into the speaking tube to the engine room. The sound and bustle of the men clearing for action already reached his ears. He grinned madly at Shepard as the latter rushed forward to his station.

"I would not be in such a rush," said Crook, standing outside the pilothouse but keeping close watch on the river and their course.

"We best get there quickly, Mr. Crook, or there shall be none left for us to deal with!"

The Union fleet was not organized, the rams thrusting ahead, the gunboats under Davis's direction forming into a line more or less across the river. *MACHINEEL* lay between the two forces, trying to keep up with the rams.

In an instant, the rebel and union forces were entwined. Two of the army rams crashed into their confederate counterparts. One sheered a complete wheel from the side of a rebel vessel. The army rams backed off, their victims already settling in the swift waters at the center of the Mississippi.

Richards tried to pick a target, but in the swirling melee of rams, it was difficult to tell friend from foe. A glance towards the shore showed crowds of people lining the bluffs and docks of the city, apparently turned out to witness this spectacle of an inland water battle. But there was no time to waste on them as *MACHINEEL* drew within the confines of the action.

A ram separated from the mass, directing its attention towards the gunboat. Richards sighted it just as quickly.

"Meet him head on!" he directed the helmsman. He faced Crook. "Have the rifle hold fire until the last second!"

The ensign left to relay this information. Richards was driven from the pilothouse by the excitement of the moment. Its confines were insufficient to hold his exuberance. He barely noted the minne balls striking the structure about him.

"At least keep moving, cap'n," shouted the helmsman. "They'll mark you for sure jus' standin' there!"

But there was little time to consider the suggestion. The ram approached and, under Richards' urging, the helmsman kept their course. The rifle fired, the shot striking the superstructure of the enemy. There was an explosion of splinters, followed by another at the aft of the boat where the round emerged. Richards cursed as the shell detonated beyond the vessel, for it would have surely finished the ram if exploded within her bowels.

The boats struck bow to bow, the ram glancing off into the river. The two deck guns, as well as Shepard's field gun, fired into the ship at point blank range. Their bow caught the starboard wheel house on the ram, smashing it to ruin.

He moved behind the pilothouse to keep watching the enemy ship. She listed to starboard and circled in that same direction due to the damaged wheel. They came broadside, and the port guns fired, two more shells exploding aboard the vessel. A fire flared forward. The ram was finished.

Richards turned to sight another target but there were none. The rest of the fleet had arrived and only two rebel ships still functioned. They were steaming quickly south, a ram and a gunboat hot on their tails. He brought himself back to their rapidly settling opponent.

"Cast her a tow!" he shouted to the men on the fantail.

He looked to the helmsman, "Steer for shore when she's grappled."

"Aye, aye, cap'n."

Brief and furious, the battle was over already. Even Richards was surprised at the speed and completeness of their victory. He noted a commotion near the field piece. A man lay on the deck. He stepped forward quickly as Crook rose from his knees. Shepard, almost unrecognizable, lay there, his face shattered by a rifle shot, a growing stain of blood spreading on the smooth, bleached white surface.

"He's done." Crook opened his mouth to continue, but closed it. With a disgusted wave of his hand, he left to supervise the towing of the rebel ship.

Richards stared at Shepard for a moment, but shook himself from the sight. He remembered his new rule and the cost of violating it.

"Take him below," he directed.

Two of the gun crew stepped forward and lifted the body, carrying it aft. Richards watched the rebel ship towed behind them, idly wondering if they were in time to save the vessel. The comments from the crewmen were barely heard.

"See the cap'n out there? Mus' be brave to ignore them rebel sharpshooters!"

"Hmph!" sniffed the other. "Just plain crazy, if you askin' me!"

BATTLE AT ST. CHARLES, WHITE RIVER, ARKANSAS.—EXPLOSION OF THE "MOUND CITY."—Sketched by Mr. Alexander Simplot.—[See Page 435.]

Battle on the White River

CHAPTER SEVEN

There were those in Memphis who welcomed the raising of the old flag, but they were a decided minority. An officer from the ram fleet was sent ashore to claim federal property and he did so, in the face of large and threatening crowds. The city was in the hands of the Union and the citizenry could do little other than accept that fact or leave.

The first few days at Memphis were spent provisioning the gunboats and claiming the booty of captured rebel rams. Between Memphis and the next rebel strong point of Vicksburg lay the mouth of the White River. Word was received of rams building along its shore, guarded by a fort. Davis wasted no time in gathering his officers aboard *BENTON*.

Richards arrived and walked up the steps toward the soon-to-be crowded ward room. Almost immediately, Erben started down the steps in the opposite direction, his face flushed red in anger.

"Henry?" asked Richards, but the other man pushed past him.

"Not now, John!"

Erben pushed past him and out onto the aft deck, shouting at the bosun to recall his boat. Richards watched him, wondering what was going on. He turned his attention up the stairs and walked into the meeting.

The officers were barely assembled when Davis came in. They rose in respect and he quickly had them return to their seats. Another officer followed the commodore.

"Gentlemen, effective immediately, Commander Johnston will take command of ST. LOUIS. Lieutenant Erben will see to the refit of the captured ram SUMTER."

There were some murmurs from the back of the room, but Richards remained silent. This was not unheard of and certainly the newly arrived Johnston held superior rank. Still, it seemed a slap in the face to his friend who had commanded the ironclad through all the fighting of the last three months.

"The White River is our next focus, gentlemen," he continued, getting straight to the point. "The secesh have at least two rams building up stream and we cannot afford to leave them in our rear.

"Two ironclads will lead the squadron. Commander Kilty will command from MOUND CITY." The older Kilty nodded to acknowledge his understanding. He was at least twenty-five years older than Richards. "ST. LOUIS will accompany and give Commander Johnston time to familiarize himself with the ship.

"CONESTOGA and LEXINGTON will support and ride herd on the army transports. The Army needs to get to Helena, Arkansas, and we will support them once the rebel rams are destroyed." Davis looked over his officers, his gaze keen. "Are there any questions?"

The room was silent, but Richards stood up quickly.

"Sir, if I may volunteer MACHINEEL for the expedition? I am still working up the crew."

Davis smiled. "You are indeed hot blooded, commander. Very well, *MACHINEEL* will be included. Anything else?" No other officers voice questions or objections. "You shall have your orders shortly, gentlemen. Dismissed!"

The expedition was a combined operation. Two ironclads led, followed by three gunboats and a like number of transports with a brigade embarked. They wound their way up the length of the White, a river as full of bends and narrows as the Mississippi.

"I do not care much for this," said Crook, pacing next to the pilothouse.

"What is that, Mr. Crook?"

"This damned river!" Crook walked to the other side of the deck, looking down at a group of men along the side. "Give me another cast of the lead!" he ordered.

There was a splash, followed by a shout. "By the mark three."

"Shoaling," said Richards.

"And getting narrower," snapped Crook. "Bloody sharpshooters will have a field day. Might as well be alone out here for all the help we could get from the others."

The observation was true enough. Most of the small squadron was invisible from the *MACHINEEL*. Occasionally, Richards caught sight of the aft end of the *ST. LOUIS*. The gunboat *LEXINGTON* lay between *MACHINEEL* and the ironclad. The gunboat was lost from view at exceptionally sharp bends in the river. One transport, and the front of the next, were usually in sight behind. The remaining ships could only be placed by their smoke columns.

"I think we can manage, unless they have a heavy battery set up."

Crook turned sharply at the roar of a cannon from

LEXINGTON. A section of shoreline was swept by grape, but there was no indication of any reason for the firing.

"Captain Shirk is just letting off a little steam," commented Richards.

He took his pipe from a pocket and lit it, walking slowly along the deck. He nodded agreeably to the gun crew standing at quarters, making no mention of their lax attitude about the gun. He, too, was adjusting to the ways of the river men.

"Why were we selected for this?" asked Crook, falling in step next to Richards.

Richards took the pipe from his mouth, regarding it for a moment while he exhaled the smoke. "We were not *selected*, Mr. Crook," he answered. "I offered our services."

Before Crook could make reply, there was a snap on shore and a minne ball screamed overhead. Another raised a splinter in the deck planking about six inches from Richards' foot. The naval man looked at it casually, and stepped over to the deck gun.

"Pass them our regards, if you please." He started moving again to make a less obvious target.

The field gun kicked, sending its charge into the dense brush a hundred yards away. The main guns followed suit, the foliage dancing and flying as the small packets of death hurled through them. There was no way of knowing if anyone was hit ashore. Either way, the cannon blasts stopped the sniping for the moment.

"You were saying, Mr. Crook?" prompted Richards, as though nothing had occurred.

Crook was shaken by the nearness of the shot. He was no coward but he lived by a different set of rules than these navy men from the coast.

"You are all mad."

Richards grinned. The thought occurred to him on more

than one occasion in the past year. "Perhaps," he returned, non-committal.

They rounded a bend and moved along a fairly straight stretch of river. Their first objective, to capture or destroy the rams, was in sight. The three ships were marked by smoke and flames. As was becoming the usual case, the rebels fired the ships themselves to prevent them from being captured.

MOUND CITY headed the small union force. She rounded to and anchored midstream. The rest of the boats did likewise. A shouted order passed from vessel to vessel and Richards ordered a boat swung out to proceed to the flag.

There was a commanders call for the small squadron. Five ship captains and three army men came across. Captain Kilty was a gracious host, setting up a tarp along with table and chairs on the deck of the gunboat so his guests would not be troubled by the staleness of the interior. A sailor of the old school, he was an officer before Richards was even born, serving in the various squadrons around the globe. The commander served his guests wine, the one beverage excused from the regularly ignored ban on alcohol within the flotilla. It was pleasantly cool, a welcome drink on a warm afternoon.

"Gentlemen," began Kilty at length, "as you can see, the first part of our job is done. Tomorrow, we shall tackle the fort. It is but two miles further upstream."

"And my men?" asked Colonel Fitch. Richards recognized the officer from the earlier engagement at Ft. Pillow.

Kilty gestured at the chart. "They shall move up and disembark here under cover of darkness. At first light, I will lead *ST. LOUIS* in and silence the batteries. When that is accomplished, you may storm the place at your leisure."

Fitch nodded. "From there, it is an easy march to Helena."

"Correct, sir."

It was strange the elder Kilty referred to the young army officer as 'sir', but it was something they all lived with. Fitch, a lieutenant colonel, outranked the elderly Kilty who was only a commander. Age and experience had nothing to do with the inter-service game of who was in command.

"And the gunboats, captain?" asked Richards, not wishing to be left out of the fight.

"Will cover and support the ground forces, commander," returned Kilty.

Richards nodded in acceptance but was disappointed. At best, it promised to be a slow day's work.

"We have done this sort of thing before, without a lot of trouble," Kilty continued. "So let's finish this wine, and toast our adventure tomorrow."

As ordered, the ships moved out in early morning darkness. Troops disembarked and moved into position before the ironclads left to begin their assault. The MACHINEEL lay down river, out of gun range. To his consternation, Richards was again just an observer of events. None the less, the crew stood to quarters and steam was up.

Following general practice, the ironclads moved close to the first fort, holding themselves in the stream with the bow armor facing their adversary. The firing became general, the gunboats making good practice. The rebel works were arranged in batteries along the river, and they were shooting rapidly.

The explosion of shells around the earthworks showed the naval fire taking effect. The return firing slowed almost to a stop, and the MOUND CITY moved forward to address a second in the line of batteries. The rebels guns fired at the ironclad and there was a shower of splinters as a shot struck the boat, followed immediately by the screech of escaping steam. The ironclad was enveloped in the white, clinging cloud of death.

"Upstream!" ordered Richards.

"Into them guns?" queried the helmsman. The look he received was a clear reply to his question.

The screams and shouts of the scalded men were heard above the continual sounds of the cannon. At the same moment, the army made their appearance, rushing over the batteries to silence them permanently in a flurry of rifle fire.

MOUND CITY was a dreadful sight as they closed on her. Men crawled from the scalding interior of the vessel, the skin scalded from their bodies. Others ran blindly, throwing themselves into the river to escape the steam. A few were organized at the rear, trying to launch the boats and get clear, but the rush of steam forced them into the water and out of harms way.

"Man the sides to pick up survivors!" shouted Richards. He ran to the hatch on the gun deck. "Man the boats! Quickly now!"

The ironclad drifted with the current, her motive power destroyed. The white cloud dissipated and Richards edged MACHINEEL next to the crippled vessel, grapnels flying to lash draw the crippled ship close. Boats from the other ships approached to help the injured as they lashed the two shipd together.

A quick word and the commander led a small force of men aboard the ship. The anchor was let go and she stopped her drifting. Searching for survivors, Richards led the way inside.

She was a ghost ship, for the only sounds were the occasional moans of an injured man. The interior of the casemate was still hot and damp from the explosion of steam. Most of the men were dead, still at their posts, the skin literally boiled from their bodies. As they found the injured, they were moved to the deck, accompanied by the screams of agony as their damaged bodies were lifted. It was an unpleasant duty.

"Set up an infirmary in the officer's mess," instructed Richards when Crook stepped aboard the ironclad. "Take as many of the less injured aboard as we can. The rest will be moved to the other ships and the transports."

"Aye, sir," he answered, regarding the suffering men laid at the stern. "Nothin' but damn steam kettles!" He cursed the ironclad under his breath as he returned to his own ship.

The interior of the vessel was dim and lifeless. The spot where the deadly shot entered was obvious, blasting through the ship's armor and oak backing. It went through the chain and hawsers piled about the engine room and laid open the boiler as if it were a tin of meat. The eight inch shot which caused the damage was imbedded in the far bulkhead.

Captain Kilty was severely wounded, so Johnston of the *ST. LOUIS* took charge of the vessel. The few uninjured men were sent back to the ship to prepare her to return north. Meanwhile, boats plied constantly to shore, adding to the line of draped bodies piled there. The river waters were too shallow to consider a naval funeral for the men.

Aboard *MACHINEEL*, eight injured survivors lay on the deck of the small mess room, a few men told off to see to their needs. Richards visited them briefly before seeing to his own vessel's requirements.

"How are you getting along?" he asked, kneeling next to a master's mate.

The man was not too badly scalded, just his arm and the side of his face showing the horrific effects of the steam. He lay quietly, staring up at the ceiling of the dim room.

"Well enough, cap'n," he said, his words low. "How are me mates?"

Richards shook his head sadly. "I am afraid many of them are dead. We are doing what we can do for the injured."

"Poor ole' *MOUND CITY's* a marked ship, I would say, cap'n. What after bein' sunk and all, you know." The man coughed slightly and faced Richards.

"Are you in pain?" the officer asked.

"Don't really feel much of anything," the mate answered. "Thinks you could give me some of them ice chips, sir? They seem to help."

"Sure, sailor."

Richards turned for the cup and brought it back to the master. The man lay there, eyes still open and mouth agape. The final moment of his last breath still issued from his lips. Richards set the cup down, reached over and closed the man's eyes.

He stood and examined the room. The other victims all had men attending to them. He returned to the upper deck and leaned against the pilothouse, slowly packing tobacco into his pipe.

"Drink, cap'n?" Crook offered a bottle of whiskey. Richards reached for it slowly and took a long swallow. "Thas' the worse thing I have seen in my life," said Crook, taking the bottle back and gulping deeply from its contents. "They say Commander Kilty will live, but he lost his left arm."

The young commander nodded. It was only at times like this when he realized death was not the only possibility in combat. He never considered he might lose a limb, be blinded, or crippled in any number of horrible fashions.

"Them ironclads have two and a half inches of iron on the front, atop of a solid foot of oak," continued the pilot. "Did them no good, 'cept maybe keepin the steam in longer."

Richards did not feel in a conversational mood, but Crook did not stir from his course. Whether it was the events of the day or the alcohol, he could not contain his anger.

"What is the point, Mr. Crook?" questioned Richards,

tiring of the intrusion into his thoughts.

"Old *MACHINEEL* has the sidings she was born with, cap'n, and they ain't no foot of oak. That could as easily been us."

"You do not understand our mission, Mr. Crook. Nor, I fear, shall you ever."

"What is there to understand, cap'n? That you jus' as soon get yourself killed as go on livin'? That you ain't afraid to take the lot of us along with ya?"

"If it achieves the purpose, Mr. Crook. That is what we are here for!"

"Purpose?" chided Crook. "What did we accomplish today? Over a hundred men dead, and what for? Some damn earthworks?"

Richards grabbed the bottle back and took another long drink. The raw whiskey burned its way down his gullet, but he did not care. He tossed the bottle back to Crook.

"How about so river men like you, who survive by taking things down to New Orleans, can continue to make their living? How about so farms in the Illinois and Ohio can continue to sell their goods? So factory workers in New England can get the cotton they need to maintain their lives and family? What of all that, Mr. Crook?"

Crook had no answer for the outburst. He finished the contents of the bottle and tossed it into the river. At length he spoke again.

"And how many of us it will cost, cap'n? How many?"

Richards snorted. "As many as it takes, Mr. Crook. Now leave me in peace!"

Crook left the upper deck and Richards went back to his pipe. He appreciated the drink. The sights aboard *MOUND CITY* were beyond his experience, and the death of the master's mate was simply the cap to an appalling day. Yet, he had wanted to come out here, to fight this war. Worse, he was more than willing to take MACHINEEL in the next day and fight again.

Only twenty-five of MOUND CITY's crew of a hundred and seventy-five answered muster the next morning. Men were taken from all the ships to crew the vessel north. Richards provided them with Keeler, along with a few seamen. The young ensign was progressing in his naval education, and it was time to give him a bit of freedom.

The wounded were removed to the army hospital ship RED ROVER which arrived from Memphis to take charge of the casualties. It was accompanied by the gunboat CONESTOGA when it left with its sad cargo.

The battered MOUND CITY, for all the death and injury suffered the previous day, was easily repaired. They naval force pressed up river, guarding the army's flank as they moved towards Helena. Fitch gained his object and the gunboats pressed forward, searching for the rebel army.

The remaining gunboats did not hold this position for long. Within two days, the river level commenced dropping. In another day, it was obvious the ships must retreat or face the prospect of being left high and dry and at the mercy of the rebel forces in the area. With the army secure in the city, the diminished fleet turned south, passing the earthworks that had cost them so dearly.

The trip down the White River was as uneventful as the trip up. A few Confederates paused to snipe, but it quickly became an unpopular activity. Whenever a musket round received a broadside of grapeshot and shells in return, the sharpshooters saw there was no chance for an even exchange. The frustrated river flotilla made sure the sharpshooters paid for their temerity. In any event, the return to Memphis proved short lived.

USS Machineel

CHAPTER EIGHT

Davis prepared to get his fleet underway from Memphis as quickly as possible. But the Western Flotilla now faced another problem, one which wore down their numbers more quickly than rebel rams. The farther south they proceeded, the more river there was to guard, and Davis had only a fixed number of boats with which to do it.

The army was still mostly north, at Ft. Pillow and Corinth. Transports brought troops to occupy Memphis, but there was a large stretch of river in between remaining in rebel hands. Gunboats were necessary to escort the transports to insure their safe arrival.

The intent of the river campaign was to split the Confederacy in two. The western shore of the river was the food bank of the new found country; the eastern was the population and production center. Driving a wedge between them might starve the more bellicose portion into submission. But the gunboats could not be in all places at all times and the rebels simply watched and moved their supplies when the river was clear. As always, there were never enough vessels to do all that was needed.

MACHINEEL steamed at a slow pace, well back in the column of ships. The ironclads were first, black gun snouts projecting from their sloping sides. Behind them were the tugs, mortar rafts in tow, three and four per vessel. Next were the transports, with a few army troops, and then the supply ships. Intermingled with them were the Army rams, staying close to their normally land locked brethren. The rams were under a new commander, though still an Ellet. The original was north, attempting to recover from a wound received at Memphis.

Last in 'line' were the wooden gunboats. There was no steaming order, so they spread across most of the river. Some darted about, sniffing along the shore for anything suspicious, sometimes loosing a broadside of grape. The latter activity was more from exuberance than danger, though there was that aplenty along the river's course.

"Man signaling from ashore, cap'n." Keeler gestured to the small figure in the distance. The young ensign disembarked from MOUND CITY at Memphis to be sure to accompany his boat south with the fleet.

Richards mopped his forehead before lifting his telescope. The heat was even more oppressive. The form swam into view, a black man jumping up and down and waving a rag to attract their attention.

"Looks like a darky," said Crook, lowering his glass. "Probably just tryin' to escape his masters."

Richards nodded. "Another reason we are fighting this war, Mr. Crook. Mr. Keeler, bend on a signal to the flag. 'Investigating Shore'."

"Aye, sir." The young man rummaged through the signals box.

"Bring her into the current and hold us out into the river, Luther," ordered Richards. "Tell off a boat crew from the starboard watch to retrieve that man."

Richards awaited the boat's return at the bow. The air was hot and motionless with little to break it except the steady slap of the stern wheels against the waters.

"Think he'll have anything important to say?" asked Keeler.

"He wants something. It is a lot of effort just to be passing the time in this heat."

"Aye, cap'n, it was never like this in Missouri. Not all the time, at any rate."

"You are from Missouri? Why did you decide to go with the north?"

Keeler shrugged, grinning broadly in his opened mannered way. "Jus' the way it worked out, I guess. Workin' on the river an' all, you know, sir. My ma, well she didn't want me to go."

"And your father?"

"He's dead, cap'n. Been dead a long time."

Richards opened his mouth, to ask the boy another question. He turned the action into a faked yawn. He did not want to know any more about Keeler. He had already heard more than he wanted.

"Where is that boat?" snapped Richards, angered at allowing himself to be drawn into the conversation.

Keeler was surprised at the sudden change. "I will go check, cap'n." He went up the ladder, his face perplexed.

It was an old man. He grinned and nodded, happy to be of service. His white hair stood out sharply against the wrinkled black skin.

"You the cap'n?" he asked in a slow drawl.

"I am." Richards glanced at one of the sailors. "A glass of lemonade for our friend. And how can we be of service to you?" he said, directing himself back to the contraband.

"No, suhs. Ize wants to helps Mistah Linkun's gunboats. I does." He drank the offered glass greedily. "They's a fixin' a gunboat of their own up San' Frans."

They were just passing the mouth of the St. Frances River. A gunboat, or ram, built further up its length would present a danger to the fleet's rear. Their supply problems were difficult enough without an enemy afloat on the same waters.

"How do you come by this information?" asked Richards casually. The blacks were always coming forward to provide information. Unfortunately, their white masters were often the original sources and sometimes the information provided were feints and deceptions.

"I sees it myself I did." The man nodded and grinned. "'Bout the size of this un. They had us stackin' cotton on the deck. Tall as me, them stacks was. And cannon. Don' ferget the cannon!"

"How many guns?" demanded Crook.

"Don't rightly knows," responded the black. "Only one on the ship yesserday. The others was sitting on the ground."

"Unmounted guns, do you think?" asked Crook.

"Probably," returned Richards. He looked back to the colored man. "How far up the river?" he asked.

"How far?" The old man stood in deep thought. "Mebe a half days walk. Mebe less."

"Give our friend another glass of lemonade," instructed Richards. He touched Crook's arm and went back to the wardroom. He brought out the rough chart of the river complex. "What do you think, Mr. Crook? Have you ever piloted the St. Frances?"

"No." It was a blunt reply. He studied the map for a

moment. "No tellin' what a 'day's walk' is. Could be ten, twenty miles for these darkies," he continued. "Couldn't be too far past here, anyway." He pointed to where a railroad bridge crossed the river. "Too shallow from there on up."

"Can you get us up there?"

Crook snorted. "Tossin' the lead the whole way. It will not be fast, I can tell you that."

Richards accepted the comment at face value and returned to their informant. "Thank you for your information," he said. "Would you like to stay with us?"

The old contraband shook his head vigorously. "No, no, suh. Ize go home. One them days, Missuh Linkun's gonna set this ole nigga free. Mebe I can help you agin."

"Set him ashore." Richards glanced up to the pilothouse. "Mr. Keeler!"

The young face appeared over the rail. "Sir?"

"Is the flag still in sight?"

"For the moment, captain."

"Signal: 'Investigating Enemy Vessel'."

"Aye, sir."

Crook stood at the side, watching the boat row back towards shore. "So we're goin' up?"

"We are, Mr. Crook."

Crook's prediction was accurate. Their movement up the twisting St. Frances was slow going, very much like the White River two weeks past. Though the *MACHINEEL* drew little water, they made their way with caution.

"Smoke ahead!" shouted Keeler, standing on the roof of the pilothouse with a glass.

"Can you tell what's burning?" asked Richards.

"All I can see is the smoke, sir," returned the young gentleman, climbing down from his exposed post.

"We go through all the trouble to get up here," commented Crook, "and they burn the bitch before we even catch sight of her."

Richards smiled, for the comment was undoubtedly true. "Never the less, Mr. Crook, we shall ascertain her destruction."

"Of course, cap'n!"

They rounded a sharp bend and their quarry lay ahead. Only it was not the boat in flames, but a large pile of cotton ashore. As they appeared, there was a blast from a cannon on the rebel steamer. The forward gunner of the MACHINEEL did not waste time asking, and a shot bellowed from the Parrot rifle. The shell struck square amidships on the enemy boat and exploded to good effect.

"Bring her broadside, Mr. Crook!"

"These waters are tight, cap'n," cautioned Crook.

The helm was put over and the port wheel backed. Another shot came from the rebel, raising a column of water close aboard. The two broadside guns replied, one raising a column of dirt ashore, the other hitting high on the stern wheel of the vessel. There was a spatter of small arms fire from shore, replied to by the army gun. The soldiers that served as their marines took positions behind the cotton piled forward and opened upon the troops. More than one man fell on the rebel side as their volleys rang out.

The guns fired again and Crook ordered the anchor dropped to hold the ship broadside to their enemy. Both shots took effect, the shells exploding clearly on the vessel. Cotton bales flew into the air at the impact, along with other debris. Almost immediately, men ran from the gunboat, and fires licked at the torn cotton.

Once more, the thirty-two's roared, and the single gun of the rebel failed to reply. The flames grew aboard the vessel, and the soldiers ashore melted into the underbrush, no longer willing to face the fire of both soldiers and cannon from the union ship.

The gunboat burned brightly, flames growing above it. There was a series of small explosions aboard, as the inferno reached some of the ammunition. Then *MACHINEEL* was rocked by a large explosion as the ship disappeared in a blast of smoke and debris. Flaming pieces fell on the ship, and men ran about to kick them overboard or douse them with buckets.

"Not a bad afternoon's work, Mr. Crook," said Richards, examining the smoldering wreckage left in the wake of the blast. "You can raise anchor and guide us out of here."

"As fast as I can," replied Crook without ceremony, a note of relief in his voice.

The first officer was good to his word, and they were quickly moving with the river's current. Crook was nervous, for the St. Frances was not a wide river, and there were many sharp turns and twists. He maintained a man forward, casting the lead at regular intervals as they felt their way.

Richards noted the other man's agitation. "We will be out of here soon enough."

"Not soon enough to suit me," replied Crook. "Them troops was headin' south when they retreated. I figure's they'll be waitin' for us somewhere along here."

There was wisdom in the words and Richards could not deny them. He had most of the crew stand down, remaining inside where they would not present a target to the rebel sharpshooters.

The prediction long in realization. A crack from shore and the leadsman fell, a hand gripping a growing red stain on his thigh. The firing increased, with shots whizzing past the ship, splatting into the woodwork, or occasionally felling a crewman.

"Load with grape and shell," Richards ordered. The

cannon quickly joined the soldiers in replying to the fire.

"Keep her in the center!" yelled Crook, turning on the helmsman as the boat swerved towards the riflemen. But the man slumped over the wheel, half his head blown away by a musket shot. Crook grabbed his collar and pulled the body clear to take the wheel himself.

"Keep her moving," said Richards, stepping from the pilothouse. "I will see to the guns!" He ran forward to the field piece, splinters rising in the decking about him as the sharpshooters tried to mark him down.

"You have got to fire faster!" he yelled. One of the gun crew yelped as he was knocked to the deck, his chest splattered in red. Richards retrieved the rammer from the dead hand.

The gun kicked again and a sailor ran the swab down the barrel. Another tossed in the charge, followed by a shell. Richards inserted the rammer and pushed it home, withdrawing it as quickly as possible. The gun fired and the procedure repeated itself, another crewmen falling to the fire from shore, but dragging himself clear of the gun. A final bend in the river, and the firing ceased all together, only the puffing of the engine and groans from the wounded were heard aboard the ship.

Richards returned the rammer to a crewman and went aft. Keeler stood at the wheel, his face blackened and hair in disarray. The commander strode quickly, wondering what would cause Crook to abandon the post. The Acting Volunteer Ensign sat in a corner of the pilothouse next to the dead helmsman, his chest torn by a minne ball.

"See where you got us?" Crook coughed as Richards knelt on the deck. His lips were lined with bright blood. "They've done for me, that's certain."

Richards was no doctor, but it was clear there was nothing to be done for the man. The bullet struck a glancing blow and ripped his chest open. White ribs glinted as Crook's chest heaved in agony. The path of the bullet had smashed his arm above the elbow, and Crook sat in a growing pool of his own blood.

"I am sorry, Luther," said Richards quietly.

Crook coughed, spraying blood onto Richards. "It don't matter," he whispered painfully. "Now ... or later." The words came in a gasp. "You was headin' us ... this way." He gulped for a last breath. "See you in hell, cap'n." His back arched in a final spasm of pain, and his head slumped upon his bloodied chest as his final breath hissed between his teeth.

"The Mississippi's ahead, cap'n," announced Keeler, his normal exuberance subdued.

"We will drop anchor when we reach the headwaters, Mr. Keeler, and see to our dead and wounded."

"Aye aye, sir."

Three smoke columns rose on the western shore of the river as MACHINEEL headed after the rest of the flotilla. The standing orders to the fleet for dealing with sniping was the burning of plantations. This was Richards first such action, and he found it distasteful.

A raiding party went ashore, Richards taking personal charge of the operation. Three plantations were reached before nightfall called an end to the enterprise. All the structures were burned: houses, barns, out buildings. If stacks of cotton were found, they also received the torch. On the one hand, it was inflicting the war on possibly innocent civilians. On the other, it punished those who allowed rebels to operate in their area.

The crew took particular pleasure at the action. Four of their number were slain, six more wounded. They approached the task with a glee for destruction Richards had rarely seen in civilized men. They were avenging their mates and, once started, it was difficult to pull them off after the third plantation was aflame.

That evening, their four comrades, bodies wrapped in canvas, were buried on the western shore. Richards read the words from the bible, thinking of Crook and the argument after the White river action. *As many as it takes.* Had he really meant those words? The proof lay before him, men filling the four graves and arranging the markers for their slain shipmates.

Crook should have been ordered to take the place at the field piece. Richards thought he was the one taking the risk by doing so. Yet Crook's body was being set into a quickly dug grave while his captain read the service. If he had stayed, and sent Crook forward, the positions would be reversed. The realization of how much death he had seen the last few weeks was hitting home to the young officer.

They steamed through the night, their speed slow. Without the pilot, he had to be careful. He looked to Keeler at the wheel.

"You have the helm, Mr. Keeler. Keep us slow and in the center of the river until we rejoin the squadron. Call if you need me."

Keeler nodded, his eyes intent on the river before him.

Richards when down to his cabin and turned up the lamp. Tossing his coat on the bunk, he sat at his small desk and pulled out a sheet of paper. It had been two weeks since he had written Becky and those words had come slowly and haltingly. Now, his hand moved the pen quickly across the sheet.

At dawn, the rear of the fleet lay before him, the shore lined with on-lookers. A few union flags waved enthusiastically at the passing force. Most were quiet and still, eyes downcast and faces clouded. A beaten people, their victors before them. Not for the first time, Richards wondered why they were fighting. He mopped his brow. The sun was barely up, and already the ship felt as if the steam were loose.

"Readiness report, sir," announced Keeler, still to be cleaned up from the previous day's action.

"Go ahead." Barely eighteen, he was, temporarily at least, the second in command of the gunboat. Down the river, there was a nineteen year old Ellet actually commanding a boat. The service expected boys to age quickly.

"All the wounded are still unfit for service. We also have five men reported sick this morning."

"Sick?" questioned Richards.

"Fevers, captain. I saw them myself."

Gunboat *TUSCUMBIA* with a mortar raft

CHAPTER NINE

Vicksburg was a city built by nature for defense. It was located at a hairpin turn in the river in the northern part of the state of Mississippi. The east bank was a mass of bluffs overlooking the water, well situated for mounting heavy guns and firing down on passing vessels. The fact was not lost on the rebels and the bluffs were lined with every bit of artillery available. Nor were they shy about using it.

Davis wisely decided not to attack this bastion. His mortar boats lined the east side of the river bend. Across this narrow, flat strip of land, they announced the fleet's arrival to the besieged rebels.

The next day, there occurred an event which swept Richards with homesickness. Across the headland appeared the ships of Farragut's squadron: five ocean sloops, with their tall sides and truncated masts. There were three smaller sloops plus a number of steam gunboats of various descriptions. Farragut also brought his own mortar fleet, a collection of reworked sailing vessels which took up positions and added their fire to the pounding of Vicksburg.

But other matters were pressing *MACHINEEL*'s captain more closely. He was still without a first officer since the loss of Crook. More importantly, the loss also deprived him of his river pilot. The sickness which began the previous week grew and spread throughout the squadron. *MACHINEEL* had lost twenty men already, disabled by the illness. Over a quarter of his crew was unfit for action, though none appeared likely in the immediate future. There was no solace in the fact the rest of the fleet was similarly afflicted.

The Louisiana side of the river was a headland separating them from Vicksburg. It quickly became festooned with army tents as General McClernand unloaded his troops from the transports. This afforded the fleet shore facilities and it was a daily effort to take the most grievously ill ashore. Richards accompanied the morning trip to the field hospital. He checked on his men, making sure they had whatever slim comforts could be provided.

He was on the way back to the boat when he encountered Erben. It was the first he had seen him since Memphis.

"Good morning," he said.

"'morning," came a low response. The other officer appeared in a surly mood.

"How are things proceeding with *SUMTER*?" Richards tried to turn the discussion to professional matters.

Erben turned on him in anger and too late Richards realized he struck a sore spot with the other officer. Still, Erben forced himself to remain cool and answer his friend in a level voice.

"It is a poor excuse for a warship, John. The rebs did not maintain her well and we did her no good by driving a ram into it and forcing her aground. But to have to take over that rotting hulk after commanding a proper warship..." His voice rose at the end, but he lowered it and leaned closer to Richards.

"I tell you, John, Davis has it in for me! The first chance he got, he took ST. LOUIS away. He gives me the worst gunboat in the squadron and the cast-offs from every other ship and expect me to turn it into a fighting ship!"

"Easy, Henry!" cautioned Richards. He, too, kept his voice low. "It will certainly do no good if you are overheard and it finds its way to the commodore!"

"I am beside myself, John," returned Erben with a sigh of resignation. "He actually accused me of failing to bring my ship into action! That maybe a new captain would make better use of the ironclad! How am I to redeem myself from such a slander with a boat I can barely keep afloat!"

Richards remembered the state in which he found *MACHINEEL* when he stepped aboard. It was working with the crew and perseverance that turned the ship into a respectable gunboat.

"Do what you can. Perhaps we can pool resources and I can send some men over."

"A decent carpenter would be of great help."

Richards shook his head. "Sadly, mine was killed in May and I have not been able to find a good replacement. I have a man that is trying to learn. You are certainly welcome to use his services if they will help."

Erben shook his head sadly. "He sounds no better than the incompetent sot I have in the position now, but thank you for the offer."

"Persevere, Henry," urged Richards. "Give the men a reason to be proud of their ship, and they will get the work done." Erben nodded, but was not convinced by Richards' advice. "I must be off to see the commodore. Do not hesitate to ask if there is something *MACHINEEL* can do to help."

Erben mumbled a parting comment before proceeding on his way. Richards watched after him, wondering what he could do to help. His ship was under-manned because of the sickness, but he had crewmen that could help paint and clean. It was hard to see his friend in such a state.

Richards steered the boat for BENTON. It was still before noon and even close to the water it was humid and stifling. The slight air movement caused by their motion provided more breeze than the nonexistent wind.

"I would like to see the commodore," he said, addressing the ship's first lieutenant. He was shown to the upper deck, where Davis and Phelps sat under a tarp strung across the open space.

"Have a seat, commander." The captain waved to an empty chair, mopping his brow with a handkerchief. "What brings you our way this miserable morning?" A steward brought a glass of lemonade, small pieces of ice still floating on its surface. The coolness was welcome.

"I still require a first, commodore." The heat did not permit the luxury of beating around the bush. "Or at least a pilot, if no officers are available. I would also like to promote Mr. Keeler to acting lieutenant."

Davis breathed heavily, the heat weighing heavily on the older man. "I have no officers or pilots on hand, commander," he answered. "And as to your Mr. Keeler, he's still a bit raw for promotion, don't you think?"

"Perhaps." Richards found breathing in the humid heat just as difficult, but he hoped he showed it less than the older man. "There are younger carrying the rank within the squadron."

"Aye, that is true," returned Davis. "You know your vessel best, Richards. Do as you see fit." He paused again, then glanced across the peninsula. The masts of the Gulf Squadron were only dimly visible through the haze. "There is, perhaps, another source for you pilot, commander. I am to visit the flag officer this morning. Perhaps you might care to accompany me."

"I would be honored."

The short land trip was like entering a different world. The army occupied every square inch of ground that could not be hit by the guns at Vicksburg. For all the men ashore, the soldiers were engaged in little practical activity, their efforts directed more towards drills and keeping the camps clear than presenting a bellicose front to the rebel army such a short distance away.

They were forced to walk for lack of other more suitable transport, and Richards found himself breathing just as heavily as the commodore after the mile trek. He was glad to settle himself in the rear of long boat for the short trip to HARTFORD.

Stepping aboard the flagship of the Gulf Squadron reinforced the feelings of homesickness. She was a larger ship than COHOCTON but similar in most other respects. An honor guard rushed forward to greet the commodore, another formality all but lost upon the river. They were directed below and introduced to the man who captured New Orleans.

"Sir, Commander John Richards," presented Davis.

Farragut, a tall, thin man who was forced to bend beneath the deck beams, stretched out his hand in greeting. Richards took the offered handshake, feeling the strength within it.

"Captain Davis, Commander Richards," returned Farragut. "Have a seat." He gestured to open chairs before his desk. The heat in the cabin was stifling but the flag officer did not appear to mind. "I was expecting a message, captain," Farragut continued, "not a visit in person."

Davis shrugged. "It was an opportune time to meet you.

Primarily, I wished to discuss our course of action. Do you have troops coming up from the south?"

Farragut shook his head. "None. They are all consumed watching over New Orleans and Baton Rouge. And your army contingent?"

Davis smiled. "On the river, sir, we are the army's *naval* contingent. I am afraid General McClernand has no more men available than you see ashore. We estimate the rebels forces enclosed around the city as two or three times his number."

The other man nodded. "A land attack is out of the question." He paused, considering the situation. "I shall run north of Vicksburg," he said at length. "We shall merge the fleets, if only temporarily."

"But why?" asked Davis. "There is little point to place your ships at risk to their guns."

"I have my orders to link our forces, captain. I shall follow them." He raised a hand at Davis's protest. "There is a benefit served by the action as well. We will show these rebels we are undaunted by any barrier they place before us. It will demonstrate the river will be open when we choose it to be."

Davis lodged no further protest. "And when shall you make the attempt, sir?

It was Farragut's turn to shrug. "On the first favorable night, captain. I may wish to run the batteries," he said, a twinkle of humor in his eyes, "but I am not so foolish as to attempt it when they have clear shooting."

The meeting was closed by Davis mentioning Richard's need for a first officer. Farragut listened and waved his flag captain over. They emerged on deck and Richards was temporarily blinded by the change in lighting.

"Commander Richards?" It was Farragut's flag captain. "I believe I have an answer to your need for a pilot. We have a spare pilot aboard *HARTFORD*."

"A spare?" It was rare in the navy to have a spare anything.

"A river man from up north," the man explained. "He was sent from New York for the trip up the river. The man does nothing but complain. Wants to get back to the right side of Vicksburg so he can see his wife and family."

"If you want to release him," Richards ventured, "I will be glad to take him in the river flotilla."

"I will arrange it with the flag." The man smiled and leaned closer to Richards, a sly smile on his face. "To be fair, Farragut finds the Irishman a complete irritation. He will be more than happy to pass him on to you."

The mail boat came by late the next afternoon. Richards distributed the personal correspondence before going down to his cabin to read the official letters. The first was a note from Davis confirming Keeler's promoting. It would make the young man happy. The second was a more serious. Davis informed his officers of a new threat beyond the illness and the rebel batteries. A short way up the river lay the mouth of the Yazoo River. Somewhere along its length, a rebel ironclad was said to be completing.

Ironclad. The term struck a note of fear in his breast. It was a reminder of the action in March and no rationale could suppress it. Their guns were not meant to destroy iron ships. His shells reduced rebel gunboats to flaming ruins in minutes but were totally ineffective against armor. Now there was another iron sheathed monster waiting to descend upon them.

He sighed. They had the advantage of numbers, that was clear. And there were the rams, something else not present in Hampton Roads. Perhaps here they stood a chance against such a beast. He would see to *MACHNEEL*'s preparation in the morning.

The last item on his desk was of a more personal

nature. He recognized the handwriting immediately: a letter from Becky. The light in the cabin grew dim, and he lit a lamp before picking up the envelope.

My Darling John:

Since our parting in April, you have been uppermost in my thoughts. Please understand, dearest, that I do not wish to prevent you occupying the position of your choice in your chosen profession. But things were different before the war, and I have seen so many ruined men in this last year. The thought of it happening to you is more than I can bear.

I have heard from father and he informs me Captain Worden is doing well. His eyesight is much improved and it appears he will soon be getting a command in the Atlantic Squadron. Father sends you his regards.

Lorraine finds her pregnancy agreeable and she appears to glow. Somehow, she has avoided the plague so many women encounter when carrying a child. We believe the baby will arrive in early December, and I trust you will be as glad to see poor Rene's child as we. She prays for your safety, as do I.

I love you, John Richards, and that is all that must matter. I shall try to get west at the earliest convenience. Pray be safe and keep yourself from harm, for it would be my death if you were killed or injured.

With Love,

Becky

Rebecca. He checked the date of her letter, but it was posted before the letter he wrote the night they buried Crook. She had not seen that yet, but she was conciliatory. He hoped his words would add to her frame of mind. She was his wife now, not merely a prospective fiancé left behind. The memory of the few nights they spent together came back, the warmth of her body. His heart beat faster at the thought. He folded the page and put it into his breast pocket. Turning down the lamp, he left his cabin for the upper deck.

His wife. It was a new concept for him, to always have someone waiting for him. The thought that she feared for his life constantly had not occurred to him for it rarely pressed on his thoughts until an action was concluded. It was the risk posed by his trade and she must learn to accept it. But Becky had a mind of her own, and she was not afraid to try imposing her will over his. That was where the two of them ran into problems.

There remained a dim light from the sun, long set. The air was still and heavy and in the west rose the towering heads of thunderstorms, their backs lit by sunlight, faces etched in flashes of lightning. He slapped the back of his neck, killing a mosquito, and raising a wet sound from the sweaty skin.

Married less than four months and already there was trouble between them. Could he expect any difference in more peaceful times? He was a navy officer, as his father before him, and his before. He had never wanted anything else from life, with the possible exception of Rebecca Welles. *Was it possible he could not have both?* Their time together over the past year pointed might indicate such an outcome. He sighed.

Things would be no easier in peace. He would be gone, for years at a time possibly. And what would she think, alone with the children? The notion had not occurred before, but the fact appeared inevitable. His agitated mind suddenly focused on Lorraine and Rene's child. The baby would arrive fatherless and could very well grow up that way. It could as easily happen to a child of his.

He leaned on the rail and studied the storm clouds advancing upon the squadron. They would bring with them a welcome wash of fresh air. Their noise and light would keep the sick men awake during the night, so they were a mixed blessing. And the storms affected the next day, adding to the humidity and misery of the past weeks.

He doubted his reasons for getting married. It was a dangerous thought, but he could not ignore it. Was what he felt actually love or simply passion taking charge? And if the latter, then what? He mulled the idea of marriage through completely, considering all the ramifications. But like the war, it was too late to draw up short.

"Good evening, captain."

Keeler's young face could not be seen in the black night. An occasional flash of lightning revealed only a portion of his features in the shifting light.

"Good evening," he returned, his mind only partially withdrawn from the reverie. The interruption made him dimly aware of the sound of distant thunder.

"Sounds like a battle, doesn't it?"

"Aye." He leaned his back against the rail. "I have some good news for you, Mr. Keeler."

"Sir?"

"An order from the commodore in the afternoon dispatches. You are confirmed as an acting lieutenant."

Keeler smiled widely, his face slightly demonic in the flicker of lightning. "Thank you, captain," he said.

Another few dollars a month and a greater chance for death or injury. Other words came from his lips. "Your welcome, lieutenant. You have been working hard, and you deserve the opportunity."

Opportunity.

"I will try to live up to your faith in me, sir."

The voice sounded very young, a boy making a promise to his father. There was only ten years between them, but the gulf of experience was much wider. At his age, mused Richards, he had been at sea for two years. Still, it was not quite the same as fighting the people who were only the neighbors across the river eighteen months before.

There was danger in these thoughts, too. Keeler was a young, likeable boy. There was an image of the youngster, his face ashen, being wrapped in canvas. Richards tried to dismiss it - think of it as simply part of his job. There was a crash of thunder overhead and the splat of large drops on water.

"I believe I shall turn in rather than get wet, Mr. Keeler."

"Aye, sir. See you in the morning."

Richards nodded. "Yes. In the morning."

The bells of the dogwatch were ringing, the sound crisp and clear in the damp, cool air. True, the sound of thunder was still in the distance but was receding. The skyline behind Vicksburg was marked by the lightning. Richards stood at the small window in his cabin, drinking in the fresh air as it blew into the stale interior. There was a flash and a roar from much closer, and it was not thunder.

Low on the river, one of the first batteries on the south edge of the Vicksburg chain was firing. It was joined by others along the bluffs, winking pricks of light, followed by the crash of a gun. And in the intermittent flashes of guns and lightning, there was a sight to hold a man speechless. The masts of the Gulf Squadron were clear, advancing against the current.

The firing from Vicksburg was ragged but general. It was easy to imagine the rebels, laboring on wet firing platforms against the weight of their weapons. Men loading and discharging the guns as fast as their strength would allow. The whole bluff was alive with the flashes. From a distance, it was like a swarm of fireflies, dancing and sparkling in the night. Richards was not fooled by the deceptive appearance.

Instead, death issued from the guns. There was, occasionally, the sight of a splash when a shell hit the water in time with the flare of a gun. More often was the deep red growl of an explosion when a shell burst in the air between gun and target. The rebels would not let this attempt go unpunished.

As for the ships, they moved steadily upstream. The entire profile would become visible, burned into the eye by the discharge of a broadside. It was even possible to discern there were two ships moving, side by side, instead of just single vessels.

The view of the river was visible for only a brief while. Smoke from stacks and guns intermingled, laying a dense blanket across the water. The wind blew towards the opposite shore, and the layer of smoke first dimmed, then almost completely hid the flash of the rebel guns.

But the lead ship (it could only be *HARTFORD*) was usually in the clear. The firing from the rebel guns stretched before it along the bank, until the sloop reached the sharp turn of the bend. It rounded to, pointing its bow at the waiting river flotilla. It was then obvious the two ships were not just near one another. The vessels were actually lashed together, making one large, strange ship to fight the flowing current.

One by one, the pairs made it around the painful curve in the river's course. Over an hour later, the first was joining their waiting comrades in the river squadron. Thirty minutes after that, the last weathered the point and the deed was done.

There was still firing from the rebels. At least one pair of ships drifted back down the river, its course marked by the explosion of their broadside and the burst of rebel shells. And then they, too, were clear. The rebel firing drifted into silence. There was only a very slight, distant rumble of thunder. Lightning was no longer visible in the pall of smoke over the besieged city. The Gulf Squadron had joined forces with the Western Flotilla.

Mortar boats both north and south of the river beat at

the fortress with little visible effect. The presence of the heavy, ocean-going vessels north of the city did not change the situation one iota.

Richards straightened his uniform coat and placed his cap on his head. He sweated copiously under the wool uniform, but had to look his best this morning. He was summoned to the *BENTON* to confer with Davis. He could not be sure why, but it probably dealt with the flag captain had offered at their brief meeting.

His boat crew mumbled complaints about the heat as he climbed down to their longboat. They quieted, but only slowly. They were afraid and it was a fear deeper than rebel cannon. A full third of the crew was ashore with the fever and several on board had it. The sailors could face a shelling like men, but this unseen killer in their midst wore them all down.

BENTON was a short stroke away, and Richards released the boat to return to *MACHINEEL*. He did not know how long the interview would take and could not see keeping the men sitting in the sun for any length of time. They were but a signal and a few minutes away, and it was best to protect those that still maintained their health.

He was greeted at the entry port and stepped aboard the flagship with a salute to the stern. Up the ladder at the rear slope of the casemate, he joined Davis under the ever present awning.

"Have a seat," said Davis, amiable even with the heat. "I have received word from Farragut that he will transfer the officer from *HARTFORD*."

"That is good news, sir." He took the offered drink from the porter. It was only water with lemon juice but it helped a bit against the heat. "I must say, though," he continued more seriously, "if losses due to the fever continue to mount, I shan't have enough hands to work the ship!"

Davis nodded in agreement. "Too true of the entire squadron." Towards Vicksburg, a mortar shell exploded close above one of the gun works. "This damnable place," he cursed. "We cannot hurt them, and they sit up there watching us die. I wish we could move back north to patrol the river!"

"I agree, sir." There was little use railing against the climate, even if it were an aid to their enemies and killing more men than the rebel shells.

"Now this bloody ram. ARKANSAS, it is called," said Davis. He waved a hand to stop Richards' reply. "I know I told you all not to worry about the damned thing, but I certainly do! Every day, I get more and more reports of how it is nearing completion; how it will take the combined squadrons and sink us all. Every story is wilder than the last!"

"Iron ships can present a terrible danger, commodore."

Davis paused, considering the opinion. "Ah yes, you have had first hand experience. Well, we have our own iron ships," he said, tapping his foot on the wood of the deck. "But no single vessel could engage this entire fleet, no matter how well built or how cleverly handled." A shell burst in the distance to punctuate his sentence. "I shall have to send a couple of the boats north to deal with this threat."

"It is a prudent course." Richards moved to change the subject. "Did the flag officer indicate when he would send the pilot over?"

"You can ask him yourself, if you like," said Davis. He pulled out his watch and glanced at the time. "He shall be here within a few minutes." Davis stood and stretched, then indicated a boat moving towards the BENTON. "Doubtless, that is him now. I am taking him to the first line of batteries to have a shoot. It will give him an idea of what we do here on the river. In fact," continued Davis, buttoning his coat and retrieving his hat, "I would like you to accompany us."

"Honored, sir."

Davis smiled. "I want to give you an idea of ironclad fighting, Commander Richards. If something should happen to one of the boat commanders, I think the posting would be more suitable to your rank and experience."

Richards could not deny the truth of Davis's statement but found himself rebelling against the idea. The homesickness brought about by Farragut's ships made him all the more determined to get an ocean assignment. Moreover, what would his friend Erben think if he received command of an ironclad that was denied to him.

"Thank you for your consideration, commodore," he answered, leaving his concerns unvoiced.

Farragut's barge bumped alongside at the appointed time. The old man was welcomed aboard with a flitter of pipes, an infrequent honor accorded in the river fleet. Davis led him to the ward room and offered him some of the lemonade.

"I have given the order to clear for action," he informed the distinguished visitor. There could be little doubt, given the amount of noise and commotion within the confines of the casemate. Farragut jumped at the sound of something heavy striking the deck above his head.

"What the hell was that?" he demanded.

"We only carry planking on the upper deck, sir," said Davis, personally refilling the flag officer's glass. "When going into action where we might encounter plunging fire, we place every spare bit of material there to help provide protection."

Farragut snorted. "Seems a damn silly waste to me."

The sounds died away and Davis led the men into the casemate. Farragut, tall and slim, was forced to bend even lower beneath the deck beams than Richards. The gun crews stood to their weapons, so still they seemed posed. After a quick review of the guns, Davis took them to the pilothouse.

The pilothouse sat well forward on the vessel. Just aft, black smoke issued from the stacks as steam was raised.

Richards gulped in excitement at the immediate prospect of action.

"Visibility is a bit restricted here, because of the iron plates," explained Davis. "It makes the position less vulnerable, which is important when the shells fly thick."

Farragut glanced nervously around the confines of the pilothouse. "Bit small in here, wouldn't you say?"

"I would prefer an open deck myself," Davis returned, "but this is where I must be during the course of the action." He pointed down the river to where the land just started curving round the bend. "We will head down there today, sir. There is a five gun battery right at water level. We will move in bow first and engage it. With a bit of luck, we might silence it in an hour or two."

Phelps got the ship under way. While so occupied, Farragut directed his attention to Richards.

"You are a salt water man by nature are you not, commander?"

"Aye, sir, and I plan to be again."

The old flag officer smiled. "Good lad. I do not trust these damned contraptions. Not the least bit. I will be glad to be retired from navy before it is taken over by their like."

The ship started down, the wheels actually moving in reverse to slow their advance with the current. To a landsman, such a vessel seemed to have only one large wheel. In reality, there were two side by side, each driven by a different engine. Though not as effective in maneuvering the vessel as side wheels, it did improve the vessel's handling considerably.

"A thousand yards, commodore," informed Phelps, before returning to his duties.

The announcement was unnecessary, for the rebels made it known. They started a slow and deliberate fire on the gunboat. Water rose in spouts alongside where shots plunged in, or splashed as others skipped past. The was a metallic crash forward as a shot hit the forward plates and ricocheted into the air. Richards had expected a feeling of invulnerability in the armored gunboat, but nothing was further from the truth.

"You may commence firing at 500 yards, captain," instructed Davis. Phelps responded with a nervous nod. "We hold the ship steady against the current," Davis explained, an instructor to two new pupils. "Backing is not the best method, but it is better than anchoring in a single spot where their gunners can mark the range."

"Of course," agreed Farragut.

There was a roar beneath them. A geyser of dirt was raised ashore near the earthworks when the shell exploded. The next three guns fired in succession, and the face of the gun emplacement disappeared in the dirt and smoke. Still, flashes from the rebel guns announced their ability to function.

"Fair shooting, sir," said Farragut, examining the target with his glass. Every three to four minutes, the guns would fire. Each time, the rebel position was smothered by the flying dirt and shell splinters.

All this while, the guns ashore were not silent. Shells fell about *BENTON*, though few struck. Those that did either hit a glancing blow on the side or simply struck the armored bow plates and bounced off.

Farragut moved nervously about the room, glancing through the slits at the action outside. Richards did not believe him to be afraid, simply confined by the limits of the pilothouse.

Suddenly, the small room was alive with noise. There was the sound of splintered metal and wood as something crashed past them. There was the whine of splinters in the air. Before any of the men could react, it was over.

The helmsman lay on the deck, screaming. His right foot

was gone at the ankle. Richards reached forward for the wheel and Phelps pulled the man back. A large hole in the side of the pilothouse and another in the deck showed where the shot made its entrance and exit.

"Are you all right?" asked Davis, stepping quickly to Farragut.

"Damned iron coffin," hissed Farragut. He wrenched the door open. "I will take my chances on the deck, thank you!" He went aft to pace before the wheelhouse.

"Relief, sir."

Another seaman was there, pointedly ignoring the injured man as he was carried from the room and taken below. Richards turned the wheel over to the waiting man.

"I will go out and keep the flag officer company, if I might," he announced, also stepping to the door.

"As you will, commander," returned Davis. He pulled out his watch. The exchange had progressed for almost two hours. Now, only an occasional shot returned from the battery that was their target.

Richards fell in step next to Farragut, dodging the material scattered about the upper works of the vessel.

"Damned silly way to fight, if you ask me!" grumbled the old man. "Never heard of such a thing for an officer. Stay in the pilothouse during an engagement! Ridiculous."

"Aye, sir," said Richards, having difficulty maintaining the pace set by the older officer.

"Out here to keep an eye on the old fool?"

"No, sir. I just thought you might enjoy my company better than rebel shells."

Farragut grunted. "Do not take my comments wrong, Mr. Richards. The flotilla has done a splendid job thus far. This is just not my style of fighting. Give me an open deck and a frigate any day!"

Richards remembered the days on the blockade. It was hot, though not this stifling blanket of heat. There was action, at least some of the time. And there was prize money to be had, a welcome addition to his meager income. Nothing similar was to be found on the dirty brown waters of the Mississippi.

"How long do you plan to stay, sir?" prompted Richards.

"I do not know. However long it takes - or until the river drops."

The land was moving past them now as Phelps backed his vessel up the river. At best, it was a difficult maneuver, but better than turning the unarmored stern towards the batteries. Once out of range, the BENTON swung with the current and faced her bow upstream.

Davis approached the two men. "That is enough of a shoot for today."

"How is the wounded man?" asked Farragut.

"The surgeon gives him a good chance. At least as good as any of us in this damned climate!"

"My men have been getting word on a rebel ironclad, commodore," continued the flag officer. "What plans do you have for it?"

Davis smiled carefully. "The young commander and I were discussing just that subject before you arrived, sir. I will dispatch a patrol up the Yazoo within the next few days to deal with this ram."

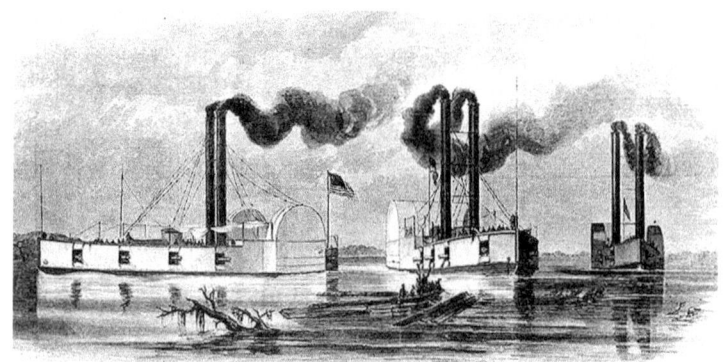

Gunboats *TYLER, LEXINGTON* and *CONESTOGA*

CHAPTER TEN

MACHINEEL slowly baked in the bright, noonday sun. The interior of the ship was an oven, hot and still. The men vacated it for positions on deck, but it was little better. Tarpaulins were rigged both fore and aft, as well as across the upper deck. The crew sat or lay quietly, keeping in the shade with little sound or movement.

"Boilers completely shut down, cap'n," said Anson. His face was pale, his brow dotted with sweat.

"Thank you, Jeremy," said Richards. He gestured to the small table. "Have a drink of lemonade, if you like. All the ice is gone, but it is still a bit cool."

Anson did not reply but reached for the pitcher. Richards did not blame him, for none of the men had energy for any but the most necessary activity.

"How long to relight if we must?"

Anson gulped down a glass and poured another. "Couple hours at least." He took another drink. "Mebe one an' a half, ifn' we push it."

"Very well."

"The temperature in the fire room's over a hundred and twenty, cap'n. An' that's with the boilers off!"

Richards nodded, his strength drained in the heat. "I will not ask it unless it is necessary."

"Any more word on that reb ironclad?" Richards just shook his head. "I hear she's got ten inches of iron plate and twenty guns."

The captain snorted. "I doubt it, Mr. Anson. She would draw about thirty feet with a load like that."

"It's what I heard, cap'n." He set the empty glass down. "Thanks." Richards waved a hand in acknowledgement as Anson withdrew.

Ironclads and heat: it was all they experienced the past week. He sat on the chair, wearing his uniform pants but no coat. His shirt was unbuttoned to the waist and he dabbed at the sweat on his face and chest with a damp handkerchief. A mortar banged in the distance, the sound was flat and strange in the still air. Any more, the sound stirred no thought of excitement. It was simply another part of this drab existence.

He roused himself to his feet, a difficult and slow process. He strolled forward, careful to stay within the shade provided by the tarp. The crew lay about listlessly, only the occasional swat at a fly or shift into a more comfortable position indicating they were even alive. Little more than than two-thirds of the men were still aboard, and many of those were unfit for duty. The rest were either ashore or dead. The squadron's burial plot on the Louisiana side of the river grew daily.

He leaned against a stack and stared upstream. If there was an ironclad building up there, she was biding her time. Whether incomplete or waiting, they did not know. The rebel captain did not have to do much. If he put off his attack for two weeks, this heat would do his work for him.

The ships huddled densely north of the Vicksburg bend,

all manner to be seen. Ironclads and gunboats, sloops and tugs, transports and rams: they all had a place. Only one or two carried steam. It was not unusual; the boiler room temperatures easily reached a hundred fifty with the fires lit. Richards had finally given up any thought of maintaining such preparedness just that morning.

The ironclad was said to be named *ARKANSAS*. The stories about the vessel were wildly divergent. Anson's thoughts were on one end of the spectrum. There were others which said the ship was still on the stocks. Most of their information came from contrabands, slaves who escaped from their masters to seek the protection of the union ships. For all their wish to help, the blacks did little more than confuse and muddle the issue.

Hampton Roads returned to his mind. It came back regularly, without conscious effort. With the exception of the eight iron gunboats, all their ships were wooden. Even their so-called ironclads were only partially so. Would they be able to stand up to a fully armored ship?

The comparison with the events in March was not fully fair. If the single rebel ship dared to appear, there were dozens of ships able to move and run it down. It was not at all like the Roads, where events left only one ship in a position to battle the attacker. He still did not sleep well because of thoughts of that one ship. What would he do here, if the rebel ship came down? The answer was clear.

"Captain?" The words took a moment to intrude into his thoughts.

"Yes, Mr. Keeler?"

"Boat headin' our way, sir. Looks like they's got an officer aboard."

He followed the young man aft. The men at the oars of the approaching boat were stripped to the waist, their backs glistening from the sweat of their exertions. They bumped up to the entry port of the gunboat and an officer stepped across, wearing the river mix of civilian and military dress.

His kit bag followed him quickly and the boat pushed off to return to the *HARTFORD*. It was not a matter of dislike, simply one of survival. The sooner the boat returned to its position at the davits, the sooner the crew would be released to the shade.

"Volunteer Lt. Morgan Woodard," announced the man after a casual salute to the stern. He touched his cap to Richards, and the commander returned it. The newcomer's voice revealed a distinct brogue.

"Would you see Mr. Woodard's things to his cabin, Mr. Keeler?" Richards directed. He did not wait for a reply, but turned to the steps leading to the upper deck. "Please join me above, Mr. Woodard."

He regained his seat, and gestured for Woodard to take the one opposite. Pouring them each a glass of tepid lemonade, he leaned back. "Your orders, please," he asked, extending his hand.

The other officer reached into the interior of his coat pocket. His coat was of a decidedly civilian cut, his head was topped by a Panama skimmer. He was older, probably in his late forties, with a close-cropped beard with gray streaks. After giving the envelope to Richards, he took the offered glass of refreshment.

"Do you mind if I remove me coat, captain?" he asked, regarding Richards' dress.

"I would think you insane if you do not." He opened the envelope. There was only a single sheet enclosed, the words simple and formal. Even Farragut must be finding the heat oppressive enough to limit the length of a dispatch in such a fashion. "Everything is in order, Mr. Woodard."

"Morgan, please," returned Woodard. He, too, produced a handkerchief to absorb the plentiful perspiration from his body. "I am not much on all your navy rigmarole."

"Indeed." The man opposite him was perhaps fifteen or twenty years his senior. None the less, he presented a straight and robust appearance. And contrasting with Crook, he was neat and well trimmed, quite different from the other men who had come with *MACHINEEL*. "I understand you have family in Missouri."

"Aye, I do." Woodard sipped at his glass. "Me wife is in St. Louis. I have been a river pilot for the best part of twenty years. Been workin' on the river since first settin' foot in your country, more than thirty years past."

"Ireland, I presume," ventured Richards, based on the accent.

"Aye, indeed."

"What sort of craft did you pilot?"

Woodard regarded his surroundings. "Nothing quite as small as this barge, captain," he answered. "Passenger boats, mostly. Gamblin' boats on occasion. That was how I ended in New York when this whole thing started."

"I do not know that I understand that, Mr. Woodard."

"Morgan, I insist." Woodard drained his glass and grabbed the pitcher. The remnants flowed into his glass as Keeler reappeared. "I piloted one of the last river steamers to New Orleans, you see. When things got hot, I took an ocean steamer east, figurin' I could make me way back home on the train. Seems the army is bein' a might particular on who gets to ride these days. Before I knew it, Captain Porter was organizin' mortar boats for assaultin' New Orleans. It seemed the best way to get back here, so I volunteered like. Then they found I was a pilot. The next thing I knows, I'm on me way up the river."

Woodard drained his glass. Richards considered interrupting the man, but several of the crewman were already listening to the tale. Entertainment in any form was hard to find, and these same men would have to depend on Woodard for their safety. It did not hurt to let him ramble. It might also save the time of repetition later.

"Runnin' those forts at New Orleans was an exhiliratin'

experience...what did you say your first name was?" he asked, pausing in mid-sentence.

"John."

"And you, lad?" he requested of Keeler.

"Cole."

"Short for Colby?"

Keeler drew himself upright. "Colburn," he responded with dignity.

Woodard nodded with a smile. "Aye, laddie. Anyway, as I was sayin'... exhiliratin'! We passed the fort with guns firin' and boats a blazin'. *HARTFORD* had a fire boat shoved up against it by a rebel tug," he said, pointing to Farragut's flagship. "But the old man, he just as coolly shouts 'Shove it away, boys. There's a hotter fire than that awaitin' ya'!' Might have been out for Sunday dinner, he might!"

He paused in the story for the expected laughter and was not disappointed. Woodard was a man with a gift of gab, and easily found listeners aboard the gunboat. Richards was not yet decided whether it was an advantage or a problem.

"Then we comes up to New Orleans," continued the Irishman. "A sight from hell greeted us, and I can say there wasn't a man in the fleet who wasn't afraid. A giant ironclad comes at us, fire a shootin' from it and guns afirin' every which way. But them rebels, they wasn't aboard. Burned it themselves, lest we take her north and turn her into a real fightin' ship," he pronounced, again raising some chuckles amongst the crew.

"We have seen a bit of that ourselves," responded Richards.

"Aye, sir, I am sure ye' have. But anyway, since then, we have just been experiencin' a pleasant summer's cruise north along the river, until we made your acquaintance. Well, pleasant exceptin' the snipers and cannon, of course."

"And how did you come aboard *HARTFORD*?" It did not

occur to Richards, as he listened to his new officer, that he failed to take notice of the heat for the first time in days.

"Well, captain, I was an extra pilot on the ol' *HARTFORD*. The main man went and got himself shot passin' them forts. So I gets to take his place, not knowin' he wasn't goin' to die on 'em, you see. Then George up and gets well, and I am second man agin and still needin' to get back north!"

Richards chuckled. "Well, Mr. Woodard, you will be the first man for *MACHINEEL*." He realized he was warming to the openness of the pilot, and he had to summon his energy to close off the feeling. "Providing we leave this god forsaken place behind and get back up north."

"Aye, captain, that's exactly why I took the position when it was offered. I would like to see the missus agin. Been over a year, you know." He chuckled to himself. "Not that I have been totally lonesome, ya' understand." Again, the remark drew further laughter. He continued in a more serious vein. "And I have got boys of fightin' age, captain. I need to know what's happened to 'em."

"We shall let you find out, Mr. Woodard, as soon as we are sent up that way."

"Morgan, please, sir," he said again.

Richards looked to his younger lieutenant. "Mr. Keeler, show Mr. Woodard his quarters and let him get settled in."

Keeler touched his cap. "Aye, sir."

Woodard shoved himself from his chair. "Thankee, captain. Lead the way, laddie!" he instructed. With his coat draped over his shoulder and his hat at a rakish angle, he followed the officer below.

Richards watched the man for a moment, unsure how to take him. His good humor was a welcome change to the dreary days they faced. At first glance, it was an immense improvement over the morose Crook. But good humor was not necessarily an asset in combat. He resolved to have a few words privately with Woodard at the earliest convenience.

The evening dinner in the wardroom was simple. Some canned meat, beans and biscuit, all served cold. Cold was not completely correct either. Rather, the food was unheated. Even emersion in the river for the better part of the day did little to reduce the canned goods' temperature much.

Woodard impressed the crewmen, raising laughter with his stories and jovial nature. Richards watched the man in action, perceiving much of it was a facade he affected, hiding feelings of a deeper nature. And those feelings were revealed in momentary glances of his blue eyes whenever the subject of his family was broached. *There* was something which affected this man deeply.

The night wore quickly and the men found spots to attempt sleep. Most did so on the forward or upper decks, leaving the interior to roast in empty silence. Even when the ever present thunderstorms roared across the river, the men remained outside, accepting the rain as a refreshing shower to cool them, no matter how briefly.

The upper deck around the pilothouse was a different matter. There, the business of the ship transpired, regardless of heat or storms, light or dark. Watches were stood and a lookout maintained. Richards led Woodard to that mostly empty space, where he could speak in relative privacy outside the stifling warmth of his quarters and the wardroom. He offered the acting lieutenant his tobacco pouch, but it was declined politely as Woodard withdrew a cigar and lit it.

"We need to speak on shipboard matters, Mr. Woodard," opened Richards quietly. He remained relaxed, leaning across the rail and observing the fall of shells above Vicksburg.

"Morgan, I insist!" he replied.

"This is the navy, Mr. Woodard. The correct manner of addressing you is as mister or lieutenant. I shall use one or the other."

"As you please, cap'n," he said, some of his exuberance subdued.

"I would also request you refer to Mr. Keeler with either of those terms. 'Laddie' does not cut it."

"But he is just a lad, sir. There cannot be no harm..."

Richards cut him off. "He is an officer aboard this vessel," he said, his words stronger. "The men must follow his orders and his lead. And since they must do as he orders, live or die, you must take him seriously also. Is that clear?"

"I believe so, captain."

The words were stern. Richards relit his pipe and held out the match for Woodard to do the same for his cigar. The man leaned forward, puffing tentatively on the tobacco.

"We are fighting a war, lieutenant. Pleasant anecdotes aside, things have been a bit rough around here of late."

Woodard drew on his cigar and blew out a smoke ring in a cavalier manner. "I have seen your type quite a bit the past year, John," he said, his voice lapsing into the easy going mannerism. "Now, I have never been one to pass up a good fight, particularly one of this magnitude. But do not ask me to do it as a gloomy sort, even if you are set on it! I haven't spent fifty years livin' that way and I do not intend dyin' that way!"

"Fair enough, Mr. Woodard," returned Richards. "You have given these men a spark of life, something they badly need against this climate. I truly appreciate that. Just make sure it does not interfere with running the ship!"

"Fair enough, captain."

Woodard oversaw the ritual of holystoning the deck. He

regaled the crewmen with his stories, raising laughter as they went about the daily chore. All were usually chuckling when dismissed for breakfast, which was little more than repeats of their previous meals.

Richards observed the process with interest. The men found Woodard easygoing, one of their own kind. The pilot was able to strike a balance between their civilian expectations and the navy lifestyle that he had not been able to achieve. It was something the gunboat needed. But despite his jocularity with the men, Woodard abided by Richards' instructions regarding Keeler. He used either of the appropriate titles, though occasionally referring to the young man by his first name. It was a lapse Richards found tolerable and not destructive of the new lieutenant's authority. The captain also found time to wonder how the new officer would deal with the deaths of some of these same men when the next battle came.

"Where they be goin'?" asked Woodard as the men went below.

Three boats moved north, breasting the current as best they could. The first was an ironclad, recognizable as *CARONDOLET* from her lack of funnel bands. Behind her was the *TYLER*, one of the original wooden gunboats of the Western Flotilla. Lastly came an army ram. The "Q" suspended between her stacks proclaimed her *QUEEN OF THE WEST*.

"To the Yazoo, Mr. Woodard. Checking on the rebel ironclad." Davis had finally ordered the ships north to confirm or deny the rumored threat.

The two officers watched the boats head up river and disappear beyond the bend. Their locations were still marked by the columns of black smoke from their stacks.

"'Appears like enough for one rebel gunboat," Woodard commented. The horizon grew brighter with each passing minute. Soon, the sun would break out and it would go from hot to miserable. "Any orders for today, cap'n?" he asked.

"What is the muster?" asked Richards.

"'bout fifty-five," responded the first. "Just half of normal."

"Exactly half." Of the other half of the crew, twenty would never return to the vessel. The rest lay ashore in army hospitals, their continued existence simply a matter of time and strength. "Keep the men rested. We might try a gun drill tonight, if it looks like the evening will be cool enough."

"Aye." Woodard touched his cap and started to turn.

"And, lieutenant," said Richards, before the man could leave, "you have been doing an excellent job. Thank you for joining us."

"I am glad I meet your *standards*, sir," returned Woodard with an impish grin.

Richards smiled in return. "Perhaps you simply show how far my standards have fallen, Mr. Woodard."

A steward appeared with a plate of cold beans and biscuit, plus the inevitable lemonade. Richards took his time with the meal. Indeed, there was little reason to hurry. The ship remained stationary, day after day. The meals were monotonous. Even training was largely forsaken to spare the men the rigors of the climate. It was not a happy existence.

He finished the meager breakfast slowly, preferring the liquid refreshment to the substance on the plate. He pushed it to the side of the table for the steward to remove. At the same instant, he became aware of a distance boom. Given the climate, he at first thought it thunder. The idea was quickly dispelled. Woodard appeared on deck, followed closely by Keeler. They gathered at the bow, facing upriver and discussing this turn of events.

"What might it be, captain?" asked Keeler earnestly.

Woodard shrugged to confess ignorance, but there could be little doubt of the source.

"Must be the gunboats," concluded Richards. "Maybe

they have run into some sniping from shore."

As with any other noteworthy event of the past three weeks, it gave the men something beyond worrying about heat and fever. Woodard and Keeler remained, each voicing his thoughts on the continued cannoning.

"One thing's certain," noted Woodard, his head cocked. "They're gettin' closer."

Richards tipped his head. It was true; the sound appeared to be growing. "That *is* odd," he commented, his heat dulled senses making no connection with the fact. "They were heading upstream, to check out this *ARKANSAS* business. Even if sniped at, they would just fire some shots in reply and finish the task."

Another, dimmer sound intruded and grew from the north. It was a shrill, high pitched screech. "One of 'ems soundin' her whistle," said Woodard. "And they're definitely headin' this way."

It was unlikely for the ships to return so quickly. It slowly dawned they must have completed their assignment, only sooner than expected. They were with engaged the rebel ironclad and withdrawing to the support of the fleet. The thoughts flashed through his mind, followed by the knowledge *MACHINEEL* was in no condition for a fight. With the crew so badly depleted, they would be lucky to work more than one or two guns if called upon. Yet, it was where the facts pointed. And with a fight rushing down on them, it did not matter to their enemy whether they were prepared or not.

"Mr. Keeler, my compliments to the engineer. Have him light off the boilers."

"In this heat?" questioned Woodard.

"If I am not mistaken, it will be a might warmer yet this morning," he replied. "Split the men between two of the guns and the boilers, Mr. Woodard. Be ready to swap them out as needed." He paused, looking to his two officers. "Get to quarters, gentlemen!"

It was a long process. Smoke rose quickly from the stacks, but it was of little use for the boilers were totally cold. In the meantime, the few men detailed to the guns went about the job of sanding the decks and storing everything they could out of harms way. They grumbled loudly at the exercise and more than one collapsed from heat prostration.

Richards kept his few crewmen at it. The big gun forward was manned, as well as one of the thirty-two's. Beyond that, there was little to be done. The rest of the guns were loaded with shot, which would at least let them fire once from each. But the activity, usually done in a few minutes, was still progressing an hour later when the QUEEN appeared around the bend, her whistle shrill in the hot air.

"Give me our status!" he demanded through the speaking tube.

Anson replied, obviously worn despite the distortions of the tinny voice. "Enough to move her, cap'n. That's about it."

"Stand by."

"What are you going to say if this is for nothin'?" asked Woodard.

"I will give the crew the rest of the day off," shot back Richards.

The sound of firing was very close, and the TYLER came around the bend, her wheels madly thrashing the water and here whistle sounding shrilly in the hot, stagnant air. A third vessel was marked by a column of thinner, whitish smoke.

"The next one is the rebel," he deduced aloud.

"How..."

"She is burning wood!" He bent to the tube. "Engage the engines, Mr. Anson." To the gun crew forward, he shouted "Cut the cable!"

"The *TYLER*'s just escorting a prize," insisted Woodard.

"The *prize* is still firing, Mr. Woodard!"

The third ship appeared, a low, brownish-red vessel of peculiar shape. Forward, two guns thundered after *TYLER*. At the bow, a flag with red and white stripes and a blue canton flew from a makeshift staff.

THE CONFEDERATE RAM "ARKANSAS" RUNNING THROUGH THE UNION FLEET AT VICKSBURG, JULY 15, 1862.

C.S.S ARKANSAS engages the Union fleet

CHAPTER ELEVEN

"All ahead!"

The rebel ship proceeded down the right bank of the river, close to the large ships of Farragut's squadron. *MACHINEEL*'s wheels turned slowly with the low pressure in the boilers. It was barely sufficient to hold the gunboat against the current. Nevertheless, Richards ordered her into the river against the oncoming ram.

There was no fear in Richards' heart at the sight of the rebel. His thoughts and doubts previous to that moment were swept away by the sound of guns firing and the pounding of his heart. He hardly realized he was outside the pilothouse, shouting orders to the men on the deck below.

The *ARKANSAS* fired steadily at the union vessels, for she was in an unenviable position. Her commander could hold no fear of striking a friend in error, for every way she faced lay only vessels of the Union fleet. Only one other besides *MACHINEEL* moved. The rest lay still, the stacks only starting to issue smoke as the engineers lit the fires. *MACHINEEL* approached the rebel bow on, the water around her rising under the fall of shots from both friend and foe.

"Hold your fire until we are upon her!" shouted Richards, using his trumpet to be heard above the crescendo of cannon fire. The forward gun captain waved a hand in acknowledgement, the men struggling to keep the gun trained on the ram as the vessels neared one another.

The air above the gunboat was alive with shot, for many of the Union ships were firing with no clear target in sight. To add to the clamor, the rebel batteries downstream commenced to shoot, even though none of the ships were within range.

The ram came on, its sides constantly marked from the flashes of her own guns and the burst of Union shells. Richards shouted for the helmsman to steer closer and the gunboat moved further into the river. They were alongside and the order to fire was all but lost in the roar *MACHINEEL*'s two starboard guns.

"Man the port guns!" he shouted above the din.

ARKANSAS scraped down their side, the top of the vessel clearly visible from the upper deck. Richards cursed aloud, for they could have boarded easily were there enough men and time for preparation. The rebel was passed, its guns silent during the entire time of its transit. Even as they cleared her stern, *ARKANSAS*'s guns roared out at other vessels. It did not occur to Richards they were spared severe punishment simply by the rebels being occupied in reloading.

"Port your helm and steer for her again, Levenson." The ship turned slowly, drifting sideways as the current caught them and pushed them along.

There was a crash forward and the starboard stack leaned drunkenly, cleanly severed just above deck level. It tilted, falling over the side and dragging the other stack from its base. Enough guidelines were still intact to keep the port from following its brother completely. The smoke, moments before sent into space ten feet clear of the deck, now swept back to surround the pilothouse in choking fumes. And the wheels, just gathering speed with the steam pressure, slowed noticeably as the draft fell off.

"What was that?" asked Richards as the helmsman called to him.

"Anson, captain!" the man returned.

He leaned over the speaking tube. "What is it?"

"The men have collapsed! I can't keep up the fires!"

"Try!" His head snapped up to the helmsman. "Steer after her!"

"I can't maintain a draft and the smoke is backing into the engine room!" continued Anson,

In confirmation, hatches opened and men stumbled onto the deck. Coal smoke came from all the open hatches and gun ports. The wheels slowed as the steam pressure died, moving only in fitful spurts. The firing moved downriver with the ARKANSAS, which was already several hundred yards ahead. The wheels jerked to a stop and the gunboat drifted sideways in the current.

"After her, sir?" questioned Levenson. He spun the wheel helplessly in both directions, but the unmanageable ship did not respond.

Woodard appeared at the pilothouse, coughing from the mixture of coal and gun smoke surrounding the deck. "We cannot give chase, captain!" he shouted, the words rising above the din about them. "With the stacks damaged, we'd never make it back against the current. Their batteries will smash us for sure!"

Richards gripped the railing and watched the ram move past the rest of the fleet. "We cannot let her go! If we do not stop her, she will be a danger to the ships below the point!"

Woodard grabbed his shoulder hard and turned him from the rebel ship. "We'd never make it!" The words were only a bit above normal speaking tones, but came clearly. Their eyes met and locked for a long moment. "We'll be killed, and that ram will be just as dangerous after we're sunk."

Richards pulled himself from Woodard's grasp. He followed the progress of the ram for a moment, watching the shells fall about the lone Union ironclad in pursuit.

"Have the engineer secure the fires," he said at length. "Drop anchor and see to the repairs, Mr. Woodard."

Woodard had not taken his eyes from the young commander and his reply was a long time coming.

"Aye aye, captain."

It was not even noon when Davis called for the captains to repair on board. *CARONDOLET* had limped in a half hour before, badly shot up. There were viible holes in her side as well as broken armor plates. The davits on the ironclad were smashed, the boats hanging from them a collection of splintered planks. *BENTON* had to send a boat to retrieve her captain.

Richards sat in the stern sheets quietly, his eyes on the flagship, as he was rowed across. Farragut's captains also proceeded to the *BENTON*. Though the senior officer, the admiral accepted the riverboat had more room for such a meeting. A glance at *MACHINEEL* showed one stack already returned to the proper location and the other being worked on. The damage, for all its dire effect on the ship's performance, would be made good before nightfall.

There was time to think of the fast action while approaching the flagship. *MACHINEEL* managed to get into the fight when only two other captains in the fleet accomplished the feat. But he wondered at his order to pursue. It was not a reasonable request: the ship was clearly crippled and incapable of complying. Yet the words came from his mouth. When Woodard grabbed him, he was ready to strike the other officer. He rubbed his eyes, mopping his brow in the heat. Perhaps he *was* still the hot blooded young lieutenant of the year before.

Aboard *BENTON*, the officers gathered on the upper deck. Erben stood to one side, a telescope trained across the headland at Vicksburg. Spying him, Richards walked over.

"Sharp action, John," Erben commented. His eye remained fixed on the rebel city.

"Aye." Erben offered him the glass. "She's right across there," he said, pointing. "Just at the main quay."

A blurred image of the ram swam into view, but it was not possible to clarify it any further. Many forms swarmed about the vessel, like an anthill someone had kicked.

"Taking off the dead and wounded, I would venture." Erben retrieved the instrument and aimed it again. "You could see the blood draining from one of her scuppers." He snapped the glass shut and turned his attention to Richards. "One of our shots went clear through the side of the beast! The one from your forward gun did the same. It burst on our side of the reb!" He chuckled at the thought. "Cut the fuse a bit shorted when you lay yourself alongside like that, John."

"I will try to remember, Henry." He collected a glass from a passing steward. Surprisingly, it was wine and it was even pleasantly cool. "Did you loose any men?"

"Nothing came near us. And you?"

"We were lucky." He paused, unsure as to what his comment referred. Was it the fact the ram's guns did not fire while they were alongside, or that Woodard's good sense prevailed at the pilothouse? "Not so much as a splinter."

Erben gestured towards *CARONDOLET*. "Old Henry was not so fortunate. Twenty dead, I hear. Fought a down river battle with the secesh shooting into his stern the whole time. The steering was shot away three times."

"And Walke?"

Erben smiled. "I do not believe these rebels have made the bullet to kill him yet, John. That ornery old man will probably see us both into our graves."

Richards took another drink of wine. "He is quite the terror of the river.

"Gentlemen, your attention." It was Wesley, Davis' flag captain, interrupting. Behind him came Farragut and Davis. The tall form of the flag officer stepped forward to address the assembled ship captains.

"The Gulf Squadron will prepare to get under way," he announced. "We cannot leave the ram as a threat to the vessels left below. We shall attack her tonight." He paused.

"We must do our utmost to destroy the rebel as we pass her!" he said, his voice rising. "I shall not rest until she lies on the bottom! The fleet shall proceed immediately."

Davis continued when no further questions were forthcoming. "The ironclads will move to the bend and provide covering fire," he announced. "Captain Porter?"

A heavy set man with a long beard straightened. He commanded *ESSEX*, and it was his ship which had chased the *ARKANSAS* into the hail of Rebel fire. "Aye, Commodore."

"Is your ship battle worthy?"

"More than ready, sir."

"Finely said, sir," returned Davis. "We shall move down at four bells in the evening watch. We will engage the north battery and such of the upper works as we can reach. Word has already gone to all the mortar batteries to provide covering fire."

"What of the rest of the gunboats, sir?" asked Richards.

Davis laughed lightly. "I would think you have seen enough action today, Captain Richards!" he quipped. The assembled officers laughed lightly at the joke. It was only polite when spoken by a senior officer. "The gunboats shall hold back. There is little to be gained at this point by risking them to the fire of the batteries."

"Yes, sir." Richards felt a sense of disappointment at the comment. He hoped it was not reflected in his voice.

"We were taken by surprise today, gentlemen," continued Davis. "With steam up, we could easily have driven the ram ashore and smashed her. But these rebels have shown themselves bold in both planning and execution. We cannot let them take their ship south. Too much is at stake."

"And another factor," picked up Farragut. "The river is dropping. My sloops must be gotten south or we shall spend the rest of the year up here!" There were a couple of snickers from the riverboat captains at the comment, but they were just as quickly stifled as it was clear the flag officer was not amused. "Aye, 'tis nothing to laugh at! If we do not destroy the ram, we shall have her at our backs clear down to New Orleans!"

Davis nodded in agreement. He looked to his flag lieutenant.

"Lt. Wesley, you may make the general announcements."

The young man stepped forward clearing his throat.

"Thank you, sir. Just three announcements today.

"First, Congress has created the rank of Rear Admiral for the navy. Flag Officer David Farragut is hear-by promoted to that rank."

There was a burst of applause at the news and Farragut was duly touched at the show of support.

Someone in the back called out. "Three cheers for

Admiral Farragut."

The cheers were lustily given, bringing the new admiral to the point of embarrassment. Finally, he held up his hand for silence.

"Thank you all. You can be sure I will do my utmost to live up to this honor."

There was another brief round of applause and Wesley continued as it died away.

"Another promotion, though not as grand, I fear. Henry Erben is hear-by promoted to the new grade of lieutenant commander."

There was another round of applause and some back slapping applied to their fellow ship captain.

"Finally, the department has changed the rank insignia to be worn on our uniforms." A general groan went through the assembled officers. "I am well aware. *Again*." Everyone laughed at the small joke. "Our quarter master has received a supply and you may draw a set before you leave." He looked back to Davis. "That is all, sir."

Davis nodded and stepped forward. "Any further questions?" None were forthcoming. "Fine, gentlemen. Enjoy another glass of my port, and then make ready. There will be little sleep in either squadron tonight!"

At the dismissal, the more senior officers stepped forward to congratulate Farragut. Richards stepped closed to Erben and shook his hand.

"Lt. Commander Erben," he said formally.

"Commander Richards," returned the other.

They stepped away from the assembled officers to where the quartermaster and a mate were waiting. It took only a minute to identify themselves and receive the new shoulder rank for their uniforms.

Richards looked at his: instead of two fouled anchors, there was now only one. However, there was a silver oak leaf on each end. Erben nodded and showed him the lieutenant commander insignia. The same single anchor, but the oak leaf was gold.

"I guess that will solve some of the inter-service squabbling," commented Richards. The new insignia's inclusion of the corresponding army rank could not be clearer.

"That it should," agreed Erben. "I best be to my ship, *Lt. Colonel* Richards."

"And I to mine, *Major* Erben."

Keeler directed Richards' barge up to the side of the *BENTON* to collect him several minutes later. The young officer sat in the stern sheets, his face flushed. Whether still from the morning's excitement or simply from sitting on the river for over an hour in the hot sun was unclear. In either case, he fidgeted with excitement when Richards stepped into the boat.

"What's to be done, captain?" he asked nervously.

"Admiral Farragut will take his ships south this evening," returned the commander. "Commodore Davis will provide support with the iron ships."

"And what are we to do?"

"Watch."

The single word answer was sufficient to cause Keeler to drop into silence. Richards glanced about the crowded waters of the river. Between the two squadrons, over fifty different war vessels were present. Yet the ram, through either luck or determination, forced his way through them. Now Farragut was taking the larger part of this force under the guns of hostile batteries in an all out effort to destroy the ironclad. Could one ship really pose such a threat?

Woodard awaited his arrival on the *MACHINEEL*. He came up immediately as Richards stepped aboard.

"Repairs completed, sir, and the crew sent to their noon meal."

"Good, Mr. Woodard. Light duties this afternoon. Did Mr. Anson check our coal bunkers?"

"Aye, as you requested. Over half full; enough for twelve days steaming along the river."

"Good." He repeated the night's plans for Woodard's benefit.

"And what is our part to be, captain?" he questioned dubiously.

"Mere spectators, Mr. Woodard. We will be unable to assist vessels disabled by gunfire. They will just have to drift downstream to get clear. We shall have a rather uneventful night, I am sure."

"Praise the lord," said Woodard, the reverent whisper barely audible.

"What was that?" asked Richards.

"Nothing, captain. Nothing at all."

The fleet raised steam late in the afternoon. Despite the length of the day, it was full dark when HARTFORD raised anchor and started downstream. Attention was forced back to the city, for the mortars opened fire at their fastest rate, followed quickly by the guns from both batteries and gunboats.

"It'll be hotter 'n hell along that stretch of river tonight," commented Woodard.

"No doubt," Richards replied.

The night filled with the flashes of guns and the burst of shells. It was impossible to hear any one gun fire, for the volume rose to a continual rumble with the number of weapons being worked.

"I would like to talk about this mornin', captain." The

tone was cautious and respectful.

"And what is that, Mr. Woodard?"

"'Bout you tryin' to follow that bastard, captain. Do not misunderstand me, sir," he continued quickly. "As I told you before, I am all for bein' involved in the fightin'. It's just chasin' a rebel ironclad under their own batteries in a crippled ship doesn't quite fit the type of fightin' I had in mind."

"It was a poor decision, Mr. Woodard." Richards strained into the night. The first of the ships were already even with the quay where the rebel was tied up, but there was no sight of the ram, unless the gun flashes on the water a bit further down came from the vessel. "Thank you for calling it to my attention."

"Aye, sir." Woodard's thoughts echoed those of his captain. "I cannot see the bastard. I doubt if they can, either." He paused as the firing became particularly heavy for a few minutes. It slacked off to the steady roar again. "I am just hopin' I will not need to do it again, sir."

Richards grew angry at the continued prodding. "I do not need any fatherly advice, *lieutenant*."

"Of course not, captain," said the other calmly, "but you be gettin' it anyway. These men respect you. The lad Keeler worships you! Do not betray their trust."

Richards feigned at studying the course of the battle. Instead, the words cut deep. The wound from Hampton Roads was still there: bare, open, painful. He was unsure how the morning's fight tied in to it. "I will endeavor not to, Mr. Woodard."

"Please, sir." There was genuine pleading in the voice. "Because if you do, I am sure I will do something stupid to stop you and end up in the stockade for it. Or I would do something even dumber, and follow along with you and get meself killed. In either case, I would not get to see the missus and the children again."

*   *   *   *   *

"Our number, captain!" reported Keeler excitedly.

It was hardly full daylight, but already the commodore called for some of his gunboat captains. The *ARKANSAS*, in spite of Farragut's efforts, still lay at anchor under the guns of Vicksburg. When her position was seen, the mortar boats started firing at her and forced a change in her position. It would be difficult them to range in on a target which could move so readily.

"Have the barge swung out, Mr. Keeler," ordered Richards between swipes with his razor. He cleaned the blade off before raising it back to his cheek. "And tell off a boat crew."

There was no question what the captains would discuss at the meeting. Richards was pleased with the summons. Davis must have some regard for his efforts to want his participation in this venture. He wiped the remaining lather from his face. It would be an interesting morning.

Aboard *BENTON*, he was shown to the wardroom. It was different from the previous meetings held on the upper deck to avoid the heat of the interior. Something was afoot. William Porter of the *ESSEX*, or "Dirty" Bill as he was called in the squadron, was already present. One of the Ellet's, the youngest, appeared shortly, followed by Erben. Davis came after the last of them, wasting no time getting to the point.

"As you can see, Admiral Farragut's attack last evening did not destroy the *ARKANSAS*. I want to make another attempt tonight." He laid a roughly made drawing on the table, one clearly showing the situation around Vicksburg.

"There was no secret, no surprise last night when the fleet ran the guns. I have yet to hear from the flag officer what the losses were in the squadron, but they could not have been light."

"But, commodore," protested Erben mildly, "can four ships accomplish what the entire squadron did not?"

"I do not know, commander," he answered. "I do know the ram is a serious threat to our control of the river. I am hoping the rebels will not expect another attempt upon it so quickly. Last night, what we tried in the open, we do again tonight with a bit more subtlety."

Davis leaned over the crude chart. "The batteries are all marked here, as you can see. *ARKANSAS* is anchored here, around the quay. They keep shifting her position because of the mortar fire."

It was an opportunity to achieve what had been missed the night before. The force was small but capable of dealing with the vessel. They would get steam up just before midnight, so as not to attract the attention of the rebels. *ESSEX* would lead and lay herself alongside. The two gunboats would follow at intervals. If they could gain positions near the ram, they would board and set her afire. The army ram would come last. If previous efforts failed, she would try to either smash in the side of the ironclad or drive her hard aground where the rebels would have difficulty extracting her from the river mud.

"The lads and I are willing to give it a go, commodore," announced Porter.

"Good, but remember you will have a current behind you." He looked to Erben and Richards. "That is one reason for two gunboats. You may find it difficult to bring your ships out of the current and next to the enemy, but you are more maneuverable than *ESSEX*."

"We shall do our best," said Erben. "*SUMTER* took a hit in the sternpost yesterday. My carpenter says she's unsteerable and will be repaired by this afternoon."

"Very good, commander."

Richards considered it. It was a bold plan and one worthy of the attempt, but the ships involved needed the resolve and the manpower to accomplish it. His gunboat had its own issues.

"*MACHINEEL* is very short of men at the moment, commodore," he said. "We shall need something closer to full compliment to succeed."

"How many do you require?"

"I need gun crews and stokers." He considered the numbers from the morning muster. "At least two gun crews, and relief stokers because of this damned heat. About thirty men, sir."

"Thirty!" echoed Davis. Given the condition of the squadron, it were as if he asked for a hundred. "We shall have to see, Mr. Richards."

"I know it is a lot but it is not unreasonable. I have but two crews for six guns now."

"Perhaps I should talk to one of the other captains..." started Davis to his flag lieutenant.

"No!" Richards interrupted quickly, not giving Davis time to complete the thought and remove his ship from the night's effort. "We can rid you of the ram, commodore. Just give me the men I need and *MACHINEEL* will see to it."

Davis laughed. "I just needed to be sure you were not making excuses, commander." He did not give Richards time to reply to the off hand comment. "After yesterday, captain, I have no doubt you are willing to take on this beast. And you, Commander Erben," he said, looking to SUMTER's captain, "will have the opportunity of testing your new ship in battle."

"Thank you, commodore." Richards was not sure, but did he detect the merest hint of hesitance in Erben's reply?

"And Captain Ellet here," Davis continued, gesturing to the army officer. The young man straightened at the mention of his name. "Speaking of hot blooded young officers, Mr. Ellet has been biting at the bit for a chance to prove his mettle."

"Aye, sir," said the youngster. He appeared about the

same age as Keeler. "I would have fought to be included in this!"

Davis smiled at the exuberance. "And you, Bill," he finished to Porter, "I thought I would give you the chance to finish what you started yesterday." Porter nodded his head, the motion mostly hidden within the beard. "And your brother is commanding the mortar boats with Farragut's ships, is he not?"

Porter shrugged. "I believe he is, but we have not spoken for years. I do not think either of us feels the need to change that."

Davis did not press the issue. "Very well. Captain Porter, two blue lights at midnight when you are ready to start. *SUMTER, MACHINEEL* and *QUEEN OF THE WEST* at intervals after that. You will have your orders by night fall."

They all stood to leave, but Davis stopped them one last time. "And, Commander Richards, I shall see what I can do about the thirty hands."

"Thank you, commodore. They really are necessary for the success of this operation."

Woodard and Keeler awaited his return. The crew was released to light duties in the growing heat. Richards took his two officers to their small wardroom to relay the information.

"Wonderful!" exclaimed Keeler. "We shall show those rebs what for!"

Woodard was not so excited. "Tonight?" he questioned. "But we have barely enough hands to work a pair of guns!"

"The commodore will be sending us some additional men, Mr. Woodard." It was clear there were other concerns, and it was no great feat to guess them. "I am afraid we shall have to delay our trip north, Mr. Woodard."

The older man let out a long sigh. "The missus has made it without me so far, captain. Another few weeks should not matter."

USS QUEEN OF THE WEST

CHAPTER TWELVE

Davis made good his promise. Two complete gun crews were transferred from within the squadron, and a number of soldiers came aboard for service in the engine room. Now the gunboat was ready for the fight, and it was just a matter of time until they started their run past the batteries.

ESSEX went first, drawing fire on her way down the river's course. The small squadron started late, well after the planned time of midnight. Richards was unaware of why the plan had gone awry.

William Porter named the *ESSEX* for his father's ship which gained fame during the 1812 war. Another Porter, David, commanded the mortar fleet attached to the Gulf Squadron. Farragut was himself a stepson of that same Porter. Theirs was a naval family, with ties running strong and deep in the history of the seagoing fleet. *Like himself.*

SUMTER followed *ESSEX* after the designated interval. Again, guns from ashore roared at the gunboat, periodically marking the ship with their flashes. Soon, the vessel was lost from sight. Whether she joined *ESSEX* alongside the ram was unclear. Further, it appeared the union ironclad was not engaged with the rebel, for no firing was seen around the ram's anchorage.

"Ahead full," announced Richards, as the time came for their departure.

"Steer small, and keep her to the right bank," Woodard instructed the helmsman. Levenson nodded his understanding. "This will be tricky, captain," he said, peering into the darkness across the river.

"Are the gun crews ready?" It was the first lieutenant's job to have the ship prepared for action. Not only would Woodard be responsible for maneuvering the ship in the confines of the river, but he also had to assure the men were ready to fight.

"Aye, sir. Solid shot, charge and a half of powder as you ordered."

"Let's just get ourselves alongside, Mr. Woodard," finished Richards. "I will see to the guns when the time arrives."

The stacks belched smoke into the night air and there was little doubt the trail would be spotted by the rebels. At least their efforts were giving the Confederates a sleepless night. The churning of the wheel sounded as if they must awaken the rebels, if nothing else did. But Richards decided his imagination was amplifying the sound beyond reasonable limits. Still, the men talked in hushed whispers, subconsciously lowering their voices in the tense situation.

"Coming up to the first battery, captain!" Keeler's voice was at odds to the others, barely subdued. He need not have bothered, for the guns greeted them with a ragged salvo. The shots flew wide and they were not given time to fire a second round at the rushing ship.

The river opened to their right as they approached the bend. The helmsman started to turn the wheel, but Woodard grabbed his hand in an iron grip.

"Not yet, laddie!" The tone was harsh, the harshest yet

heard from the Irishman. The point of land to their starboard slipped past until it was well astern. "Now!" demanded the officer. Woodard made some amends by helping the man spin the wheel.

They were around the bend, Woodard's delay using the current to help them make the turn faster. Guns fired from above now, but they were not used to firing at quickly moving ships in the night. Columns of spray rose around them but nothing hit the vessel.

"Can we move into the left bank?" asked Richards.

"Whatever for?" demanded Woodard.

"Spoil their aim! They might not be able to depress the guns that far!"

A shell roared close overhead to explode on their right. All three men in the pilothouse ducked at the sound and then the rattle of shrapnel on the roof. Richards laughed as they straightened.

"A hell of a lot of good that would have done us! Move her to port if the river's safe!"

Woodard nodded and the helm was moved a couple of spokes. The city was difficult to discern but the general location was marked by the lack of gun flashes from the hillsides. They were upon it quickly, the two officers on the upper deck trying to determine where their target lay.

"Hard port," instructed Woodard. His finger stabbed into the night. "There! By the quay!"

Richards was overwhelmed by the excitement surrounding him. His heart beat so quickly, he felt it surely must burst. But Woodard's eyesight was good. The rebel lay bow into the current, and they headed straight for her.

"Man the port guns!" he shouted. "Fire at my order!"

Woodard worked the engine repeater madly, first reversing one wheel to tighten their turn before ringing for full stop as they hit slack water around the quay. After the mad rush of the past minutes, it became deathly still when the wheels slowed and stopped. They coasted forward, the bow swinging with the current.

"Hold her into it, man!" Woodard grabbed the wheel himself, pushing Levenson from the spot.

They smashed against the bow of their target and slid down her side. No cannon fire was received from the rebel ship but bright stabs of musket fire were clearly visible.

"Boarders stand ready!" Keeler had his men assembled at the bow.

"Fire!" shouted Richards, their ship laying full along the iron ram.

The three cannon fired as one, the space between the two vessels glowing bright orange in their flare. But already, it was clear they were not as near as they had hoped. The force of their guns pressed them farther from the rebel.

"Boarders away!" yelled Keeler.

"Belay!" ordered Richards immediately. Already, Woodard was spinning the wheel to starboard to keep their ship from piling headlong into the city's wharfs.

"Give me some steerage!" Woodard demanded.

"Full astern!" shouted Richards into the speaking tube while jerking back on the telegraph. The wheels turned at once.

At Keeler's order, a half dozen grapnels had flown towards the Rebel ship. Because of the sudden increase in distance caused by firing the guns, all splashed into the river. Now the gunboat lay with her stern directly in the rebel's broadside, but still no shots rang out; no shells tore into their poorly protected machinery.

"Give her some speed." Woodard was still fighting with the wheel; it was clear the ship was caught in the current.

"Ahead one half, Mr. Anson," said Richards in a more reasonable tone. The ship came broadside to the current. If they did not move quickly, they might be pushed onto the western shoreline. "Ahead full," he added immediately. He faced Woodard. "Can we have another go?" he asked.

Woodard laughed, but with little humor. "I do not think these rebs are going to let us, Richards!"

True enough, they were within range of the guns south of the city. Shells fell about them or exploded overhead to rain shrapnel on the upper deck. Richards swallowed his disappointment.

"Steer south."

"Full and bye, captain!" replied the river man. The gunboat accelerated with the current.

"Everyone into the gun house!" ordered Richards. "Work the port guns, Mr. Keeler."

"Aye aye, captain." Keeler's chagrin was evident in his voice, even though the lieutenant was not visible.

"Into the gun house?" asked Woodard. Another shell burst over head, the splinters rattling on top of the pilothouse as if going through a sudden squall. "I see your point, sir," he added with a wink.

"Damn!" Richards faced astern, watching the city fall behind them. "It will be up to the QUEEN now," he said.

Woodard laughed again, this time with genuine humor. "The young pup the army's got on that barge will not do any better'n us, captain." He grabbed the helmsman and placed him back on the wheel. "You have got to learn to use the current, boy. Otherwise, you'll end up on the bank!" Keeler appeared, and Woodard gave him a large grin, also. "Sorry to spoil your fun, laddie. Pardon, Mister Keeler."

Richards smiled ruefully. "I believe I can forgive the lapse just this once, Mr. Woodard."

"Why did you countermand my order, sir?" The voice cracked, heavy with emotion. "We could have taken her!"

"We were already too far off, lieutenant," Richards

returned. He laid a hand on Keeler's shoulder to reassure the boy. "I could not let you go for a swim now, could I? We would not have had time to pick you up."

The Vicksburg guns fell silent behind them as they turned the next bend.

"But we could've taken her!" protested the young lieutenant.

"Listen to the captain, Mr. Keeler." Woodard's words were stern and paternal. "He knows what he's doin'." He straightened to face Richards. "Most of the time, anyhow," he added. He gestured over his shoulder towards the bow. "Comin' up on the fleet, captain."

"Very good. Find us an anchorage not too far from the flag, and then join me in the wardroom. I think we deserve a drink after this night's work."

"More of your wine, captain?" asked Woodard in distaste.

"I think we can both use something more substantial, Mr. Woodard."

"Aye indeed, captain." Keeler turned to follow Richards, but Woodard caught him by the collar. "Not so fast, Mr. Keeler. As a young gentleman, I am about to see to some of your education at boat handlin'!"

Dawn grew in the east and another burst of fire erupted from the batteries north of the city. Richards did not believe the army ram was actually attempting to make the run in the daylight. What had Woodard said? *Young pup.*

Farragut looked at the three captains gathered on his quarterdeck. He regarded each carefully, from Porter, the senior, to Richards, then Erben. Ellet was not with them, taking his ram back north of the city when his attempt at the rebel ironclad failed.

"A bold attempt, my lads," he said. "I wish it were more

successful."

"As do we," said Porter, speaking for the group.

The flag officer faced up river, shaking his head ruefully. "Mr. Erben."

"Sir?"

"Why did you not get engaged?"

Erben burned hotly at the question. "Caught in the current, sir. Then the sternpost gave way."

"Hmph." The flag officer was unimpressed. "I would find myself another carpenter, captain."

"Already done, admiral." Erben disliked being belittled in front of the other officers, even if the rebuke was so mild.

HARTFORT's captain approached and saluted Farragut. "Down another half foot," he announced.

"That's it then!" Farragut's temper rose at the announcement. "We cannot destroy the bloody ram and if the river falls much further, we will be left high and dry! Damnation!" He calmed himself visibly, then spoke directly to the officer. "Make out the orders. We shall leave as soon as word is passed." He brought his attention back to the men from the gunboat fleet.

"We must move south, gentlemen. For now, I think you shall accompany us. We have troops at Baton Rouge that might use the support of some gunboats."

"Aye, sir," responded Porter. The man was more taciturn than usual at the announcement, glowering darkly at his step-brother.

"Do not worry, Bill," continued Farragut, touching his adoptive brother's shoulder. "I will inform Davis of the change in plans and, with any luck, you shan't have to meet with David!"

Richards proceeded to the entry port, wondering about the Porter family. Williamn's brother David commanded the mortar boats attached to Farragut's fleet. Richards thought if he had a brother he rarely saw because of the service, he would quickly find a way to see him if they were so close. It was a strange family who did not have any dealings with one another even on professional plain.

Heading south with the main fleet was a pleasant cruise. With so many guns, the rebels thought better than to bar their progress, particularly as they were withdrawing. Port Hudson, Natchez, the mouth of the Red River were each passed in turn. When arriving two days later at Baton Rouge, the flag officer immediately departed to consult with the army troops ashore.

Richards fiddled near the pilothouse, unable to decide on a course of action. Going south with Farragut was not what he had in mind when running the batteries at Vicksburg. At the present, there appeared little work below the city, while the river north held open immediate prospects for fighting. The response from the flag officer was not what was expected.

Farragut intended to proceed south with the major ships, he was leaving the smaller ones were left behind to bolster the defense of the city. Rebel troops were maneuvering to retake the place and it was felt the gunboats would provide much needed support. Along with the gunboats from Davis' command, three others were also detailed to the duty. But for all the preparation, the result was to sit in the heat for another week and maintain their inactivity.

"Porter's calling again," observed Woodard, not even permitting Keeler time to check the book.

"Call the barge crew," returned Richards. These conferences occurred every other day or so, and it was no longer surprising to see the signal. Still, the net result was usually to sit and await events.

"The rebels are making a heavy push from the east,"

informed an army officer sent to brief them. "We are holding at the moment, but they are threatening our northern flank."

"Get 'em close to the river," growled Porter. "We'll see to 'em."

"Yes, sir." The officer was unconvinced. "We took some captives. They say the rebels sent for their ram at Vicksburg. It could arrive any day."

The ship captains traded glances. The major did not understand the significance of the comment.

"That will be our first order of business then!" snapped Porter. He may have been a brooding sort, but there was never a hesitation when action was necessary. "Okay, lads. We will head north to meet the ARKANSAS. Mr. Erben and Mr. Harrison." The two officers stood. "You shall provide support for ESSEX."

"Captain!" Richards was taken aback at the thought of MACHINEEL being left out of the fight.

"Do not fret, Richards. MACHINEEL will help the rest of these boys cover the army's flank for them. We do not want their bare ends hanging out now, do we, commander?"

The assembled ship captains laughed at the joke. The army major did not find it so funny.

"You are taking half your ships to pursue one ram?"

"That I am," returned Porter, nonplussed. "This one ram passed both fleets north of Vicksburg. I think we will be doing well if we manage to stop it with the boats I have got!" The major opened his mouth in further protest, but Porter would have none of it. "It is either that, sir, or you may watch after your northern flank yourself!"

The army man was convinced by the threat. "Yes, sir. As you say."

"Damn right!" Porter looked back to Richards. "Commander, you are senior after me. You will take command of the remaining gunboats. Do your utmost to bedevil the rebels."

"Of that you can be sure, captain."

"I have no doubts, John." Richards nodded to the gruff old captain. It was the first time he could remember the man using his Christian name. Porter turned to Erben and Harrison. "Gentlemen, we leave at first light!"

Richards felt a keen disappointment at *MACHINEEL* being left behind. It did not occur *MACHINEEL*'s shallow draft would be more useful supporting the troops along the shore. There was a pain at remaining, not being allowed to help administer to the rebel ironclad. It was not until he was on his way back to the gunboat that it dawned it would be his first time commanding more than one vessel.

With the exception of Keeler, the crew of the gunboat felt differently. They had dealt with troops ashore, and to them it was only slightly more dangerous than a turkey shoot. After the wild night passing Vicksburg, they believed they earned a break from laying alongside the ironclad yet again. Of course, they could not voice this opinion openly to their captain. Woodard, on the other hand, did not feel a need to hide his true feelings.

Woodard eyed Richards carefully. "I am surprised you didn't *volunteer* us again."

Richards still felt a vague sting at staying behind, as if he was shirking his duty. It left little room to treat Woodard charitably. "Captain Porter felt those ships were sufficient."

He closed the conversation by raising his telescope. The shore to the east was held by union troops and they remained anchored near the front lines of the force. Somewhere to the north of those men lay a rebel division waiting to attack. The closer inspection in that direction did not reveal any sign of their enemy, however.

"We shall keep half steam up," he said. "Always maintain a watch on the shore for signals from the army."

"We're goin' to spoil a perfectly nice day by fightin'," lamented Woodard. Indeed, it was cooler than it had been for the last several weeks.

"That is what we are here for, Mr. Woodard."

It was not long before the sound of rifles firing was heard from up river. The union sailors could only guess at its meaning, but it did not last long. A column of smoke was seen in the distance to mark the probable sight of the engagement. Richards could guess a ship was aflame, but whose? Shortly thereafter, soldiers appeared on shore, signal flags waving frantically.

"Take a boat, Mr. Keeler," Richards directed. He pulled back on the engine room telegraph. "Raise full steam, Mr. Anson. We shall be under way in a few minutes."

The reply was lost in the sound of the boat splashing into the water. Richards picked up the megaphone and shouted orders to the other three gunboats lying nearby. The coal smoke poured freely from the stacks of each ship.

It was several minutes before the boat returned. When it did, the army major from the previous day was the passenger. Richards directed him to the wardroom.

"Get us moving and clear for action. Load with shell and canister. Pass the word to the other ships." Richards did not wait for the reply. Woodard was capable of seeing to it.

Below, the major already had a map spread on the table. Hastily drawn lines marked the face of the chart. "Now, major," asked Richards, realizing he did not even know the other man's name. "What is happening?"

The soldier was excited, gesturing quickly at the table. "The rebels cavalry is massing," he said, gesticulating wildly across the map. "They mean to move down and cut us off from the river."

Richards glanced at the chart, trying to compare it to his memories of the actual shoreline. The major's excited hand motions had revealed nothing of the exact situation.

"Just where, exactly?" he asked, calmly.

"Here!" The finger stabbed hard on the paper. "Two full brigades we think. We have nothing to stand in their way!"

Richards judged the distance. "I think we can do something about it for you." The indicated place was a flood plain. The large flat expanse was an ideal location to prepare a cavalry unit for an attack against the union left flank. Most of the area was within sight of the river itself.

"You are sure?"

Richards thought of his little squadron. Four gunboats did not seem like much, but between them they carried twenty-two heavy naval guns and nine army field pieces. Army men rarely appreciated the difference between a six pounder field piece and a thirty-two pounder naval gun.

"They will not want to stay on that plain too long once we reach them," he assured the major. Woodard entered the room and he pointed to the map. "Just about here, Mr. Woodard. What is that, three or four miles?"

"Closer four I should think, cap'n." He looked up from the map. "Rest of the boats are in line astern, sir. I would guess about an hour to reach that point."

"Very good."

"Excellent," said the major, grabbing up his map. "I will pass the word to the general when I get ashore!" He spun towards the door, but Richards touched his arm and stopped him.

"I am afraid that will not be possible."

"What?" he responded in confusion.

"We're already under way." Woodard smiled at the army man's discomposure. "Tain't possible to put you back ashore."

"What!"

"Make yourself comfortable, major." Richards was

unsuccessful in hiding a moment's pleasure at the turn of events. "Maybe one of the stewards can find you a glass of wine. I am sorry, but I must see to the squadron." He left before the major could do more than sink uncomfortably into a chair.

"A nasty trick for our friend, Mr. Woodard." He did not look at the other officer directly but kept his attention on the passing shoreline.

"A might, sir, but I figured you'd want to hurry." His voice indicated he took the comment as a rebuke.

Richards glanced at the Irishman and smiled. "The major needed some time to relax. And that was more in the line of a commendation, lieutenant."

Woodard laughed out loud. "Oh, I see, cap'n!"

The other three gunboats followed in single file, the *VIRUNA* directly behind them and two others from the Gulf Squadron further astern. Richards looked over the vessels. They were all ocean going ships, converted from yachts. Narrow and long, they contrasted sharply with the boxy *MACHINEEL*. What was clear was the other captains were looking to him for direction this day.

"How close can we get to the shore?"

"Maybe fifty yards, cap'n. Closer, if you want a man swingin' the lead."

"These other gunboats are not river craft like *MACHINEEL*, Mr. Woodard. They can draw as much as ten feet."

The first officer nodded. "Fifty yards it is, then."

"I propose we pass north, engaging with the starboard, then swing with the current and engage with the port as we head south. If possible, and depending on the return fire, we will anchor and have a proper shoot."

"Reasonable, given the river at that point," replied Woodard.

Richards pulled out his watch and checked the time. Just twenty minutes since they up-anchored. At best, they were making three knots against the river's flow, and the other boats kept their spacing at that speed.

"There, cap'n," said Woodard, as they rounded the next bend. "That's the ridge. Them rebels should be on the other side."

"Raise 'Enemy in Sight', Mr. Keeler." The flags squeaked up the aft signals mast. "Now down below with you. Take charge of the gun deck."

"Aye, sir." Keeler touched his cap and left. Woodard's eyes followed him briefly.

"Lot of enthusiasm, that one."

"Aye, Mr. Woodard."

The land crept slowly abeam, the ridge drawing closer and closer. There was a glint from the crest. Someone was watching them with a telescope. There was no doubt who it would be.

"Stand ready," shouted Richards, his voice raising as the ridge sat full to the starboard.

The flood plain beyond opened before them, the Confederate cavalry arranging themselves in neat rows as they prepared their attack. There was the sound of someone entering the pilothouse: the major had come to watch their progress. He stepped close to Richards, wine on his breath.

"God!" The word voiced awe and reverence at the sight.

"Fire as you bear!" ordered Richards.

The cavalry held their ranks. The rebel officers were clearly observing the advancing gunboats, but they took no action. Whether they thought the warships presented no threat, or simply were incapable of engaging the cavalry was not known. But the neat lines of mounted men stayed in position as the first gun fired from forward on *MACHINEEL*.

The shell exploded in their midst, horses rearing and

falling, men thrown and blown to the ground. The canister preceded the shell only slightly, scattering men and animals before it. The broadside guns discharged immediately, adding their loads to the death ashore.

Firing came from astern as *VIRUNA* added her weight. The boats behind her joined in, spreading havoc through the massed horsed troops. Another broadside erupted from *MACHINEEL*, echoed as it was repeated down the line. A third followed before they drew out of range on the northern leg.

"Wonderful!" The major was jumping up and down in positive glee. "Marvelous!"

"Bring her around, Mr. Woodard. Have the other boats follow." Richards stepped from the pilothouse and shouted down to the casemate. "Prepare to engage to port!" The order was not necessary, for he could already feel the boat shift as the guns were run out on that side.

"Cap'n!" It was Levenson, pointing towards shore. "Over there, sir. They's settin' up some artillery of their own!"

Four horse drawn guns and caissons moved to the river's edge, the men working feverishly to unlimber them. The Parrot fired, raising a large column of water within feet of the guns. The thirty-two's roared and the shells exploded amongst them. There was a larger explosion as one of the ammunition caissons was struck by the naval fire.

"Keep at it, Mr. Keeler!"

Even the upper deck gun was firing, the small six pounder adding to the chaos. Officers rode about, trying to rally their men and keep them in formation. One was decapitated by a shell, the body riding upright on the panicked horse for several seconds before slumping to the ground. After the second pass, the cavalry unit was mass confusion. Their artillery was never deployed, laying in wreckage at the point where they tried to set it up.

"Another turn north," Richards instructed. The pilot

hesitated, his gaze riveted on the shoreline. "North, Mr. Woodard," he repeated, raising his voice. The other shook himself from the sight.

"They's runnin', cap'n. We can let them go."

"Bring the boats about!"

They stared at one another for a hard second, the helmsman glancing from one officer to the other. Then Woodard nodded, and the wheel came over. Again, the forward and broadside guns shifted to bear on the disorganized enemy.

The smoke from their guns and fires drifted across the flood plain obscuring their view of the field. As they watched, the wind dispersed the haze and the effectiveness of their attacks became visible.

The field was strewn with casualties, both men and animals. And, as Woodard observed, lines of riders were fleeing. But still there were men trying to regroup, to hold their discipline in the face of the withering fire. The guns roared out again, the line of gunboats firing straight across the level plain. At this last onslaught, all sense of order broke. The survivors, men and officers alike, fled from the field, trying to get as far from the gunboats as possible.

"Anchor us in mid-river, lieutenant. Pass word to VIRUNA to scout around the bend. She can fire a rocket if the rebels try to regroup. The other ships will follow us."

Woodard's words were weak and subdued. "Aye aye, sir."

"Well done, captain!" said the major as the guns were secured. "Well done indeed!"

Richards nodded in reply. As the ship lapsed into silence, sounds drifted from shore. The squeal of injured horses mingled with the cries of wounded men. No individual screams could be heard: just a constant cacophony of pain and fear. Another sound rose as the shouts of victory reached them. Union soldiers poured down the face of the slope and onto the plain.

"You can place me ashore here, captain," said the major, his tone much more respectful of the navy officer. "Be assured I shall mention your courage to the general."

"Courage?" snorted the commander. Despite the necessity of their mission, the ease of their attack preyed on his conscience. "Courage be damned! You cannot call this slaughter courage!"

The major was shocked at the reply and opened his mouth to respond but Keeler's arrival forestalled an answer.

"Report on the men, captain," interrupted Keeler, his breathing heavy.

"Yes?" demanded Richards.

Keeler shrunk back a little at the sound. "One injury, sir. A minor burn from brushing against a gun."

"Very well, Mr. Keeler." Richards took a deep breath to regain some of his composure. "After he is treated, you can send the surgeon's mate ashore with the major. I think they shall need some extra hands there."

"Not happy when we lives; not happy when we dies," whispered the pilot, just loud enough to be heard.

Keeler twisted his head to Woodard in anger, but replied to Richards and ignored the remark. "Aye, sir."

"Pass the word to the other ships to do the same!"

Keeler stepped back, his previous enthusiasm visibly drained. "Aye, sir," he repeated.

There was a sound of firing ashore, intermingled with the cries of men and animals. "What the devil's going on? Are the rebels attacking again?"

"No, captain," replied Woodard. "The soldiers are just relievin' the injured horses of their misery."

ESSEX and her consorts appeared, all intact after their brush with *ARKANSAS*. That evening, Porter brought all his captains ashore to meet with their army counterparts. It was Richards' first opportunity to find out what had occurred in the clash.

The plain was still littered with the bodies of horses, though the troops butchered some to supplement their rations. Others were engaged in moving the bodies of the troops to a large, mass graves. The graves were shallow, little more than four feet deep before water was struck. But the rebel dead were tossed in, the sounds of splashes as their corpses struck the muddy earth a continual backdrop to their surroundings.

"How did it go?" asked Richards, as he spied Erben near one of the tents.

Erben waved off the whole affair. "Damned boat was grounded when we found her. We commenced firing into her and she took flame, but I think the rebs did it themselves."

He was eating from a plate provided by an army cook, and one was thrust into Richards hands as well. Whatever it was, it smelled better than the normal tinned rations. Oddly, Richards could not find an appetite.

"Looks like you had a much more exciting time here," Erben commented between bites of food.

"There was nothing exciting about it," returned the other coolly. "It was murder, pure and simple."

"That may be, old man," replied Erben. "But if you hadn't done it, they would have done the same to our lads."

"I know. It is what I keep telling myself." He saw Erben's plate was clean. He handed the other officer his own. "Here, you seem to relish this much more than I."

Erben took the plate before it was dropped.

Capt. William Porter's ironclad, the *USS ESSEX*, with ships from the Gulf Squadron behind.

CHAPTER THIRTEEN

A hand was on his shoulder, shaking him awake. Richards' eyes opened, his vision still blurred by sleep.

"What is it?" he asked dully.

"Wanted on deck, sir. Captain Porter's callin' for ya'."

The heat had finally broken, making it possible to get some semblance of sleep. It appeared he was not destined to get any. He arose, wondering what lay behind the summons.

The last of the Gulf Squadron ships departed south at dusk, leaving only the gunboats from the river flotilla around Baton Rouge. And Porter's last comments were he would start north the next day. Richards was only to happy to oblige. Now he came on deck, Keeler pointing south.

"Firing, sir." he said. The noise could barely be heard in the distance.

"Richards!" Porter's voice rang hollowly across the space separating the vessels. He lifted his speaking trumpet in return.

"Sir!"

"Get up steam and move downstream to check that out!"

"Aye aye, sir!" He yawned as he replaced the trumpet in its holder. "You heard the man, Mr. Keeler. Rouse the crew and get her under weigh!"

"Yes, sir." Keeler almost collided with Woodard as he left the pilothouse.

"What's happenin'?" asked the first officer.

Richards shook his head. "Firing to the south. Porter wants us to check on it."

Woodard allowed a disgusted sigh to escape. "We're headin' the wrong way, cap'n. Me missus is north, at St. Louis."

Richards ignored the complaint. It did little good to want to go somewhere. In the navy, they went where they were told.

MACHINEEL moved quickly, the current adding considerably to the slow turning of the wheels. The firing died off, and there was no further reoccurrence of it. But then, in the distance, rose the orange glow of a fire and a column of thick smoke. It grew brighter as they neared, resolving into a ship on the shore when they rounded the last bend.

"My god!" said Woodard, regarding the vessel and the flames leaping high into the air.

"That's *SUMTER*!" Richards observed. He glanced down the river. "Take us downstream, but keep us clear."

"Aye, sir!"

The ship exploded as they passed her, debris hurled

high into the air and falling around the smoldering remnants of the vessel. A few moments later, a man on the bow called back.

"Boats ahead!"

"Dead slow," ordered Richards, ringing the repeater. "Let her drift down to them on the current." He cupped his hands to yell forward. "Prepare to throw them a line!"

The evolution of passing a light line to the cutters was easily accomplished. Erben came aboard first, followed by his officers and crew. Richards guided the officers into the wardroom, while the remainder of the men were sent into the gun house and upper deck. After ordering Woodard to rejoin Porter, he met with the ill-fated vessel's officers.

"What the hell happened, Henry?" he asked, a steward distributing wine to the men present.

"Damn sternpost gave way and we grounded," said Erben. The words were hurried, rushed as if Erben was trying to convince himself of the fact as much as Richards. "She was stuck fast, and there were rebels ashore. We took some small arms fire..."

"Well, maybe it was firin', sir..." ventured another of the officers.

"Of course it was firing," shouted Erben, rising to his feet. "Damn your eyes!" He cooled a bit, but remained standing and downed a whiskey in a fast gulp. "They were around us, and the other boats were out of sight below. We fired rockets and guns to signal them, but they must have misunderstood. Finally, I gave the order to fire the ship to keep the rebels from capturing her. We took to the boats to catch up to the others."

Richards was unwilling to believe his ears. Erben had set his ship aflame to avoid capture, a necessary act at times. It was occurring at regular intervals along the Mississippi, no doubt because of the narrow waters. But Erben's first officer was questioning his own captain. And even Erben's story did not state clearly there was an enemy threat. Had the ship's captain been too hasty in this case?

"We are heading north to rejoin our squadron," said Richards. "Make yourselves comfortable here for a few hours. "

"Take us down to the other gunboats!" demanded Erben. His voice was panicky. "They will confirm there were rebels ashore."

"Not tonight, Henry. Captain Porter is expecting us to return. You may put the matter before him."

Richards excused himself and returned to the deck. Taking a position away from the pilothouse, he paced slowly in the darkness. Erben was his friend and they had shared a few adventures together. But this did not seem the same man he had met at Pensacola. Richards could not imagine *that* Henry Erben destroying his ship because of shadows in the night. But this same man also failed to engage the ARKANSAS on his run past her. He had shown something like relief when the rebels burned the ram themselves.

Dawn was breaking as they rejoined the depleted squadron. Richards wasted no time getting to Porter. Porter, after listening in detail, found the story no more convincing than Richards.

"*SUMTER's* orders were to join the Gulf Squadron operating from New Orleans because Admiral Farragut needed a ram," announced Porter idly, after only a short deliberation. The weathered faced turned to Richards. "Obviously, that will not happen now. Still, SUMTER's crew is re-assigned. I will write orders for MACHINEEL to proceed south, commander."

"We were due for a break, captain," returned Richards. "Heading north for a refit."

"We all are, commander. Yours shall just have to wait a bit longer." As usual, the gristled officer was in no mood for discussion.

"Aye, sir. It should only take a day or so to get down to New Orleans. We could be back within the week."

"True, lad," returned Porter. "But you will find us gone. I intend to head north as planned."

"Aye, sir." There was no use in arguing. He did not relish the prospect of informing Woodard of the change in plans. Further, there was no telling what Farragut might decide, once the gunboat was five hundred miles from its proper command. "We will depart as soon as we get the orders."

"You will see them within the hour, commander." The interview was over.

"What do you think will happen?" asked Erben as they left the *ESSEX*. "I mean, about the *SUMTER* and all?"

Richards regarded the other carefully. He was not used to Erben in such a rattled state. It was quite different from the cocksureness displayed on previous occasions. But the thought of similar days he experienced in March sobered his attitude.

"They will have to examine the loss of the ship, Henry," he said, trying to sound supportive. He laid a hand on the officer's shoulder. "Then it is up to the board. It is not pleasant, but the waiting is worse than any possible outcome."

"Bloody hell!" Erben let the oath burst forth without effort to suppress. "My first command, and it ends like this!"

"It could be worse, Henry," returned Richards.

"How?" At first, the word was a challenge. But as their eyes met, Erben realized from where Richards was speaking. He faced the water, letting the question go unanswered.

They bumped next to the entry port of the *MACHINEEL*, and Richards immediately stepped onto the deck. "Mr. Woodard," he called, stepping quickly to the chart room.

"Sir?" asked the officer as he appeared.

"We are to head south." Richards continued quickly, before the other had a chance to comment. "A further delay, I know, but it was none of my doing. New Orleans. If we can catch Farragut there, we can turn around and come home."

"Yes, cap'n." The words held resignation.

"I was planning on the trip north also, Mr. Woodard," said Richards. He suddenly found himself in the role of consoling all of those about him. He did not care much for it and he continued in a harsher note. "Check with Mr. Anson on our coal stores, and then find something for all these idlers to do."

"Yes, sir."

Damn commodores and flag officers, thought Richards.

The trip to New Orleans took just over a day but the effort was for naught: Farragut had already left for the Gulf. *MACHINEEL* was immediately dispatched to the Head of Passes with her extra crewmen, reaching there only to find *HARTFORD* had proceeded into the gulf. They continued down river, the wide waters of the Gulf of Mexico opening before them.

If Farragut's sloops caused Richards homesickness when they were at Vicksburg, the sight of them afloat in the unrestricted waters beyond the river's mouth was almost more than he could bear. The *HARTFORD* was finally found, a new broad pennant at the aft.

"Steer for the flag, Mr. Levenson," ordered Richards.

The *MACHINEEL* met the easy swells and immediately displayed a much more lively nature than her commander would have imagined. It was her shallow draft, of course, combined with the top weight of artillery. Still, she rolled from side to side like an unfettered barrel, and more than one crewman was at the side with his head hanging over the rail.

"This is no ocean boat!" announced Erben loudly, his

hands gripping the rail about the pilothouse.

"Never meant to be," replied Woodard. He replaced the helmsman from the wheel and steered the ship himself, though struggling to maintain his footing.

"Let's discharge our passengers quickly, Mr. Woodard." He gaged the distance and the motion of the respective vessels. "Can we lay her alongside the flag?"

"I might be able, cap'n," Woodard returned.

"The sooner we are done, the sooner we will be pointing north."

Woodard smiled, but did not voice a reply. Instead, he gripped the wheel firmly, and commenced changing the speeds of the two engines, working them down as they closed with the warship. The crew aboard the flagship sprang to work, producing poles to fend the impertinent gunboat from the sides of their vessel. Most of the efforts were unnecessary. Woodard rang full stop, and their entry port lay next to that of the sloop.

"Fine bit of work, Mr. Woodard."

"Thank you, cap'n."

Richards made his way with Erben up to the deck of the flagship. They were met by the ship's first lieutenant, then passed onto the flag lieutenant before finally sent to Farragut.

The old officer sat in his cabin, drinking a glass of wine. His sleeve glistened with two extra bands of gold, their color contrasting with the duller bands which occupied it previously.

"Captain Richards; Captain Erben." He gestured to seats. "Nice to see you again." He looked at Richards more closely. "Fine bit of boat work there, captain."

"My first officer, sir." His glance stole to the extra bands on the admiral's sleeve.

"I am deeply honored," said Farragut, tugging at the

cuff. "Our navy's first admiral should be more elegant, I think. But at least now we can give some of them damned generals the what for!" The small group laughed lightly before Farragut turned his attention to Erben. "I take it we have lost *SUMTER*?"

The officer shifted uncomfortably under the gaze. "Aye, sir."

Farragut nodded. "We figured as much, when she did not show up with the other gunboats. There shall have to be a hearing."

Erben straightened, unflinching under the eyes. "Of course, admiral."

"And you, Mr. Richards? What is your part in this?"

"Transport only, sir," he answered. "We have *SUMTER*'s crew aboard. I would like to transfer them and get headed back to the flotilla."

"Would you want to spend a few days in deep water with us?" queried Farragut.

Richards saw past the old man at the broad expanse of ocean beyond. He could not deny he was tempted by the offer, no matter how lightly given. "I am afraid not, admiral. Half my crew's seasick already, and we are not even in the real ocean yet."

"Of course, commander." Farragut considered things for a few moments. "Send the *SUMTER*'s aboard. We will see to spreading them throughout the squadron."

"Aye, sir," replied Richards, fighting an impulse to jump out of the chair and get started immediately.

"And I will have cut orders so you can coal at New Orleans before heading north."

"Thank you, admiral. And congratulations on your promotion."

Farragut smiled, a friendly gesture. "And you can relay my gratitude to your father-in-law next time you see him."

"Yes, sir."

It was just after dark when the *MACHINEEL* re-entered her home waters, the river men aboard thankful to be off the sweeping gulf. Richards watched the river close about them with reluctance, again feeling the call of the sea. Gunboats were small and dirty little ships in his opinion and nothing could change it. But the ship headed against the current, and by daybreak they were coaling at New Orleans, preparing their return trip.

The layover was short, only long enough to refuel. *MACHINEEL* started her trip accompanied by two gunboats from Farragut's force. They were replacing those which had been left at Baton Rouge. They stayed astern of Richards' command, and little communication passed between them.

The trip down the river was made in just over a day with the aid of the current. Now, fighting it as they headed upstream, the return to Baton Rouge took over four. When the city came into view, the sight confirm what Porter had said before their departure. The ironclad was no longer present. *MACHINEEL* did not stop at the city but kept right on going. Her two consorts were left behind.

Late in the afternoon, they approached Port Hudson. A jeering crowd greeted their approach, citizens lining the shore to shout and defile them. An occasional shot rang out, but Woodard held them to the center of the river, and the musket rounds fell short. Still, it announced they were now in an area no longer controlled by the union, army or navy.

"Can we keep going?" asked Richards as darkness closed about the vessel.

"Aye, we can," responded Woodard. "We are makin' good time for headin' up river," he expounded.

Richards accepted the observation without comment. The dark waters around them with even darker shore lines in the distance emphasized the solitary nature of their trek. "I do not think I have ever felt quite so alone as now," he said idly.

"It would be nice to seein' one of the ironclads out front there, wouldn't it?" returned the first officer.

"Yes, it would." There was a shuffle on the deck behind them and they both faced Anson as he approached.

"Captain," greeted the engineer.

"Ensign."

"It's about the fires, sir. They need raking real bad."

To keep the fires burning at their best, it was necessary to remove the ash and cinders which accumulated in the furnaces. It was usually carried out about once a day. But while it was performed, the boilers would lose pressure.

"How long?" asked Richards.

"'Bout an hour, cap'n."

"Can we hold an anchor set here in the middle of the river?"

Woodard took a moment to consider the option. "Suppose," he answered. "Might want to drop two to be safe."

"Let's be at it then. Mr. Anson," said Richards before the other could leave. "Make it quick. I do not like sitting around out here."

The engineer touched his cap. "Aye, sir."

The gunboat took on an air of hushed silence as the wheels stopped and the throb of the engines died. The men moved about quietly, speaking to one another in whispers. Even the boat's captain felt the subdued atmosphere. It was strange, considering their trip down this same stretch of water just three weeks before. Then they had no fears, no need for silence. Now, everyone realized just how hostile the shores surrounding them were.

At length, the smoke rose from the stacks in greater

volume, and the engine room telegraph rang to show full steam was available. The anchors were raised and Richards moved the repeater to full ahead and the wheels slowly beat against the water once more. It would be a long trip north.

"That'll be Grand Gulf up ahead," pointed out Woodard, his hand stretched towards the next bend.

Smaller than Vicksburg, the city was arranged in a similar fashion. There was a sharp turn in the river, with the eastern shoreline marked by tall bluffs.

"We can be anchored on this side of Vicksburg within six hours," commented Richards upon examining his watch.

"That's true, captain. How's the coal holding out?"

The commander shrugged. "Another ten hours of steam, I would guess. We will replenish when we rejoin the flotilla." He picked his telescope from the rack and observed the rebel city.

They made no secret of their allegiance. Confederate flags were visible at several spots. Farragut's hard fought trip to Vicksburg was of little consequence, for the navy only controlled those sections of the river where it had ships. And at the moment, the only ship from Vicksburg to Baton Rouge was *MACHINEEL*.

"Better call to quarters," he said, returning the glass.

"Think they've set up some guns?"

"No telling, but they have certainly had the time. Those flags show they have the inclination!"

The men moved rapidly about their work. The boat was back in fighting trim, the last vestiges of the fever disappearing on their way to New Orleans. And though it was late August and still quite warm, it was a drier heat and easier to withstand.

They drew closer to the city, and a cannon fired from atop a hill. A second, then a third joined, the shells falling ahead or behind the boat.

"You may reply if you can hit them," directed Richards to the gun deck.

Only the rifle fired, smoke and dirt exploding well down from the crest where the guns were mounted. The rebels, even with their advantage of height, were unable to make good on their threat, however. The lone battery could not place a shot within a hundred yards of the slow moving gunboat. And after two unsuccessful attempts at reply, the Parrot fell silent on the ship.

"Vicksburg will not be so easy," observed Woodard.

"We can bide our time," said Richards. "We will anchor south of the city, and wait for a stormy night to make the run."

"Do we have the coal for that?"

"Maybe our friends in the army can move some across the point if we get desperate, Mr. Woodard." Despite his resolve and continued formality, Richards found he liked Woodard. He hoped he would not rue the day he made that decision.

They were only forced to wait three days for a break in the weather. All day long, the clouds were low and threatening, rushing out of the southwest with mad fury. By nightfall, they were surrounded by flashes of lightning and the crash of thunder. It was just the event Richards was waiting for.

The days at anchor were not wasted. Their starboard side was piled with cotton bales obtained from the army. The upper deck, too, was equally encumbered, the space around the stacks, the field piece and the pilothouse all similarly cotton-clad. Further, with few exceptions, the top deck was strewn with all manner of cotton bales, chains and hawsers to impede shot from passing through and into the crowded gun deck below.

"Full steam," reported Woodard as the rain drummed

against the sides.

"Let's not keep our reb friends waiting, Mr. Woodard," announced Richards. "All ahead!"

They moved against the current, even more slowly than usual with all the extra weight piled upon the vessel. Still, the night was dark and visibility poor. The gunboat stood a good chance of passing the rebels unseen. The men waited expectantly, ready to reply to any fire received. Then, when the storm reached its peak, the ship betrayed herself.

A column of flame shot from one stack, flaring high into the night. Before Richards could order something done about it, the other funnel did the same. Two bright tongues of fire announced their presence clearly, and the rebels were not hesitant in opening upon them.

"Damn," cursed Woodard. He ducked, a reflex move to the roar of a shot above.

"Keep us at it," said the captain. He shouted below to the gun deck. "Reply as you can!"

The thirty-two's fired, their sound all but lost in the din of storm and shell about them. A bundle of cotton bales exploded forward from a strike. Richards tried to observe the damage, but the dark and rain obscured the view.

"I will be back!" he said, leaving the pilothouse and going forward.

The makeshift armor was scattered, but little real damage was done. The field gun crew squatted behind the bales, unable to bring their small weapon to bear at the range from shore. Richards confirmed they were uninjured, then returned to the helm.

"That was damned stupid!" cursed Woodard.

"What?"

The Irishman ducked again at the sound of an explosion overhead. Shrapnel rattled on the roof above them. "Going up there. We'd be notified if the damage were serious!"

There was a crack astern and they spun at the sound. The flagstaff was shot through halfway up its length, the colors falling over the side. No one ashore could see the flag in the darkness, so it made little difference to Richards. He faced back around to check their progress when Woodard grabbed his arm.

"Look at that!" he shouted.

Keeler was shimmying up the remaining part of the staff, the slim length swaying with the wind and the motion of the ship. At its end, he unwrapped a flag from his waist and tacked it to the pole. He slid back down the pole as a shell exploded over the stern, splinters tearing tufts from the cotton bales piled there. Keeler fell to the deck, and Richards thought him wounded. But before the commander could rush out, the young man was on his feet and dashing into the gun deck.

"You are all crazy!" concluded Woodard.

The flaming soot from the stacks died out, and the firing from Vicksburg with it. *MACHINEEL* rounded the bend with only one other hit when a shot struck a stack of cotton at the side. Richards received the personnel report of only two minor wounds gladly. But he thought about the action further. Woodard was right, for his trip to check the damage from the first hit was unnecessary.

He considered Keeler's actions aft. It was an axiom within the navy to keep the colors flying, but they made little difference in a battle such as this. The rebels would not have seen them strike, even if they had felt the need. Equally, there was no danger in the confederates assuming they had struck when the flag was blown away. So what was Keeler's justification in risking so much to replace them? Was he living up to the unspoken rules or simply indulging in a bit of bravado? Another, more dangerous idea occurred to him. Keeler made no secret of his hero worship of the ship's captain. Perhaps he was simply trying to live up to the man's standards. It was not a thought which gave Richards particular relish.

*   *   *   *   *

Two days later, *MACHINEEL* lay at anchor near Memphis. *BENTON* and two other boats were there also. A few more remained at Vicksburg with the mortars, but the rest were either on patrol or gone north.

"I heard about your run past the batteries, commander," Davis congratulated when Richards came across. "Well done."

"Thank you, commodore."

Davis passed an envelope to him. "Here are your orders for the refit I promised. Take her north to Cairo and release the crew for a few weeks."

"How long shall we be?" questioned Richards.

"You will find the refit a bit more extensive than you thought, commander. We are introducing a new type of gunboat." He chuckled slightly. "Everyone is already referring to them as 'tinclads'."

"Tinclads?"

"We are cutting down the more shallow draft boats and *MACHINEEL* qualifies. The exterior is covered with half-inch plate. It will not stop rebel shells but it will stop small arms fire."

"Aye, sir."

"Do not worry, commander, they will get you back here in time to see plenty of action."

"I was going to request an ocean assignment, captain," said Richards.

"I cannot blame you: feel free to make the request. But until then, I need you out here. Damned rebels are building ironclads up every stream and river wide enough to float a log! If they managed to get half the ships they start finished..." He let the comment die. "We sank another and burned two just last week."

"Oh?"

"They had one afloat but not plated just up the Arkansas. I sent three of the boats to deal with them. Some brash young lieutenant was not content to just burn his boat and make off like the other two. Had to have a regular shoot with him. Sank one of ours too, by God!"

"As I have said before, these men do not lack bravery."

"No, they do not," agreed Davis. "The man was navy, though. It always gives me pain to face them. We captured a few of the builders. They said his name was Caldwell, or something like that."

Richards felt a twist of pain at the name. "Judson Caldwell?" he asked.

"I believe you are right, Richards. A friend?" Davis's voice was not unsympathetic.

"Aye, sir. A shipmate."

Davis shook his head sadly. "Too bad. We heard he was killed, or at least badly wounded. His crewmen carried him off before we could capture him."

"Yes, sir. Too bad."

"I am sorry, Richards. We all have friends on the wrong side of this war. Oh, one more thing." He handed the officer a telegram envelope. "Well, you have your orders. See to your ship."

Richards saluted and left, opening the envelope as he came on deck. It was from Becky.

John:

Received word you are being sent to Cairo. I shall try to meet you there.

Rebecca

He had not expected this. In his heart, he doubted she would actually come. He expected there would be a telegram excusing her absence when they reached Cairo. Given his mixed feelings from the past weeks, he wondered what would happen if she actually showed up?

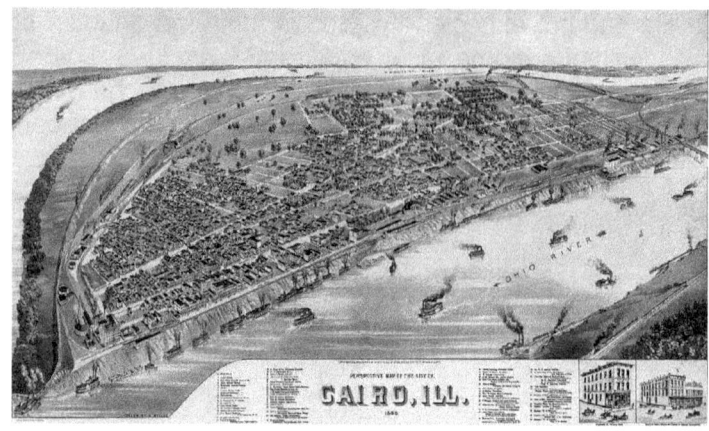

Cairo, Illinois

CHAPTER FOURTEEN

The trees around Cairo were starting to change colors when the *MACHINEEL* dropped anchor in the navy establishment. After the heat of the summer, the cool air of early fall was a pleasant experience for the crew of the hard worked gunboat. The naval yard, a scene of fevered activity in the spring, was positively frantic.

Two large ironclads lay on the stocks built about halfway up from the keel. Gunboats lay in almost every available slot, workmen swarming about them like bees in their hives. Richards was not even given time to send a boat to report when a steam launch approached and a civilian jumped onto the deck.

"This here *MACHINEEL*?" the man demanded loudly as he gripped the ladder to proceed to the upper deck.

"Yes," returned Richards. He stared down the rungs at the interloper. The newcomer did not waste time as he climbed up.

"Get the anchor back up agin," he directed. "We got your slot awaitin'."

D. A. Joy

Richards could not decide how to take the command. Normally, he was used to things done in a much more orderly fashion. Of course, he also recalled incidents where he railed against the slowness of the bureaucracy.

"You heard the man, Mr. Keeler," he responded at length.

"Get her ahead slow." Without so much as asking permission, the newcomer elbowed Levenson from the wheel. "She'll be laid up over there, cap'n." He pointed to an empty quay on the east side of the yard. "We have got a crew ready to start on her and she'll be done up in 'bout three weeks."

"Do you have our orders?" he asked, still trying to catch up to the speed of occurrences.

The man shrugged. "You can talk to the yard commander about all that navy stuff, cap'n. I just makes sure the ships're finished when they wants 'em." They drew close to the wharf, and the constructor stuck his head from the pilothouse. "Man the lines, boys! The sooner you are tied up, the sooner you'll be ashore!"

For a moment, Richards feared one of the men might be trampled in the rush to toss the lines to the waiting dock hands. But no one was seriously injured in the melee. He recalled his orders. The men would be released for two weeks when they made the yard.

The engine repeater was moved to stop and the pilot leaned to the speaking tube. "Secure the boilers and clean up down there good! You will not recognize the old girl when you sees her agin!"

Keeler was as dazed by the rush of events as Richards. He returned to the pilothouse, his face quirked in question.

"Assemble the crewmen aft, Mr. Keeler."

"Aye aye, sir," he replied, touching his cap.

Again, the men rushed to their places at the stern. The

whole ship was alive with the sound of feet on deck planking. Richards reviewed the assemblage from his vantage above, careful to confirm the boat was pulled tight to the wharf and lashed securely in place.

"You have got you orders," he said, noting most already carried their kit bags. "We are to move out in two weeks. Off to the paymaster's and you are free until then. Dismissed."

With shouts and hollers, the men streamed from the vessel, not even waiting for a gangway to cover the short stretch of water between them and the dock. Their captain watched them go, feeling relief for the first time in weeks at not being responsible for their lives.

Levenson touched his cap to the captain and was gone, following his mates ashore as quickly as his feet would carry him. Keeler waited on the deck and Richards found himself alone in the pilothouse with the man from the ship yard. There was plenty of noise and bustle along the quay, but MACHINEEL was strangely quiet with most of the crew already ashore. Steam hissed as Anson and his crew released the pressure from the boilers. It sounded like a heavy sigh of relief from the hard-worked vessel.

"That'll do her, cap'n," announced their visitor.

"What is your name, anyway?" demanded Richards before the man could escape back down the ladder.

"Jones, cap'n. Quinton Jones." The presence which had exploded upon them was as quickly gone, back to his steam launch and heading for another part of the yard.

"Welcome to Cairo, Mr. Keeler," announced Richards as the junior officer rejoined him at the pilothouse. Already, the ship sounded dead, most of her crew gone ashore not to be seen for at least two weeks. Noise still drifted up from the boiler room, but it would not last much longer either.

"Aye, captain," responded the other. For the first time in a long while, Keeler relaxed. He pushed his cap back on his head and leaned against the side of the pilothouse. "What are you going to do for the next two weeks, sir?" he asked.

"My wife is supposed to meet me here," Richards returned. He found himself enjoying the pleasant conversation, this sharing of unimportant thoughts with Keeler. He failed to remember it was in violation of his rule on getting too close to those about him. "I will stay around, and keep an eye on the old *MACHINEEL*. Make sure they are treating her right. What about you, Mr. Keeler?"

The boy shrugged. "Headin' home to see my ma," he returned. "She's up in St. Louis. I will be leavin' with Mr. Woodard."

As if on cue, the older man shouted from the fantail. "You comin', laddie? Me missus don't want to wait forever!"

"Take care, Mr. Keeler," said Richards.

The young man hesitated, glancing first down to Woodard, then to his commander. "Captain," he said, the word bursting forth. "Are you sure your wife is comin'? I was hopin' maybe you could come with us? My ma, she wouldn't mind."

Richards smiled and touched the lieutenant on the shoulder. "Thank you for the offer, Mr. Keeler, but I shall stay here with the ship. Now get going. Mr. Woodard is anxious!"

He touched his cap again. "Aye, sir."

Keeler went down the steps. Woodard placed his arm around the boy's shoulder, and they left the ship that way.

Even in the heat of summer, with half the crew sick and the rest lying about, the ship was never so quiet. The only sounds came from the work progressing in the yard, the rasp of saws and the puffing of steam engines. There was the bang of metal on metal, or the shouts of laborers about their work. All normal to them, but so different for the naval officer.

He walked about the mid-deck, taking in the silence of the vessel. She was strange and mute. He expected voices in conversation, the laughter of men at work or relaxation.

There was only still air and deathly hush. The gun deck was no different. The guns and accouterments of battle lay at the ready - solid shot, rammers, buckets for water and sand. But no roar filled the room; the breeches were cold to the touch. Even the engineer and coal heavers were gone, the boilers only slightly warm as their heat radiated away. The furnaces were clean, the ashes raked clear and dumped.

It was a rare experience, to roam a ship alone. He could only recall it happening to him once before, two years previous in December. The sloop COHOCTON was waiting to be guided into dry dock. The crew was paid-off and sent away, the war yet to start. But she had this same feeling of death about her, the air of a living thing no longer breathing. Richards tried shaking the sensation away, but it was no use. Instead, he went to his cabin to collect his belongings and the vessel's orders. The civilians might have their way of doing things, but he still had to report to the yard's commandant.

"Welcome back, commander," said Evans, returning Richards' orders after reviewing them. The commandant's secretary scratched his chin. "Surely there was something else for you?" continued the officer. He stopped in thought. "Of course, commander." The man searched through the mound of paper on his desk. At length, he produced a small yellow sheet with a hastily scribbled note. "Here it is!" Richards was surprised at the handwriting on the page.

John:

I arrived yesterday. I have taken a room for us at the Allwyn Boarding House. Please meet me there.

Becky

His heart skipped a beat at the message. He had wondered if she would actually come, or if there would be a last minute excuse offered to decline. Did he really want to see her? Their letters had been conciliatory but neither of them was willing to surrender their main point.

There was a stop at the paymasters to collect his back salary, then he found a ride to the boarding house. He knocked on the door, and was greeted by an older, heavy set lady.

"John Richards, ma'am," he said, introducing himself. "I believe my wife has taken a room for us."

"Of course, commander." She smiled broadly, throwing the door open for him. Rebecca was not there, but Mrs. Allwyn took him to their rooms, closing the door behind her as she withdrew.

The building had once been a private residence in finer times. Now, the three floors were converted into rooms for boarders. The one Becky had chosen was large, constituting half of the upper floor and had two rooms.

The first was a dressing room by all accounts. There was a sofa, and a stove in one corner. There was also a tub for baths, with a drain to let the water run outside the house. Even stranger was the pump for water, unusual because most homes would only have pumps in the kitchen. The second room held the bed and a dresser. He entered it, setting his bag on the bed.

He emptied the contents into the dresser. The room had a small window, which faced back towards the river. The navy yard was just in sight in the distance. He took his telescope from the drawer where he had lain it and turned it south. The view was not clear but *MACHINEEL* was discernable, the small blots of workmen already moving about her decks. He replaced the glass in the drawer.

The door to the room flew open and Rebecca swept in like a storm. They stared at each other for a long while. Even though he was waiting for her, he was still surprised at her arrival. He walked over and placed his arms around her. She gave him a kiss on the cheek.

"How as your trip?" he asked.

"Miserable," she answered in a huff. "Lorraine couldn't come, because of the baby and all. None of the servants seemed willing either, so I just left them there.

"Trains are horrible things," she complained. "Dirty and drafty and uncomfortable. Last night, we stopped at Mound City." She shuddered at the thought. "What a filthy place! I hope to never see it again!" She removed her light coat, and sat down on the sofa.

"I spent most of the day looking around Cairo. There is no entertainment, unless you frequent saloons. And the restaurants! There must be a better place to build these damned ships of yours." All in all, the impression given was the whole affair was for no other purpose than to inconvenience her.

"I am sorry," apologized Richards coolly. "I shall try to do better next time!"

At first, her eyes were angry. Then their look softened as she considered what she had said. "I am sorry, John," she said finally. "I realize it is none of your doing. And Mrs. Allwyn's is a fine place." She swept a hand across the rooms. "Much better than any of the others I have seen here."

For all their time apart, it seemed they had little to speak about. She talked mostly of Lorraine and her pregnancy, while Richards spoke little of the river and the MACHINEEL. She had read much about the goings on along the river, and it was evident in her replies. But she did not ask for elaboration on his activities, apparently still upset about his leaving her. And that night, after a fine dinner from Mrs. Allwyn's kitchen, Rebecca simply excused herself to bed on the protest of exhaustion from her trip. It was almost exactly what Richards had expected from the reunion.

The next morning, Richards ate a quick breakfast before

leaving for the yard. It was his ship which lay there, and he planned to keep an eye on the work performed. Though a long walk, he strolled the streets to get there, taking in the brisk air.

MACHINEEL's looks were already altered. Workmen swarmed over the vessel, and her sides were all but gone. It appeared the men were more bent on her destruction than the promised refit. At first sight of the stripped hull, Richards was forced to restrain himself from immediately rushing down to the constructor. Instead, he strolled up the line of ships and observed the changes wrought to each.

The removed siding was not gone for long. New sides grew to replace them, extending the enclosed gun deck even further forward on the bow. The pilothouses were moved and lowered, and new guns brought aboard. Finally, sides were plated with a layer of iron to keep out rifle shot. One of the tinclads moved into the river, her bow headed downstream. There was no doubt the ship presented a more military appearance than the gunboats before conversion, but it was yet to be seen if the changes improved their fighting qualities.

"Get out of the way!"

He jumped at the shout and moved to one side as two men walked past carrying a long plank. He thought of searching out the constructor, but the civilians in the place wanted nothing to do with their navy customers. They were dealing in a volume business, and the sooner the vessels were converted and back on the river, the larger their profit would be. Richards only watched the work on his vessel for an hour before heading back into the town.

He stoked the stove carefully against the chilly night. Rebecca sat on the sofa, her hands darting across some needle work. It was a small garment, apparently something for Lorraine's child. He closed the door on the stove.

"How were things at the ship?" she asked idly.

"Busy," he answered. "They do not need a naval officer underfoot."

"I have not received many letters from you these past months." The observation was pointed.

"I am sorry. After we parted in April, I was not sure what I would say. I did not see a great many coming from the east, either."

"I was angry," she answered. "Angry with you and with father." She set the sewing down. "I do not like being abandoned in that fashion, John."

He stepped across and sat next to her. "I did not abandon you, or at least I never meant to do so. There is a job to do."

"You can do it from Washington," she ventured. "Father can use you in the navy department."

He shook his head. "I belong afloat," he responded. "it is what I trained for; what I want to do."

"And what about me?"

"Becky, I was alone on the river. Your letters were a touch of friendship, companionship."

"Companionship? Is that all I mean to you? And how can you be alone in a fleet full of ships?"

"It is very easy to be alone," he returned. "You managed it by running off to Hartford. A ship, or even a fleet, is no different." She was still so beautiful. He reached out and touched her cheek. She did not draw away. "I have never meant to hurt you. You know that."

She rubbed her cheek against his hand before leaning over next to him. "Yes, John, but it is just not the way I thought it would be." She stared into his eyes, and he brought his lips down to hers. "What are we going to do?" she asked, as their lips parted.

"I do not know, Becky. I really do not know."

*   *   *   *   *

The next morning was a fresh Monday, and Richards walked briskly down to the navy yard. *MACHINEEL*'s shaped changed considerably in the past week. Her mid-deck was mostly open, just a small area in the center remaining enclosed. The pilothouse was further forward and smaller than the previous one. The main deck sides were sloping and angular, extending most of the way forward on the ship. The gun deck extended aft also, leaving just a small fantail to serve as a receiving area for the gunboat.

But her sides were still wood, the timber still green. Richards went aboard the vessel, wondering how she would differ. Another navy officer was already there, and Richards was surprised to see the stripes of a rear-admiral adorning his sleeves.

"And who might you be?" asked the admiral. He was a middle-aged man, probably in his early fifties. His face was covered by a luxuriant beard which hid most of his features except for a pair of bright and questing eyes.

"Commander John Richards, sir," he returned, surprised at finding an admiral aboard his vessel. "I am commanding the *MACHINEEL*."

"Richards." The voice was clipped and gruff. "Of course. Pensacola and Vicksburg if I am not mistaken."

"You seem to have the advantage of me, sir."

The deeply buried mouth turned up at the corners. "I know because I was there too, commander. David Porter." He extended his hand.

"*POWHATAN* at Pensacola," commented Richards, shaking the firm grip. This, then, was the brother of Dirty Bill. "And the mortar flotilla. Congratulations on the promotion. I thought David Farragut was our only admiral!"

Porter chuckled. "Not any more, it seems, but I am only an acting admiral. A month ago, I was just a commander like yourself. Gideon Welles has sent me to take command of the Mississippi Squadron."

"The Western Flotilla surely, Admiral."

Porter smiled again. "Not for long, my young friend."

"And Captain Davis?"

"He is to receive his stripes also," replied Porter. "Taking over the Bureau of Navigation."

"I see." Richards stepped aside to avoid a hurrying workman. Porter commanded a certain presence, however. The workmen avoided him. "What are you doing on my ship?" he asked.

"Just noting how the construction is going, commander." The admiral regarded him keenly, his eyes narrowing to slits. "There is one thing I have questioned, Commander. How does an observer from Washington can command an active vessel?"

Richards straightened at the remark but did not hesitate in his reply. "It is where I am most effective, admiral. I will leave the observing to the war correspondents."

Porter chuckled with real humor. It was clearly the answer he wanted to hear. "They tell me she'll be ready to leave by next Sunday. May I request a ride south with you?"

It was Richards' turn to laugh. "I cannot turn an admiral down, sir. Even an acting one."

"No, Richards," replied Porter in all seriousness. "You cannot."

"I met the admiral today," he said that evening, as he stoked the fire carefully.

"That's nice," she replied.

Their conversation dwindled, little more than an exchange of pleasantries on how each had passed the day. But when it came time to retire, there was no hesitation in either of their minds. In bed, their naked flesh entwined, he had no doubts or questions about their relationship. But when the passion died, the same thoughts would reoccur, as if nothing would banish them. It was a question of balance, and Richards did not perceive how to meet her halfway.

"The train leaves tomorrow," she said, leaving the bed momentarily to put on her night gown.

"So soon?" he asked. "But I am here through the rest of the week."

"I know, darling," she said, her endearment ringing hollow. "But Lorraine is due within the next six to eight weeks, and I want to be sure to be there. If I wait, it will be two weeks for the next train."

"You could take a river boat in two days," he suggested. "We could spend more time together. You would get to Washington only 4 or 5 days later."

"The train is faster," she answered. She returned to the bed, but lay on top of the covers. "The timetables are set."

"Of course," he relented, agreeing to her excuse.

Their conversations were all like this one. If anything seemed at all confrontational, they would both sheer off, afraid to broach the problems between them. But he found he could no longer live with the uncertainty.

"Our marriage was very sudden, Becky. Sometimes, I fear I let you rush me into it," he said, unable to stop the flow of words. "But it is a fact in our lives, and we must both confront it. Our relationship has not been what it should or could be, and this failing concerns me. We cannot run from it forever."

She paused before answering. It seemed a long while before she spoke.

"I admit I, too, share some of those feelings." She dabbed at the corner of her eye with a handkerchief. "What are we to do?"

Now given vent, he could no longer contain his feelings.

He pressed ahead, as if he was driving his ship into action.

"What *are* we to do, Rebecca? Are we to spend the rest of our lives hiding from one another? And now you are leaving early to even avoid the subject."

His voice was calm and did not reflect the emotions that stormed within him. He could see the tears in her eyes now, but he steeled his heart against them

"We have had such a short time together these past two years. I reread some of your letters from before the war, and I recalled why I fell in love with you." She dabbed at her eyes again and there was a slight quaver to her voice. "When we are together, at night when I lay next to you, I can only think of holding the feeling forever. Yet in my heart, I know your duty calls and you will always leave to answer it."

He shook his head, for this was always the heart of the problem.

"The life of a naval officer is not an easy one. I am well aware of this. You were not ignorant of it before we wed. I spent over a year in the Mediterranean, and you waited for me. You knew this is my life and how I chose to live it."

With each passing word, he felt a weight lifting from his heart. The message was not pleasant, for either him or Rebecca. It made the words no less necessary.

"We both have our lives to lead," he continued. He could no more stop than withdraw from an engagement. "Mine is as a naval officer. Risk of death and injury is part of my oath as an officer. I could not live with myself, or anyone for that matter, if this conflict passed and I did not feel I executed my duty. Whether you wish to admit this or not, you know it to be true.

"I love you. If you believe this and feel it, we must find a way to make our lives together work. If you cannot accept this or my chosen profession, we must end our marriage - now, before any further commitment is made." Her tears flowed freely, but he could not stop now. "I am aware these are harsh words. But they are true words. What is our life together to be, Rebecca?"

She shook her head angrily. "We have been married such a short time," she protested. "To suggest annulling the vows is outlandish!"

"When is the right time, Becky?" he asked softly.

She rolled over to lay against him and he could feel her tears on his shoulder. Still, the covers of the bed separated them.

"I love you more than I care to admit," she said. Her arms gripped him tightly, echoing her words. "I will not let you go until we are both sure our marriage cannot survive. If that comes to pass, I shall release you, even if it breaks my heart."

He slipped his arm around her and could feel her sobbing quietly as they lay in the dark. He stared straight ahead into the darkness. After their words, he found his heart beating as fast as if he were under fire. In effect, he was. The turmoil of the thoughts expressed did not let sleep come to him. It was a small price for seeking the resolution to the rest of one's life.

The following morning, he saw her to the station, carrying her bags aboard the car for her. They kissed, the touch of her lips reawakening his passion, but there was no delaying her departure.

Their conversation only solved half of his problems, however, and he knew it. It was clear some of his actions the past six months were foolhardy. He would address that issue on the river, in the face of the enemy.

By Friday, *MACHINEEL* was looking like a ship again. Her sides were dull black, and the barrels of guns were visible at the gun ports. He nodded with approval. Before, she appeared only as any other riverboat used for hauling supplies along the water. Now she was different, lower and deadlier. There was now the aspect of a proper warship about the small vessel.

The crew was reporting back and, upon confirming with the yard's superintendent, he was able to let men stay aboard the ship. The interior work on the ship was completed, and there were only a few iron plates to bolt to the sides to complete her transformation. Before, where Richards could barely get aboard without being trampled by workmen, it was now possible to move about the decks in relative freedom.

The upper deck still held the pilothouse, but it was now directly behind the stacks instead of just forward of the wheels. The height of the entire vessel was lower, and the pilothouse was no exception. It was wound round with hawsers and chains to provide some measure of protection for the occupants. No longer was an "N" suspended between the stacks. The white painted sides of the pilothouse, all four of them, sported a large "37" to announce their identity. Even the tops of the stacks were different, though it was not noticeable at first. Instead of the normal, pointed flares of metal so common to the river ships, they now carried cylindrical caps. Also, their lone six-pounder was sited a deck down.

The middle deck was open, leaving a wide walkway all around the enclosed center section. Officer's country was still at this level, the enclosed area holding the wardroom, with the tubes of the two stacks running through it, as well as quarters for the officers. There was a considerable deck forward of the old end of the superstructure which formed the roof of the gun house. This was just planking, however, and now carried the field piece.

The gun deck was the most noticeable change on the vessel. Extended forward and aft, the sloping sides carried the dull glean of iron upon them. There was very little open space at either the extreme bow or the fantail. Most activity would be kept within the gun house confines.

Inside, the center was still occupied by the boilers and engine rooms. The furnaces remained forward, directly beneath the stacks. The boilers lay next with some open space behind them. The engines lay dead aft, the pistons needed to drive the stern wheels given a large amount of clearance. The bulwarks of the engineering space were strengthened and chains wound round to serve as a mail armor. About that were stacked bales of cotton, further protection against their most deadly enemy: steam.

The armament changed considerably to match the other alterations. Gone was the massive gun forward, a weapon too large to be fired quickly. Instead, a pair of sixty-four pounder cannon pointed across the bow. Still heavy pieces for so small a ship, they could be fired much faster than the monster carried previously. Down each side were five gun ports, and they carried two types of guns. Immediately behind the sixty-fours were a pair of army field guns on both sides, though they were twelve pounders instead of the smaller six pounder carried above. These were for attacking personnel ashore, for they were much too small for ship work. Aft of them lay three thirty-two pounders per side, the standard weapon of any naval vessel.

For all the modifications, the ship actually drew less water in the new configuration. Everything had been done to reduce weight as the iron and guns were added. Where she took close to five feet before, she now drew just over four. The first year on the river showed it was necessary to get the ships into all sorts places, and the less draft the vessel carried, the more she could meet those needs.

Before, Richards had thought the vessel barely tolerable. Now these changes brought her more in line with what a warship should look like. There was a whole different feel to the gunboat, and it was a pleasant change.

Along with the increased artillery came an increase in the crew. On the average, it took eleven men to serve each of the weapons on the vessel. Whereas she carried five big guns before, there were now eight on the vessel. With a crew of five for the twelve and the six pounders, their gunnery compliment had changed from requiring sixty men to over one hundred twenty. And as the old crew returned over the course of two days to see the changes wrought to their ship, additional new men came aboard and had to be told off into gun parties, watches and all the other necessities of ship board life. Richards, left to handle most of this with only his petty officers for help, was more than glad to see Woodard and Keeler walking across the gangway.

"Welcome aboard, gentlemen," greeted Richards.

"I didn't recognized the old girl!" said Keeler enthusiastically. He hardly remembered to salute the stern of the vessel as he stepped aboard.

"Aye, lieutenant," agreed Woodard.

There was an easy-going familiarity between the two, a change brought about by their trip together. Could there be any doubt it was the first time Woodard had addressed Keeler by his rank since stepping off the vessel two weeks previous? Still, Richards had come to know Woodard fairly well over their three month association. There was something troubling the man. The easy going charm and wit was slowed, kept in check.

"Store your gear and meet me in the wardroom," directed the captain, regarding his first carefully. "I have much for you to do if we are to up anchor on Monday."

"Aye, sir."

Four officers for close on two hundred men was not unusual. With the petty officers, they still had a controllable crew. Each gun crew contained a gunners mate, and that left the chain of command the same numbers of layers. With Anson seeing to his engine room crew, Richards assigned his other two officers to storing the supplies which were being stacked on the dockside. It was dark, the late fall evening robbing them of light shortly after five o'clock, before the crew was released for the evening. A few stayed aboard, but most went into town seeking other diversion for their last night's leave. The next night, all would be aboard. At first light on Monday, they would be steaming south, with the current at their backs.

"Not going ashore, Mr. Woodard?" asked Richards, noting the man at the rail outside the wardroom.

Woodard did not bother to turn to greet his captain. "Not this evenin', sir. I have other things on me mind."

"Is everything well at home? Is your wife alright?" questioned Richards. He regretted it immediately, for it did not matter to their job. But he did await the reply.

"Aye, cap'n. The missus is fine." Woodard spat over the side, his eyes pointed south. The Mississippi opened beyond the confines of the yard, and the shore of Kentucky was just a black mass in the distance. His shoulders were slumped, but his face turned to Richards as he continued to answer.

"It's me older boy, cap'n," he said sadly. "Run off to the army, he did."

"I see," responded Richards. "There is a lot of that these days, though. How old is he?"

"Seventeen. Just seventeen."

"I am sorry, Mr. Woodard. If we had been north, maybe we could have taken him aboard here. At any rate, if he's joined, he was able to take his choice of units. Surely that's better than letting him be drafted."

"You do not understand, cap'n." The words were bitter, but not directed at Richards. They were aimed at the shore across the river. "He joined the *rebel* army."

It was still dark Monday morning when Porter came aboard. Richards quickly introduced his officers before sending them to their duties. The admiral accompanied him to the pilothouse as the ship prepared to get underway.

"Looks like a beautiful morning, captain," observed

Porter. "A good omen for starting our work against the rebels!"

"Aye, sir."

There was the sound of the anchor being raised, the shouts of men as the cables was hauled inboard. Porter roamed the confines of the pilothouse, pacing its dimensions like a caged animal. He pointed out one large ship to their beam.

"The *BLACKHAWK* will be joining the squadron soon. That will release the *BENTON* for service with the other ironclads."

The large ship lay there, her sides marked with the lights from lanterns as workers continued their labor in the darkness. She would definitely dominate the rest of the squadron when she joined them, for she was one of the largest river vessels Richards had yet seen.

"Ahead slow, Mr. Anson," said Richards to the speaking tube, pulling back on the repeater. There was a moment before the slow splash of the wheels reached the bridge. "Hard port, Mr. Weaver."

The tinclad moved clear of the other vessels, nosing out into the river proper. Woodard joined them at the pilothouse, noting their position and grunting with satisfaction.

"A brilliant morning to be heading out against the rebels, eh Mr. Woodard?" commented Porter, in a truly jovial mood.

"Aye," came the dull reply. "Brilliant." He looked to Richards. "I will be below if I am needed, cap'n." He did not wait for permission and went back down the companionway.

"Is he always so taciturn?" asked Porter.

"No, sir. He's just found out his oldest son has run off to join the rebels."

Porter took a deep breath, realizing what his words had done to the man. "I must apologize to him later, but I did not know. Still, the rebels must take their own chances. We are here to save the republic!"

"Aye, sir."

At the moment, Richards thoughts were not on the war. Instead, he was staring east and thinking of the letter he had mailed to Rebecca.

A Mississippi Squadron tinclad

CHAPTER FIFTEEN

The *MACHINEEL* made a quick passage to Memphis. With her new lighter weight, the vessel gained nearly a full knot of speed through the water. And with the aid of the current, she made a respectful showing on the trip.

Porter was a different sort than Davis, a different sort entirely. Whereas the old commodore was willing to let each captain run his vessel with a minimum of interference, the new admiral was constantly giving Richards suggestions on how to handle the gunboat, or methods of organization, or just about anything else that crossed the quick and fertile mind. By the time *BENTON* came into view, Richards was more than happy to turn his charge over to the flagship.

Still, the vessel spent a day languishing under the eye of flag before receiving orders to proceed. In this case, there were three army transports waiting to move south. *MACHINEEL* was to see them safely to their destination north of Vicksburg before patrolling the stretch between the Yazoo on the south and the White on the north.

MACHINEEL led the column, the three transports trailing in a ragged line behind. Their decks were crowded with blue uniforms, the soldiers moving from the interiors of the vessels whenever possible. The weather was pleasant, but it was still mid-autumn. Likely, it would change as winter approached.

Unlike his first time down this stretch of river during the summer, the trip took almost five days as they were slowed to the pace of the vessels behind. A collective sigh of relief went up from the gunboat when the transports anchored off the mouth of the Yazoo with the growing army forces there.

Woodard was no longer the wit of the vessel, and the men noticed it quickly. Before, he had spiced their days with yarns and laughter, but now the man withdrew within himself. There was no doubt as to the cause of the change, but there was also nothing to be done about it. A soldier, especially a rebel one, was lost in the masses. The chances of tracking one down without even knowing where to start were all but impossible. And even if Woodard was to find the boy, what was to be done about the situation? There was surely no way to release him from the confederate service.

For the rest of the ship, the river became an old home as they cruised back and forth in their designated strip week after week. Occasionally, a shot would ring out from shore, but they stayed well to the center of the flow, and the shots generally fell short. If not, it was just as likely to glance from the new iron plating attached to the vessel. Those shots always drew a load of grape from the field guns on the gun deck, which were primed and ready to sweep the shore with a scythe of death if one were foolish enough to fire upon them. It did not take long for word to spread, and the incidents became rare events.

At night, the vessel anchored near mid-stream but clear of the main channel. It would not do to have other traffic run them down in the middle of the night. The crew stayed within the gun house, out of the crisp night air of mid-November. Richards still appreciated it was warmer than a night farther north, say in New York or Connecticut.

"Captain?" Keeler shook him awake.

"Yes?" His eyes snapped open, and he forced himself to complete wakefulness.

"Boats upstream of us." His words were hushed, as though someone might overhear. There could be little doubt as to their meaning.

"Get the crew to quarters," he instructed, pulling on his clothes. "Quietly!" he emphasized before Keeler could leave. "Make sure the muskets and cutlasses are within easy reach."

He went into the night air, making for the bow. It was dark with rain falling, but the sound of slow oars reached the gunboat. A white line of splashes was visible, little more than twenty yards away. Richards quickly went down to the gun deck.

"Load with canister!" he ordered, forgetting all pretense at quiet. "Standby to repel boarders!"

He cursed himself for not rigging boarding nets outboard of the vessel, but it was too late for recriminations. Already, one of the boats was rushing up alongside.

"Captain!" The crewman pointed to the boat through a gun port.

"Fire as you bear!" At the order, one of the thirty-two's fired; splashes from the canister swept across the waters. But the boat was not within the line of fire and no damage was done.

The crew moved forward to reload the weapon. Outside, a yell arose from the boats, a scream of a terrify, almost inhuman nature. This was the rebel yell they had heard about, but there was no time to consider it.

"What the devil's happening?" demanded Woodard as

he arrived half dressed. Men leapt onto the open space on the bow of the gunboat, and a gunner pulled a lanyard on one of the sixty-fours.

The screams which followed were filled with pain and injury. Only two or three forms were left moving, and these fell motionless very quickly. There was a rattle of musketry, and a sailor fell near a gun port. Soldiers fired back, one leaping out of the way just in time to prevent injury as a cannon fired. The boats, for there were surely four or five of them, were all about them, and another gun fired from astern.

"Marines!" shouted Richards, looking for their sergeant. He was nowhere to be seen. "Follow me!"

With his pistol in one hand, he snatched a cutlass from the wall and headed up. He emerged into the night on top of the gun deck. Rebels clambered up the side, the dark forms hiding their numbers.

There was no time for Richards to think. A hand appeared near his foot as someone grasped for a hold to make the middle deck. He slashed it through, hearing a scream of agony followed by the splash of a body into the water. The hand, grip slowly relaxing, still lay on the deck.

He pulled back the hammer on his pistol and gripped the hilt of the saber tightly. With a yell, he ran towards the rebels, emptying the pistol into the bunched mass.

One victim fell, half his face blown away by the shot, but the rebels held their ground, unwilling to fall back down the side. Three more lay on the deck when the pistol clicked on an empty chamber. Richards hacked at one as he tried to raise a pistol.

He pulled back, blinded by the flash of a pistol in the night. He swung the cutlass, feeling it bite flesh as a man screamed at the impact. There was a warm wash of air past his face as another gun exploded in his direction. He continued to hack at the rebels, but their combined weight began to push him backwards. He felt panic at the thought of losing the ship, the imminent loss of his life not registering in the heat of the moment.

There was the sharp crack of a musket, followed by two more. His eyesight returned in time to see three of his marines run into the crowd with their bayonets fixed. One grabbed his collar and pulled him inboard. As he cleared the rebels, a ragged volley of musket fired from astern and several more of the rebels dropped. The remainder fell back, jumping over the side or down to the main deck. The six soldiers formed a rough line.

"Fire at will!" ordered Richards.

At the bow, a boat tried to pull off towards shore and was raked by canister from one of the cannon. Downstream, another drifted, only one or two oars fighting the flow. Another was slightly ahead, pulling steadily. The enemy fire died away to nothing. Two men left standing on the bow dropped their weapons and held up their hands in surrender.

"Cease fire!" ordered Richards. He let out a long, heavy sigh.

"Mr. Keeler?" he called. The lieutenant appeared, his face blackened by powder. "Two more minutes, and we would be spending the rest of this war in a confederate prison camp!"

"Aye, sir."

"Secure from quarters. Bring me a list of the dead and wounded."

"Yes, sir."

Woodard appeared, his night shirt torn, his hand holding a pistol. Richards became aware of the cutlass, still gripped tightly in his left hand. He had to pry his fingers from the hilt. The weapon was covered with blood, and he was spattered with the substance.

"Bloody fools!" cursed Woodard. He kicked at one of the

bodies at his feet. "This isn't some damned transport waiting as easy pickings!"

"We might well have been. We have been laying up every night for the past two weeks in this stretch of the river. It takes no great genius to see I set us up for this! Damn me as a fool, too!"

"If you insist, cap'n."

Richards gave him a hard look. At least it was some return of the humor he had always shown. "Get this mess cleaned up! I want her looking proper in the morning!"

"Aye, sir."

Richards returned to his cabin. He found their sergeant was one of the first casualties, cut down at the stern by the boarders. He sat on his bunk, chastising himself for placing the ship in such a position. It was not the first time the rebels had tried a boat action against a vessel anchored in the river, and he had given them plenty of time to make their plans.

He opened his revolver and drew out the empty casings, returning them to the ammunition box. All six chambers were expended, but he did not recall counting that many. He reloaded the weapon, and returned it to the box. He walked to his washbowl to splash some water in his face.

His left hand touched the water and it immediately began to stain. He glanced down. His hand and arm was covered with blood. He only remembered using the cutlass twice, but surely all of this could not be from just two cuts? He had never used a sword in a fight before and it was a new experience. He washed his arm, recalling the jar of the impact, the scream of the injured. It was a very personal kind of killing, not like standing off and mowing down soldiers with artillery.

He finished cleaning himself, then got properly dressed. It was just before one bell in the morning watch, and there was little use in returning to sleep. Instead, he went back onto the mid-deck, watching the crew remove the bodies of their assailants.

A few injured were taken down to the surgeon, but most were already dead and several more would follow. Their own losses were relatively light: only two dead and eight wounded. It could have been much worse. The line of bodies at the stern grew as they were wrapped in canvas. Eighteen of the rebels were found dead aboard. Ten more were tended by the surgeon. Many more were blown over the side by the blast at the bow, while still others were shot or hacked into the water. It was an expensive proposition. Their losses must have amounted to forty or fifty men.

"Get up steam when you are finished there, Mr. Woodard," instructed Richards. The first officer did not notice him standing above them at first. Instead, he examined the faces of each of the rebels before replying to the captain.

"Aye, sir."

"We will stand back down to the mouth of the Yazoo today, I think." He did not wait for a reply, but walked forward.

The six pounder sat in its normal position, and Richards regarded it dully. It was already loaded with grape. Instead of using the marines, he could just as easily pointed it down the deck. True, they would have torn up some of their own woodwork, but what of it? The blast of grape would have succeeded in one or two shots, with fewer men at risk. The thought never not occurred at the time. Yet he clearly recalled noting the weapon as he came onto the deck. *Why hadn't it registered?*

He mulled it over repeatedly. Was the need for fighting so great it drove him to perform it hand to hand? True, he had succeeded, but what if the rebels had managed a concerted rush? The eight marines could not have reloaded fast enough to stop them. Bayonets and his cutlass would have been insufficient against the press of men. He could now be lying down there, wrapped in canvas and waiting to be taken ashore and buried. It was sobering.

*   *   *   *   *

A group of gunboats were gathered at the mouth of the Yazoo as they neared it. One of them was the *BLACKHAWK,* the large black ship and its white stripes standing out among the smaller vessels of the squadron. There were ironclads and tinclads, as well as regular gunboats. There were transports, which was not surprising since they had seen them passing down river for days. Richards made his report to Porter and was more than happy to find out what was happening.

"We are forcing our way up the Yazoo," related Porter in his clipped fashion. "We will flank Vicksburg and force them to quit building ironclad rams to boot!"

Richards understood the concept. But the Yazoo was a narrow and twisting river, and the rebels were as aware of its significance to Vicksburg as the Yankees.

"In the meantime," continued Porter, "I have work for you to do. The river is too low for the ironclads just yet, so take MACHINEEL up and see what there is to find. I will detail two other tinclads to accompany you."

"Of course, admiral."

"I need to know where their batteries are, what sort of defenses they have prepared. Do not lose the ships to find out, though. We will need you later."

"I will see to it."

"I have no doubts, captain," returned Porter. "That is why you are in command."

The Yazoo River carried barely six feet of water, though rising daily under the repeated downpours. Rain had been plentiful since the first of the month and rivers were showing the influx. While the extra water beneath their keels was welcome, it added to the danger from hidden snags below the surface. More than one ship had been damaged already by the submerged tree trunks.

When he returned to the ship, he found the mail had been delivered. On his desk, there was a letter from Washington, the first since he placed Rebecca on the train in October. He withdrew to his own cabin, finding his hands shaking slightly as he opened it.

John:

Cherish my thoughts, John, as I cherish yours. There shall be no more excuses for not seeing you. I am your wife and that is all that can matter. Please, come home to me.

Lorraine is calling and I must go to her. She shall be having the baby soon. Father is sending us to Connecticut so that she may have the child away from the war. I shall write again as soon as we arrive there safely.

With All My Love,

Rebecca

He read the words two or three times before dropping it on his desk. Rebecca was a proud woman, and it would not come easy to her to admit a mistake. Yet she had done so, willing, to maintain their relationship. If her commitment was there, surely he must return and live up to his. He went onto the deck, leaving his coat open to the cool night air. There was much to consider as he paced slowly, composing his response as he walked.

The next day, *MACHINEEL*, followed by *RATTLER* and *MARMORA*, crept into the river and headed up its course. There was plenty of evidence of rebel activity, from burned piles of cotton to columns of smoke rising in the distance.

For over a week, they cruised the river, alternating between quiet times of inactivity to more exciting moments when the rattle of muskets heralded an attack. But as they moved further north, they found the true defenses of the river.

"That's Drumgould's Bluff up there," pointed Woodard at

the ground rising before them.

"No doubt they've sited a battery upon it."

"No doubt," agreed Woodard.

"Captain, something in the river ahead," said Levenson.

Richards brought his attention to the indicated direction. Sure enough, there was a swelling in the waters, where they swept across something. The sight was familiar and he connected it with the Potomac the year before. It was another of the rebel torpedoes.

"There's one," said Woodard. "And another! What the devil?"

Richards spoke to the helmsman. "Keep us clear. Ring up stop!" As the wheels slowed, he studied the objects more carefully. "Torpedoes, Mr. Woodard. Judging from the size, between fifty and sixty pounds of powder."

"Glory! That'd blast old *MACHINEEL* to splinters!"

"Exactly what they have in mind, I am sure." The ship started drifting backwards with the current. It seemed prudent to proceed no further.

Richards examined the crest of the bluff with his telescope. Sure enough, he could make out the sharp lines of a battery there. He noted its size and location on the chart.

"I think we are ready to speak to the admiral. Get us back down to the fleet."

"Aye, sir."

He retired below, taking a few minutes to rest in his cabin. Somehow, this brought him back to the night of the attack.

It was not just that night, though he was reluctant to admit it to himself. He was aware of any number of things done the past eight months which were more than questionable. He could have died a dozen times during the period. He wondered again. Were his actions the result of a true need, or simply bravado? There was a knock at the door.

"Enter," he said.

Keeler stepped into the small room. "Sorry to bother you, sir. *MAMORA* in sight below us."

"Signal her to follow. The same when you sight *RATTLER*."

"Aye, sir."

By nightfall, they would rejoin the squadron. The river had risen steadily and their soundings showed the ironclads could get as far north as Drumgould's at least. But now there was the question of torpedoes.

Richards stood and donned his coat. He went through the wardroom to the steps leading up into the pilothouse. But he was stopped by the sound of voices from above.

"...good man," finished Keeler. "He knows what he's doing, and I trust him."

"Aye he is, Mr. Keeler, but that don't make him god! You keep followin' the cap'n's example, and you'll be relayin' my blasphemy to the almighty in person!"

"We're expected..." Woodard let him get no further.

"You are expected to be brave, lad." The words were soft and consoling. Richards had heard words in that tone from his father, and later his uncle. The lapse in courtesy did not even matter. "But don't be pressin' your luck. Be stalwart, Mr. Keeler, and we'll all be proud of you. Get yourself killed..." His words choked and there was a long silence. "Anyway, lad, I would be sorry to lose you."

Keeler laughed, but the sound was forced. "I am not planning to leave just yet, Mr. Woodard."

It was Woodard's turn to chuckle. "Best be tellin' them rebels, Mr. Keeler, not me."

Richards moved on. There was really no such thing as a

private conversation on a ship. Still, he was sure his two officers had not intended for him to listen to their discussion. It was sobering to listen to Woodard's advice to young Keeler. In his heart, he felt Woodard was right. He would try to take the words and apply them to himself.

"*MAMORA* and *SIGNAL* will lead," explained Porter to the ship's captains. "Boats out, you will drag grapnels along the bottom and fish out these infernal machines.

"Commander Selfridge," he said, glancing to the officer in question, "you will support with *CAIRO*. The *QUEEN, MACHINEEL* and *RATTLER* will keep watch astern."

"Yes, sir," answered Selfridge strongly.

"When we reach the battery, *CAIRO* will engage. If possible, the tinclads will move past to enfilade from the north. Questions?" None were forthcoming. "Godspeed, gentlemen. Expect to see the army in a day or two."

Richards was not happy with their position in the rear of the line. Of course with the way things went along the river, the rebels were just as likely to attack there as forward. Still, he believed in being at the forefront of a fight.

That next afternoon they pressed forward per their instructions. The boats from the two forward ships were out, pulling up an occasional keg from the water, or finding a firing line and cutting it. There was a volley of rifle fire well ahead, and *CAIRO* put on more steam to got to their aid.

Richards watched the ironclad advance, ringing down for half speed from his own vessel. What happened next came quickly, in the roar of exploding powder and the rush of water.

The *CAIRO* was bodily lifted from the surface, even her hidden paddlewheel momentarily visible. There was a second explosion just aft of the first, and the ironclad fell back, her gun ports level with the water and sinking fast.

"Get us up there, Woodard!" ordered Richards.

"We'll be sunk, too," protested the pilot.

"We must rescue her crew!" He went down to the gun deck, ordering crews to their two boats.

The tops of the *CAIRO*'s pilothouse and her stacks were the only things remaining of her above the water. Sailors struggled into the ironclad's own boats, trying to release them from the davits holding them to the sunken vessel. More men struggled in the water while others simply held onto whatever part of their ill-fated ship still provided a hand-hold. The boats from the two forward tinclads converged on the scene of the disaster, and all were busy collecting men from the cold waters of the Yazoo.

As the last of the men were taken from the wreckage, a cannon fired from the bluff. The shell landed among the tinclads, and Richards immediately ordered them downstream.

"Why are we retreating?" demanded Selfridge, dripping and shivering as he came to the pilothouse.

"One disaster a day is sufficient, commander," returned Richards. "We will come back when we have enough ships to force the issue!"

He joined the other ship captain later in the wardroom. The man sat at the table, naked beneath the blanket wrapped about him. He drank hot coffee provided by the galley. He was very calm for just having lost his ship.

"She is not the first I have gone down with," explained Selfridge. He poured another cup from the pot, and refilled Richards' when he extended it. "I was acting commander of *CUMBERLAND* at Hampton Roads!"

"I remember," replied Richards. The same scene was being played over multi-fold on the gun deck, where the bulk of the ironclad's crew was held. Considering the suddenness and violence of the CAIRO's destruction, it was surprising all her men were accounted for.

"Miserable fight. Kept the guns working until the cartridges were swept away by the water!"

"I know. I was there."

"I remember," said Selfridge. "COHOCTON."

The single word awoke a host of memories. "Yes, COHOCTON." Richards felt the loss of the sloop as if it were an open wound. "If you are comfortable, I must see to my ship," he said, excusing himself.

"Of course."

He went on deck, walking briskly for a few moments to clear his mind. Too easily, it could be MACHINEEL lying on the bottom from any of a half-dozen engagements over the summer. That was an even more unpleasant thought.

"Inquiry be damned," shouted Porter. "I have no time for inquiries. Is there another ship you want?"

"CONESTOGA has only an acting lieutenant..." ventured Selfridge.

"You will have the orders within the hour! Anything else, Richards?"

"No, admiral. We need to destroy the torpedoes, and we will need ironclads to engage the batteries. It will be difficult to do both at the same time. We will not be able to sail past the point, because they have sunk pilings straight across the river."

"But we *will* manage, will not we, commander?" returned Porter, his expression hard

"Undoubtedly, sir."

The interview ended with the suddenness so typical of Porter. The admiral explained he did not hold the commander accountable for the loss of the CAIRO. He made it clear he accepted any actions which placed a ship alongside the enemy. Still, the sad joke already about the fleet was that Selfridge had removed two torpedoes by the simple expedient of placing his ship over them.

For over a week they waited, until Porter felt he had sufficient ships to force his way north. On the twenty-first, they entered the Yazoo again, several wooden gunboats out front dragging grapnels to break the firing lines of any torpedoes present. The method caused them to proceed slowly, and it was six days before they reached the spot where the CAIRO was lost. The vessel apparently slipped into deeper waters, for there was no longer any sight of her. But there was no intention of salvaging her, as they had the CINCINATTI and MOUND CITY. Selfridge had explained the entire hull was crushed by the force of the explosions. There was nothing left to salvage.

The ironclads immediately engaged the battery, but it was situated well up on the bluff. They had a hard time elevating their guns sufficiently to deal with the rebel works. They kept on and fired a good deal of shot at it. Never the less, the fire from the battery hardly slackened during the course of the day.

It was another day before the army troops caught up to their progress. They quickly overran the firing stations for the torpedoes and a lower battery. But the upper works seemed unassailable. The redoubtable Ellets came up with a solution.

Aboard the BLACKHAWK, Richards listened to the plan in wonder. The ram LIONESS would be fitted with a sort of rake at her bow to dredge up any of the deadly weapons she encountered. In fact, her captain already had the army troops busy constructing the device. On one side, she would tow a barge filled with powder. The ship would advance to the pilings sunk across the river, and tie the barge to them. When a safe distance, the barge would be detonated, and the way made clear to advance past the battery. Once troops were landed north of the position, the rebels would have to evacuate or be overrun.

The first of January, 1863 barely dawned at all. The river lay covered by a thick blanket of fog, so thick one could barely see the bow from the pilothouse. This was the day the *LIONESS* was to advance and earn her place in history. But the morning wore on, and there was no break in the fog. And given time to think, Porter apparently saw the danger and foolhardiness of the plan. By mid-afternoon, word passed the action was cancelled. Late in the day, the fog thinned and it became evident the army troops were withdrawing. Without the army, there was no point in the navy staying.

Richards watched as they steered the familiar twenty miles back to the Mississippi. Again, the rebels had thwarted the advance. It was a poor start for the year. He paced the upper deck, from bow to wheels and back again. The entire effort was a total waste for the cost of an ironclad. At the mouth of the river, word awaiting them was no better.

The rebels were very active in the area of the Arkansas river. Two supply ships had been lost, the stores gone to the south. Porter gave Richards orders in his usual curt fashion for *MACHINEEL* to deal with the situation. There was time for the mail boat to pass them a packet before they raised anchor and headed north against the current.

Tinclad on river patrol

CHAPTER SIXTEEN

They moved north in the rainy night, but Richards had time to see the mail distributed. It included a letter from Rebecca. He went to his room to read it. No sooner was his lamp lit than there was a knock on the door.

"Enter."

Keeler opened the door, but did not bother coming in. "Mr. Woodard's respects, captain. He wants to secure for the night."

He tucked the letter into his pocket. It would have to take second place to running the ship.

"Where are we?" He looked into the gloom outside his window, but there was nothing to show their location.

"Mr. Woodard says about five miles south of the mouth of the Arkansas."

Richards considered their position. Rebel supplies came down the Arkansas and crossed the Mississippi at several points in this area. With such poor visibility tonight, they would seize the opportunity to move as much as they could.

"Tell him to anchor, but not to secure the boilers. Do not bother with the boarding nets, either."

"Sir?" queried the young man, not understanding the change in routine.

"We will get underway again after midnight. The rebs will be moving supplies tonight."

"Aye, sir." Keeler saluted and left.

Richards returned to the letter, opening it quickly.

Dearest John:

Rene's child is here. Lorraine brought a baby boy into this sad world on the 5th. Mother and child are both doing well. It has been a while since there has been a baby in this Connecticut home, so the arrival has brought all manner of disruption.

I trust you are doing well. I pray daily for God to protect you. I am glad you are writing more regularly now and I will endeavor to do the same. I think of you every day and am yearning for our next chance to be together.

Mother and child are calling to me, so I must see to their needs.

Be safe, my love.

Becky

He folded the letter and placed it in his breast pocket. He remembered her letters and their time together. He resolved they would work out their differences.

Now, prospects of action along the river drew him. There was no doubt rebel boats would be crossing the river in the darkness. He would try to catch them in the act.

Woodard said barely a word when he came to the

pilothouse. Though slowly returning to normal, thoughts of his son still plagued the first officer. The Irishman left the bridge, and Keeler watched him depart.

"I feel very sorry for him," said Keeler, leaning on the rail and watching him depart. "His son and all," he explained further.

"It cannot be easy, knowing his son might be in the next stand of infantry we fire upon, or upon some gunboat we sink. We must keep our resolve solid, our hearts as oaks against the pain." Keeler looked at him quizzically. "Some more of our admiral's words, I am afraid," commented Richards. "He occasionally says something with the ring of truth to it."

"Woodard's wife is a lovely person," continued Keeler. "Truly beautiful." He smiled. "For all his talk about not being lonely when he's away from her, he would never think of being unfaithful. It would never even occur to him."

"Probably right," returned Richards. "There is much more to our Mr. Woodard than he is generally willing to let on." Richards produced his pipe and filled it, taking a grateful draw from the stem. For the first time in months, he did not even think of cutting off the conversation. "And your mother, Mr. Keeler. What of her?"

"Doing well, sir. Most of my pay goes to her, you know."

"I did not," returned Richards. "You said your father was dead?"

"Aye, sir." Keeler continued quickly at the concern which crossed Richards' features. "Do not worry, captain. I barely knew him, really. He died when I was only two or three in a riverboat explosion. My mother raised me and my sister by herself."

"That cannot have been easy," observed Richards.

"No, sir. But she's wonderful. I will never understand some of the things she has endured to provide for us."

"You almost make me sorry I did not come with you."

"It was a pleasant trip, at least until Mr. Woodard received word about his son. Maybe next time."

Richards nodded. He actually meant it when he answered. "Yes, Colburn. Maybe next time."

It was after four bells when Richards gave the word to move out. The guns were loaded with canister and the men stood to quarters. He took only a moment to think he would look rather foolish if their expedition did not turn up any rebels. He also thought of the letter he wrote in answer to Becky's. It was on his desk, ready to mail if this were his last night. She would at least know his final thoughts were of her.

The wheel churned slowly, making slow progress against the current. After two hours of travel, the river widened where the Arkansas joined it.

"Ahead, cap'n." It was one of the crew from the six pounder. "Boats in the water!"

A veritable flotilla of small boats lay ahead, their black hulls and all but invisible against the darker waters. White lines of oar splashes marked their locations.

"Round to starboard," instructed Richards. "All guns, prepare to fire," he relayed to the crewmen, ringing up 'all ahead'.

Quickly, they were upon the eastern shore. It was lined with boats, and the forms of men moving the supplies from them. Then they were among the boats, the men afloat raising the alarm too late to prevent the damage they would wreak.

Guns exploded from all sides of the MACHINEEL, for there were targets in every direction. Along the shore, men scrambled and returned fire with small arms, but it could not deter the gunboat. In the water, boats were torn up by shot or run under the bow of the warship, with men left screaming and thrashing in the waters about her. The guns fired again, and the resistance ashore dissolved into the night, stacks of crates and bushels abandoned where they lay.

The boats used in the enterprise were left to their own devices. Many of the men threw up their hands in surrender to the passing gunboat. Others pulled downstream, followed by the shot and shell of the vessel. More headed for the opposite shoreline, their paths marked by the supplies they dropped over the side to lighten their load and speed their progress.

"Bring us about and anchor near the shore," directed Richards. "Standby the starboard guns. Mr. Woodard?"

"Yes, cap'n?"

"Launch our boats. Use the men from the port guns, and any they can spare from the engine room. Collect as many of those boats in the river as they can."

"Aye, sir."

The tinclad nosed into the shore, and crewmen dropped a gangway across to the solid land. The marines stepped across the distance as the quarter boats touched water. Richards raised his megaphone as the soldiers formed up under their corporal.

"Secure this place as best you can! There is work to be done across the river!"

He did not await a reply, ringing the vessel into slow astern. They backed off as sailors scrambled to move the gangway inboard. The ship swung with the current, and Woodard closed his mouth before commenting on the maneuver. There was a grudging approval on his face for the deep water sailor's handling of the river boat.

"Keep us straight across, Mr. Levenson. Mr. Woodard, man the port batteries."

"They will not be around the boats by the time we get there, captain," he pointed out.

"Yes, but we will smash the boats and destroy what supplies we can."

True to Woodard's prediction, the boats upon the western shoreline were unmanned. There were stacks of goods piled on the ground, awaiting transport to the population centers of the Confederate states. Broadside after broadside from the union vessel scattered both boats and goods, until a brightening dawn announced the end of the operation. They headed back across the stretch of water, finding their boat crews and soldiers with a large number of prisoners huddled under guard.

"What are we going to do with them?" asked Keeler, surprised by the few number of men detailed managed to keep control of them.

"First, have them start loading all these supplies into the boats. As each boat is filled, lash them astern of us. We will take them down to the fleet anchorage."

"Then what?"

Richards eyed the prisoners: there were between sixty and seventy. Far too many to trust under guard on the crowded gun deck. A concerted rush, and the rebels might succeed in seizing the tinclad. With the boats filled with supplies, there was no room to carry them there. He considered the space forward of the stacks.

"Set up some rope railings around the upper deck," he instructed. "Have the six pounder moved up there and loaded with grape. That should keep them in line until we can turn them over to General Grant's army."

MACHINEEL took her pick of the winnings before turning the balance over to the quartermasters. It was only fair since they had procured it. It was a good haul and the men of the fleet would eat well for the next week.

The next few nights, they patrolled the same area, but their success was sufficient to scare the rebels to other parts. Still, the mouth of the Arkansas continued to be a matter of concern for the fleet, attested by the number of ships moving up to a rendezvous at the White River for a punitive expedition against Arkansas Post. For once since the start of the war, Richards was glad not be detailed to the operation. He had seen his fill of trading cannon fire with forts.

A week after their adventure, he was awakened by an excited Keeler. A steamer was visible off their port beam. There was a moment of panic, assuming she was a rebel ram or gunboat upon them. But no cannon fired and a voiced hailed them through the night.

"Ahoy. *EUREKA* out of Cairo."

The captain touched Woodard's shoulder as he cupped his hands to reply. The pilot glanced at him questioningly, and he spoke in a low voice.

"Don't identify us by name. Get out where they can see your civilian coat."

Woodard nodded his understanding and stepped out of the pilot house.

"Aye, lads," replied Woodard in his best brogue. "We've been expecting you!"

Richards smiled. Woodard understood the situation and gave the perfect response. He gave him a sharp nod of approval and ran forward where their marines were gathered.

"We're ready for you to come aboard!" called the voice from the *EUREKA*.

The young captain reached the marines as Woodard maneuvered the two ships closer together. He stripped himself of his uniform coat and stuck his pistol in his belt.

"Quickly, boys!" He spoke rapidly, keeping his voice low. "Get rid of your caps and rifles! Does everyone have a pistol?" The men all murmured their affirmation. "Follow me, do not take action without my order. They think we are rebs and I want the to keep thinking it." He looked to the corporal. "Give me a ten count before following."

The boats banged together and a gangway was laid across to connect them. Richards did not delay, hastily stepping over.

"Caldwell," he said, introducing himself to the officer which greeted him. He followed him the short walk to the vessels pilothouse.

"Captain Anderson," said the ship's commander, touching his cap to the other. "We have got quite a load for you. Guns and ammunition, even a few cannon with shot."

"I am sure we will put it to good use," replied Richards. He kept his words non-committal. "How do you want to handle this?"

"Oh, I can steer her north," replied the captain, lowering his voice. "I know the Arkansas from before the war. But we have got to get guards on the crew. They will not be so happy 'bout be taken prisoner."

"Very well, captain," returned Richards. "Just who can we trust?"

Anderson smiled broadly. "Myself, and me second here. And of course, Johnson." The river captain gestured at the helmsman who smiled broadly in return. "He's a southern boy clear through. The lads down in the engine room, and that's about it."

There was the sound of feet coming across the gangway. Anderson turned to it. When the surprised southerner looked back, a pistol was aimed at his face.

"There does seem to be some confusion as to our identity, Mr. Anderson. Richards, commanding the gunboat *MACHINEEL*."

Anderson spat on the deck. "God damn you lyin' Yankees!"

"No more so than a man who would turn his own crew over to the enemy." He looked to his men who had closed about them. "Corporal, I will have these men in irons."

"Aye, sir." The soldiers came forward for them.

"There are more in the engine room. And find the first officer and get him up here!"

Woodard came across, waiting while the captured officers were ushered to the gunboat.

" 'Tis a bit nippy this evening," he observed. "How'd you know, cap'n?"

"How many ships want to be boarded in the middle of the night, Mr. Woodard?" he asked in return. "And the reports on the previous captures implied they were surrendered rather than captured."

"What do we do now?"

"They were expecting to meet another boat. My guess would be a gunboat from further up the Arkansas." Richards watched a blurry eyed man approach them. "Are you the first officer?" he demanded.

"Yes..." He got no further.

"Roust out your crew and lay on some steam, man. I suspect we will have a rebel gunboat sniffing around here shortly."

"Where's the captain?"

"In irons, along with the men who were helping him to turn your ship over to the rebels," snapped Richards. "Which is where you will be if you do not jump to it!" The officer fairly ran forward, shouting to his crew to get the transport moving.

"Back to *MACHINEEL*, Mr. Woodard. This night's work is not yet finished!"

The gunboat pulled away from the transport, heading back into the stream to circle near the Arkansas. The men fidgeted at their posts, wondering what else they would encounter. But at length, the form of another boat hardened in the drizzle emerging from the mouth of the Arkansas river.

"Prepare to fire!" shouted Richards. There was no way to identify the vessel, but only a rebel vessel would be coming from that direction. "Port guns, fire!"

If the rebel gunboat was surprised at encountering a union vessel, it did not show in their actions. They replied immediately but only three cannon were revealed by their flashes. There was a crash from the impact of a rebel shell below, but there was little time to worry about it. The enemy was close alongside, the two warships running parallel, their sides banging and bumping one another as they raced through the night.

"Pour it into them!" shouted Richards, as the space between the vessels lit by a broadside from *MACHINEEL*'s guns. For ships as small as both were, the five gun broadside of the tinclad was wreaking terrible damage aboard the rebel. But she held her position, returning as much as she could.

"What's he up to, Woodard?" demanded Richards.

"Tryin' to hold on 'til he can run us ashore captain!" returned the first officer wildly.

"Keep at him!"

The broadside fired again, and the rebel ship began to list into the union ship, leaning against her side. Whatever her plans, her captain was losing his ship. Immediately after the sound of the guns, there rose a scream from forward, and the dark forms of union sailors swarmed across to the rebel. The night was pierced by the crackle of muskets and pistols, the clash of steel blades.

"What the devil?" said Woodard.

"They are boarding!" Richards was as surprised at the action as his first officer. There was no doubt who led the assault. "Damn Keeler!" cursed the captain. He took only a moment to relay instructions to Woodard before sliding down the railings to the middle deck.

There was no time to lose. Their adversary was grievously hurt. Flames were visible through a window at her stern, and Richards had seen too many such vessels explode without warning during the course of the conflict. He did not waste time going to the gun deck, but instead headed forward. His men aboard the confederate were in as much danger from their own guns as the rebel's, and both groups were threatened by the flames aboard the rebel.

He slipped down the front armor plate, landing harder than he would have thought upon the foredeck of the tinclad. Pulling his pistol, he jumped the distance separating them, sprawling headlong across a body there. Others lay about, twitching and groaning. Too many of them were union sailors.

The scene of the fighting had moved within the confines of the rebel vessel. The guns aboard MACHINEEL fell silent for fear of striking their own men. The rebel guns were not so deterred, though only two were still firing. The hand to hand fighting pushed about the third, most forward cannon.

"Where's Keeler?" yelled Richards, pulling one of the boarders to him. The man pointed to one side, where Keeler sat behind a cotton bale, reloading his revolver.

The captain moved to the younger officer, followed by a brief fusillade of shots. But the situation on the rebel gun deck was a standoff. The rebels used their cannon as a strongpoint, the iron weapon deflecting the union shots. The federals crouched behind cotton bales, the enemy balls absorbed by the material. Meantime, a dense smoke drifted forward from the flames.

"What do you think you are doing?" yelled Richards when he reached Keeler's side. He did not give the young man time to answer. "We have got to get these men off this boat before she sinks or blows up!"

"We can take her, captain!" protested the boy.

"She is on fire! Pull the men back to the foredeck and move our wounded across." Richards glanced around, trying to assess the situation in the dark and smoky gun deck. He saw three of his soldiers together, muskets propped atop cotton bales and firing back at the rebels. "Leave those three and get moving!"

Keeler opened his mouth to protest again, but there was no questioning the look in commander's eyes. He tapped two of the men and the withdrew to the open deck. Richards watched him leave, and observed the movement of the other sailors towards the door. He nodded with gratification, then slid quickly across to the soldiers.

"Keep it up, boys. We cannot let 'em know we are leaving this wreck!" It was thin enough humor, but raised a slight chuckle under the circumstances.

Richards stood next to them, firing his pistol to keep the rebel sailors back. One of his soldiers fell, his shoulder smashed by a minne ball. For all the need for haste, things seemed slow and drawn out. The flames aft grew brighter, the light within the gun deck growing with the heat and the smoke.

"All across, cap'n." It was Keeler, returned to inform him the men were back aboard the gunboat.

"Help this man, Mr. Keeler." Richards saw a movement across from them, and fired his pistol. The form dropped without a sound. "We will be across in a moment."

"Aye, sir." Keeler helped the injured man to his feet and the two struggled from the room. When they were clear, Richards nodded to the other two and they went out the door. The officer emptied his pistol at the rebels and followed them.

"Quickly, captain!" It was Woodard, his voice hollow through the megaphone. Astern, the rebel gunboat was a mass of flames, and there was fire licking hungrily across the space to MACHINEEL.

"Over you go, boys!" shouted Richards.

The two soldiers jumped the distance. Richards stood on the bulwark of the vessel, preparing to do so himself. He felt the air stir from a musket ball close to his ear, and one of the soldiers dropped. He heard the shot as he leapt across.

Woodard did not wait for orders. As the captain reached the foredeck, the helm was put over hard, and they turned away from the gunboat. The port side of their ship was in flames, and sailors trained a hose on it. The rebel gunboat lay astern, an inferno in their wake . Richards watched her moving through the water. But without the support of *MACHINEEL* alongside, the vessel started to roll. Just as she reached beams ends, there was a series of explosions. A final detonation was huge, filling the air with flaming debris and exploding ammunition. Only a pall of smoke and scattered wreckage marked the spot.

Richards knelt down next to the soldier. The ball hand taken off the top of his head, scattering brains about the deck and killing him instantly. He took a deep breath at the sight. If the shot had been three inches to the left, it would have caught him squarely. It would be his brains on the deck instead of the soldier's.

He rose from the spot and entered the gun deck through one of the forward ports. It was the method used by Keeler to lead the men from the ship. The space was occupied by wounded men, and several bodies. The surgeons mate was working over one of the more serious cases, but the man expired even as he withdrew the ball from his chest.

"Mr. Keeler?" The lieutenant stepped forward, his face and hands smeared with powder, his coat ripped across the back. A droplet of blood progressed slowly down his cheek from a slight gash below one eye. "May I see you in the wardroom?" Richards started up the stairs. The steps behind his were slow and hesitant.

"What ye' think ye' doin', laddie?" Woodard exploded before Richards could say anything. The anger stripped away the years of practiced speech, and the Irish brogue was deep in his voice. "Ye' could have gotten us all kilt! I have half a mind to turn ye' over me knee!"

Keeler was shocked by the outburst. He and Woodard had grown very close over the preceding weeks, but it was clear he did not comprehend what he had done.

"We were going to take her, captain," he said, his eyes pleading. "She would have made a fine prize!"

Richards held his breath, calming himself before speaking. Woodard was angry enough for the both of them. "Colburn," he managed slowly. "I appreciate your enthusiasm, but you completely misjudged the situation. Our men were in more danger from our own shells than the rebels, and the rebels had hardly had the fight knocked from them. They were already aflame before you crossed."

"But we were alongside..."

"And what if she had turned off, Mr. Keeler? There was no preparation, not grapnels to hold the ships together, You and your men would have been left aboard a hostile ship, and one that was already in flames to boot!"

"I didn't think of that," replied the lieutenant.

"You did not think at all, Mr. Keeler." Richards did not know what else to say. He let out a deep sigh. This was adding to the heavy weight placed upon the young shoulders. "Get below and see to the men, Mr. Keeler."

"I ain't done wit him yet, cap'n," started Woodard.

Richards continued to Keeler, not allowing Woodard time to speak. "Carry out your orders, lieutenant."

"Aye, sir." He left, his shoulders slumped and his eyes downcast.

"Cap'n!" protested Woodard. "The boy got three men killed and another dozen wounded, not to mention nearly loosin' the ship! Ye' just cannot let him go like this!"

"I will talk to him again later, Mr. Woodard."

"But..."

Richards spun on the officer, his anger at Keeler venting in a new direction. "I find it difficult to blame an officer who is merely trying to get at the enemy, Mr. Woodard! Further, I am commanding this boat, not you. Discipline will be meted out as I deem necessary. Is that clear?"

"Aye, sir." There was both hurt and anger in the reply.

Richards let his shoulders sag, some of the ire and frustration leaving with the motion. "I am not through with him yet, Mr. Woodard. I will have a long talk with him again, after everything has had time to sink in." He gripped the pilot's shoulder firmly. "You will have time with him, there is no doubt. But he is not a child who pulled some foolish prank. He is a naval officer who needs to be taught."

Woodard's tone was conciliatory. "Yes, captain."

Richards nodded, sharing the other man's feelings. "I know you are worried about him. So am I."

Porter's fake ironclad, the *USS TERROR*

CHAPTER SEVENTEEN

Four weeks passed after the fight with the rebel gunboat. Yet as Richards watched Keeler drill the gun crews, it was evident the lieutenant still took the incident as a personal defeat. Woodard talked with him on several occasions, and his initial anger had ebbed with time. That anger was not so much directed at what Keeler had done as Keeler himself. Woodard showed a paternal concern in the boy.

Events still proceeded quickly. The river, swollen from the continual rain, appeared as a huge lake. Water covered much of the land as far as the eye could reach. The previous day, *QUEEN OF THE WEST* ran Vicksburg to blockade the mouth of the Red River to the south. Word was received from Farragut that he was again heading north along the river, his ships just below Port Hudson and prepared to run their gauntlet.

General Grant was finally given control of all army forces assaulting Vicksburg. Porter, for his part, continued to press in every possible direction to find some way for the navy to aid in the encirclement of the bastion. That very morning, a levee was cut several miles north in an attempt to bypass the Yazoo batteries and assault Vicksburg from the north. It would be several days before sufficient water flowed through to make it possible to float the gunboats, however.

MACHINEEL was still on river patrol, and Richards did not care for it. Half their time was spent on the Yazoo, making sure the length between the Mississippi and the batteries remained free of Confederate torpedoes. The other half of the time was spent on the Mississippi, fighting the current and a flood of debris carried into it by the continual rains.

He sent another request to the navy department for a command along the coast. Whether Welles stopped them at Rebecca's request or the navy department simply chose not to give him a command was unknown. Meanwhile, his expectations about the marriage grew as the letters fro Rebecca showed she accepted his role in life and the war.

But Keeler was having trouble with his temper and Richards stepped into the gun drill, getting the captain's to take over while he maneuvered Keeler clear. He hoped it was not too obvious, as it might hurt Keeler's ability to continue to deal with the men.

"You must maintain a firm hand, Cole," explained Richards, as he walked around the mid-deck with the other. The rain drummed on the upper deck above them, and mist swept across them to keep things cool and clammy. Spring was three weeks away, but winter continued to press as it had since October. "Firm, but understanding."

"I just cannot do anything right!" responded the youth.

"No, you do many things very well," replied Richards, trying to bolster some of his lagging confidence. "You are just pressing too hard right now. Ease up a bit, mostly on yourself."

Keeler nodded. "I think I will take a turn up at the wheel, captain."

"Go ahead."

He went up the steps. It was a transparent escape, but Richards had no issue with it. He remembered times as a young lieutenant when he wished his captain had released him so easily. Keeler almost collided with Woodard as the other man emerged from the wardroom.

"Lieutenant."

"Mr. Woodard."

The exchange was cool and professional. Keeler pushed on towards the pilothouse and Woodard's shoulders slumped visibly as his eyes followed the young officer. As time passed, the Irishman was less obviously distracted about his son. But while he became more open, he never returned to his carefree attitude from the summer.

"How many more days along this blasted river?" he asked.

Richards sighed. He shared the feeling with Woodard and the rest of the crew. "As many as it takes. The ironclads and gunboats started through the levee at first light, at least if all went according to plan. Maybe they will have some success in that area."

Woodard shrugged. "The Yazoo Pass hasn't been used for years. I have seen it: overgrown, a real tangle of branches and limbs. They'll find the going difficult when they finally get into it."

"Let's not give up on them yet."

Woodard gestured south, towards Vicksburg. "And they let that Ellet boy take a ram past the batteries. Does Porter really think he'll succeed by himself in that stretch of the river?"

"Are you second guessing admirals now, lieutenant?" The older man gave him a poisonous glance, and Richards continued. "You seem in rare spirits. Anything we can attribute this to?"

Woodard bit back a retort. Instead, he lowered his voice and suddenly appeared very old. Though in his fifties, he seemed in his sixties or seventies.

"Still worried about me boy, captain," he said. "And Keeler, too. I really like that lad. I do not want to see him hurt or killed."

Richards considered the words a few moments. "It is a poor place to be having those thoughts, Mr. Woodard. We could strike a snag and sink as easily as being blasted by rebel shot. In either case, the dangers are tremendous."

"I know that, cap'n. Why do we have to be fightin' this damned war anyway? And what we be usin' children for?"

"The older I get," Richards replied, "the younger the others appear. It must be doubly worse on you. On COHOCTON, there was a twelve year old powder boy killed. But he was a sailor, just like you and me. He took the same risks."

"Seems you are takin' more than your share, captain," responded Woodard. "That's part of young Keeler's problems. He sees you as the example to follow."

Richards felt a flush of anger at the comment. "I will endeavor to set the young man a better example, lieutenant."

He turned away to walk around the deck. The worse part of Woodard's accusation was the element of truth to it. The mention of COHOCTON brought him a glimmering of that truth. His thoughts of the dead ship were buried deep, but were not forgotten. Keeler and his guilt over the boarding incident was one thing. His own guilt over the COHOCTON was something much deeper.

But little occurred to the gunboat over the next weeks. She made her patrols, exchanged ineffective fire with an equally ineffective rebel battery on the Yazoo, fought the elements which continued to storm about them. For the rain continued to fall, sometimes so heavily they could see neither shore from a position in midstream. For Woodard and the bulk of the crewmen, it was simply February along the Mississippi. For Richards and the few deep water sailors aboard, it was a dull, depressing time.

New ironclads appeared from the north. They were large, shallow draft ships with strange shapes. Their bows were low, with casemates for two or three guns and topped by a pilothouse. Midship were smaller casemates, narrower than those forward and carrying only one or two guns per side. Two stacks stuck up from here, tall and narrow. Then the decks spread again, a third casemate just before the large hump of the wheelhouse, the tops of which were eight or ten feet above the upper decks of the vessels. Then aft yet another casemate, usually with two guns pointed dead astern.

There were three of these monstrosities, silly looking vessels when compared with the simple lines of the Pook turtles they accompanied. Guns pointed every which way from the vessels, but most had limited fields of fire. Not only was their appearance strange, but the method of propulsion was also different. With the large humps of wheelhouses towards the sterns, they were obviously wheel driven vessels. But below the waterline and out of sight, they also used screws, their primary intent to help steer the beasts in the limited waters they would encounter.

If Porter had any doubts over the capabilities of these vessels, he did not show it. One was immediately detailed as part of the Yazoo Pass expedition, joining the ranks of gunboats and transports which were preparing for that endeavor. Another, the *INDIANOLA*, was immediately sent south, running Vicksburg with coal barges to help the *QUEEN OF THE WEST* and Farragut in their operations between Vicksburg and Port Hudson. The odd vessel made the run easily, but Richards was not impressed. She was an ungainly looking contraption, and he equated balanced looks with proper handling.

*   *   *   *   *

"Captain, wake up!" Richards forced his eyes open, unable to focus them on the crewman which shook him. "Mr. Keeler sent me down. There's firing from down south."

"I will come."

In the pilothouse, the dull irregular boom of heavy guns could be heard drifting upstream from south of Vicksburg. There were only two Yankee vessels in that stretch of river, and only one carried guns as large as those firing: the *INDIANOLA. But what would be down there to threaten her and the QUEEN?*

"It's been going on for about thirty minutes, captain," reported the young officer. "Hard to tell, but I would guess at fifteen to twenty miles."

There was another burst of firing, but that was the end of it. Only silence followed.

"I think your guess is accurate, Mr. Keeler."

There were no reported rebel ironclads building in that stretch and it was unlikely they would attack an ironclad as large as *INDIANOLA*, no matter how ugly or ungainly, with a mere gunboat. There was talk of a rebel ram being outfitted. She might be willing to take the risk. But that was strange also, for there would be the additional threat of the *QUEEN*. Unless, of course, the *QUEEN* were lost. Or worse ...captured. That would certainly fit Woodard's analysis of Ellet's ability. Two rams, even if lightly armed, might threaten an ironclad, particularly one as clumsy as the composite *INDIANOLA*. Richards glanced across the water. Lights were burning on the *BLACKHAWK*: the significance of the firing was not lost there.

"Call away my boat, Mr. Keeler. I am going to see the admiral."

"Aye, sir."

Keeler may have been unable to follow the twists of logic, but he did not hesitate to execute the order. Richards went below to finish getting into his uniform, and was aboard the *BLACKHAWK* within a half hour of the end of the firing.

"What brings you across so early this morning?" asked Porter. The admiral was fully dressed, as if he had not slept at all.

"The fighting downstream, sir. I fear *INDIANOLA* and the *QUEEN* may be lost."

Porter nodded in agreement. "It is likely, captain Richards. I suspect the ram was taken and used against the ironclad. But why do you think she too is taken?"

"Admiral, do you think that ship, able to fire a heavy gun just every five minutes, could ward off the attack of two determined rams?" Porter's face revealed his answer. "As I thought, sir. I can have steam up within an hour to get by the batteries. With luck, we can be moving while it is still dark!"

"Not so quickly, my energetic friend. I have no wish to send another ship south to deal with a pair of rams and an ironclad. If *INDIANOLA* is captured, the rebels will use her against us. If I send you down, I could just be adding to their growing strength!"

"Then what, sir? We must do something, and quickly!"

"Aye, and we shall. Prepare to move *MACHINEEL* north of the bend, Mr. Richards. I intend to ask General Grant for the use of his army, and your ship's carpenter will be an inestimable value."

Richards did as instructed. By daybreak, he and Porter were seeking out Grant. In the meantime, his crew were busy felling trees at Porter's order, and bringing spare planking ashore from the tinclad. It was a wild scheme, notwithstanding Grant agreed to help immediately.

A large, flat bottom barge was located, a hundred feet long and forty wide. Fore and aft, rafts were constructed to extend its length to fully three hundred feet. While the army cut down small trees to bend and form into the frame for wheel boxes aft, the ship's crew were busy building a large casemate and superstructure down the center. Out of this projected the noses of guns, which moments before were trees in the forest.

As the "vessel" progressed, Richards shook his head in wonder. He felt like calling Porter a fool for the idea, but one did not question the directions of flag officers. More of his crew were busy arranging barrels into stacks, the lowest ones filled with pitch and rags. When tall enough, Porter declared them finished. By then, the wheel boxes were closed up, and every available man was put to work with tar and brushes until the whole ridiculous affair was black, gleaming slightly in the afternoon sun. Some soldier, caught up in the spirit of things, painted words on the side of the wheelhouse.

Deluded people - cave in

"Captain Richards," said Porter, as he approached.

"Aye, sir."

"Our new ironclad deserves an appropriate name, wouldn't you think? How does *TERROR* strike you?" Richards did not answer immediately, and Porter went on. "Get her launched. Attach a line to your gunboat and tow her into the current. We will see her safely to the northern batteries before letting her finish the trip on her own."

"Aye, admiral."

The barrels of pitch were lit and large black columns of smoke rose from the "stacks". Woodard stared at the contraption behind them, the corner of his mouth turned up.

"Does the admiral really think this will scare anyone?" he asked, his voice low so Porter would not overhear.

Richards chuckled. "You must admit, Mr. Woodard, even at this distance it is fairly convincing."

For all the roughness of construction, the raft did appear as a huge *MONITOR*, even though only about fifty feet astern. And with six or seven visible guns projecting from the "casemate", there could be no doubt she was heavily armed.

"Still," continued Richards, his voice also very low, "one hit from the batteries, and the whole mess will come apart. If it scares them, it will not be for long."

"Let's hope it is long enough, captain." Porter's voice was close behind them, and Richards grimaced involuntarily at the sound. It was not a good idea to ridicule the ideas of flag officers, no matter how strange they seemed.

"Aye, sir," he replied, feeling rather sheepish.

"Stay out of range of the batteries. Cast her off when you are sure it is in the current."

"Yes, admiral," responded Woodard, vacating the upper deck to release the line. He, at least, seized a valid reason to escape Porter's possible wrath.

"As I said this morning, captain, I cannot spare enough ships at the moment to deal with the *INDIANOLA*, the *QUEEN* and a possible rebel ram. The gunboats are entering the Yazoo Pass this day, and the rest of the ships are spread along the river. Those I have here must be ready to support the army." The admiral nodded with finality, his decision sure. "We shall try this first. If it does not work, then I will consider something with a bit more daring."

"Aye, sir."

The *TERROR* was cut loose, drifting past as they headed against the current. As it neared the city, the batteries opened a terrible fusillade against the intruder. Richards and Porter stayed on the deck, watching the water spouts grow about the fake ironclad as it proceeded by at the leisurely pace of the current. The rebel fire was terribly ineffective for so large a target, and most missed the construction. Richards held his breath as one shot did plunge home, raising a shower of splinters from the deck. But the makeshift *MONITOR* held together, and was soon beyond the range of the guns. Smoke still poured from the stacks and she continued along the river.

"Very impressive," said Porter, nodding with satisfaction.

"They just watched a ship pass them in broad daylight, and so unconcerned about their guns it did not even bother with replying. What would you think, watching her from the city?"

Richards shrugged. "Tough ship I guess, admiral."

"Tough indeed, captain. Even as we speak, the telegraph lines are aflame to points south of here. They will have the word on the approach of our monster, and if my surmise about the *INDIANOLA* is correct, our rebel friends will see to her destruction for us."

"But why?"

"As you pointed out, the *INDIANOLA* is an ungainly vessel. If, somehow, she is holding them off, it will appear we have sent heavy reinforcements. On the other hand if she were not sunk outright, the rams must have damaged her severely so she is captured. They will be trying to repair her. And we have seen how handy the rebels are with fire and ships! Now if I might borrow your boat, there is other work to be done this day."

The boat was called away to return Porter to his own vessel. Richards watched after the man, wondering at such an imagination. He did not believe for a minute the rebels would be fooled by such a ruse. *And even if they were, what of it?* They would simply hold the torch until the *TERROR* approached, preparing to beat this new attacker as they had the previous. The first shot or the touch of a ram would show the *ironclad* for its true nature, and the whole attempt would collapse.

"What now, captain?" asked Keeler.

Richards chuckled, shaking his head in disbelief. "Who knows, Cole? Maybe the rebels will die laughing at us!"

He retired to his cabin to reclaim some of the sleep lost by rising so early in the morning darkness.

If he thought the plan foolish, he had to change his mind

the next morning. Army scouts on the west side of the river reported the outcome of the deception.

The *INDIANOLA* had indeed been taken, and her captors were busy making good the damage they inflicted. As the *TERROR* approached, first the two rams left the scene of the action, fleeing south before an impregnable enemy. When the raft rounded the last bend towards the ironclad, the rebels put the torch to the ship to prevent her "recapture".

As the flames rose above the union ship, the *TERROR* grounded on the east side of the river. And the confederate soldiers, at first cautious, moved forward to inspect this apparition. Upon discovering her true nature, one of them applied a torch to her in spite. A column of smoke to the south testified to the truth of the whole episode.

The captain of the *MACHINEEL* did not believe the story, for it sounded more like one of Woodard's yarns. That officer swore never to repeat it, for he claimed he would be called a liar ever after. For the total absurdity of Porter's plan, it worked exactly as the admiral intended.

It was almost two weeks later when Richards called for Woodard several times, but the officer failed to appear. Things were moving again, and Porter had shifted his flag to *CINCINNATI*, signaling several of the ironclads and tinclads to follow. Along with transports, tugs and mortar rafts, they started up the Yazoo. He sent Keeler to find the pilot, and the boy returned in just a few minutes.

"He's down in his cabin, sir," reported Keeler. His face was strained. "Perhaps you'd best handle this, captain."

Richards was perplexed and angry at this course of events. "Take over!"

He went below, moving quickly through the wardroom and back to Woodard's cabin. He knocked on the door twice, but got no response. On opening it, he found the officer propped in his bunk, an empty bottle of whiskey gripped in one hand. The place smelled of stale liquor and vomit, for Woodard had been at it all night.

"What is the meaning of this?" he demanded.

The drunken eyes turned to the captain, the slurred voice formed words. "Well, my friend, the captain! Come in, come in." The words were slow, and the hand waved only weakly to invite Richards into the room. "I would offer you a drink, cap'n, but the bottle seems to be empty."

"What is the matter, Woodard? You are supposed to be on duty!"

"Nothin' much. Jus' a letter from home." Tears welled up in the old eyes, running down the man's cheeks. "Ye' try all your life to make somethin' for your family. Your whole life, man!"

There was no point in questioning him further. He heard little, if any, of what was addressed to him.

"Your whole life..." The words faded to a whisper. "Then the boy runs off because his father is on some damned fool river expedition!" He gathered strength as he continued. "I was in New Orleans! Cannot very well stop him from a thousand miles away now, can I?"

He threw the empty bottle across the cabin, smashing it against the wall. It was not directed at Richards. Woodard was no longer aware of the presence of the other man.

"Michael!" he yelled, suddenly bolt upright in his bed. "Michael, where are ye'?" He slumped back, his head falling forward on the dirty, stained front of his shirt. "Where are ye'?" The voice faded out entirely.

"Woodard?" asked Richards again, kneeling down next to him. The man was passed out, a combination of alcohol and exhaustion. Michael was his eldest, the boy who had run off to the rebels.

He looked about the cabin, wondering what had brought

this about. It was true he pined for his son since fall. But why now, almost six months later? He spied a crumpled piece of paper in the corner and retrieved it. The mail barge had come the previous day and it was an easy connection.

The letter was from his wife, the words short and direct. Their son was dead, taken by fever at an army camp in the later part of summer. He had never seen combat, had never had involvement in battle. It made him no less dead. Word was slow reaching them, almost eight months passing before the letter found its way past the Yankee gunboats to St. Louis. Richards started to crumple the paper back up, but thought better of it. He spread the page out, folded it and placed it in Woodard's bible. The man could decide what to do with it when he was in better condition. He returned to the pilothouse.

"Mr. Keeler, go down and see to Mr. Woodard."

"What's wrong with him, captain?"

"His son is dead, Mr. Keeler." There were few secrets aboard a ship. There was little point in keeping it secret, but Richards was unhappy to make the announcement. "Just see to him. Clean him up, and make sure he's got no more whiskey stashed in his cabin!"

"Yes, captain." The lieutenant left to follow the instructions.

Richards allowed a deep sigh to escape him. There were so many ways the conflict found to injure people. He thought back to his friend LaForge and a realization struck.

"What day is it?" he asked the helmsman.

"Monday, sir."

"The date, man!"

Levenson thought for a moment. "I think the ninth, cap'n. March ninth."

Richards bowed his head and said a small prayer. One year ago, he set *COHOCTON* against *VIRGINIA*. He raised his head to look out across the open waters, but a shower swept across obscuring his view. Mist drifted into the open pilot house and he felt a slight shiver at their touch. One year ago this day, he walked those shattered decks without so much as a scratch. *How was that possible?* He felt a foul mood descending and he shook his head hard to ward it off.

"Damn this war!" he cursed.

"Sir?" asked Levenson.

"Keep you eyes on the river!" barked Richards.

Porter played his fleet like a river gambler his chips. Forces were spread throughout the Mississippi-Yazoo basin, seeking any advantage to avoid the fortifications around Vicksburg and ease the army's assault on the city, but efforts to proceed directly up the Yazoo were stymied by batteries and the torpedoes.

The army's canal failed, despite the height of the river, in an attempt to render the city impotent by completely bypassing it. The Yazoo Pass expedition proceeded slowly, deterred much as Woodard predicted. Further news was sent of a hastily built rebel fort in their path, which they must reduce or be turned back. Meanwhile, Vicksburg remained dominant, blocking the Mississippi.

But Porter was a man of considerable energy and imagination. Word was passed that much of the flooded land in the area contained by the Yazoo and the Mississippi was deep enough to float a gunboat. After sending a tugboat to investigate, he gathered his remaining forces to press off in this new direction. *MACHINEEL* joined the force.

Over what had been the shoreline and through a gap in the trees, the line of gunboats moved at a leisurely pace. The *CINCINNATI* and a tug led the fleet through wide lanes with trees on either side, though only the tops projected above the waters. More than fifteen feet lay beneath, more than enough to float the heaviest ship in the squadron.

The ironclads led the force, winding through the lanes. When a line of trees blocked any further progress, the old Pook turtles moved in and rammed them, uprooting the tall, old oaks from the mud by their weight and force. When the trees were pulled clear, the gunboats proceeded again.

It was more of a pleasant country stroll as they progressed, but for the hiss of engines and the thrash of wheels. For over fifteen miles, Porter went cross country, finding the Army unloading transports on the first stretch of solid ground. Their further passage was clear, an old bayou meandering northeast. He quickly hailed his vessels, establishing a sailing order into the narrow canal. *MACHINEEL* was again last in the line.

The canal was narrow, barely enough for the widest ships, though with enough water to float them. They moved ahead, the *CINCINNATI* smashing through the occasional bridge until a large cloud of smoke rose in front of them. The shore on either side of their path was aflame, large stacks of flaming cotton barring the way. But Porter would not be turned back, and the lead ironclad ran the flames. Ship by ship they followed, *MACHINEEL* last through.

The heat and smoke of the fire was tremendous, and both Richards and the helmsman crouched behind the slight bulwarks of the pilothouse for protection as they made their run. The heat drew the breath from them while the smoke tried to suffocate the entire crew. But they passed, coughing and wheezing in the cool air beyond. The paint on the side of the vessel was blistered, peeled by the heat from the fires.

Porter called a halt for the night, the boats closing up the gaps which had opened between them. Richards took off along the road next to the canal to find Porter, and determine their plans for the continued advance. It was not difficult to find the lead ship and the admiral on the deck.

"Captain Richards!" he exclaimed. The ironclad was strewn with her own wreckage, smashed boats and stacks a-kilter from the low hanging branches across their course. None had sapped Porter's enthusiasm. "Come up and have a glass!"

There was a gangway rigged from the upper deck to the upper edge of the dike bordering the bayou. Richards crossed it, a steward handing him a glass before he barely stepped aboard.

"Quite an experience, to be locked in land within feet of the ship," commented Porter.

"Yes, sir. I wanted to talk about the placement of my vessel."

Porter laughed. "I can hardly let you bring her forward, can I, commander?" A couple of the other officers chuckled at the joke. "Seriously, I placed you where I needed you. I am forward and am sure of our front. I needed to be equally sure of our rear."

Richards saw the compliment was genuine, and felt somewhat foolish at questioning the other officer. "I apologize, admiral," he said, gesturing a weak toast with his glass.

"Do not worry, John," commented Porter. "I needed a man back there, one willing to face whatever odds he confronted. You are that man." Porter changed the subject.

"Quite an adventure, wouldn't you say?" he asked, but did not wait for an answer. "About sixty miles along this ditch, and we will come into the Rolling Fork, then into the Sunflower. We will be around the Yazoo batteries."

"I see, admiral." He sipped his wine, somewhat surprised at the excellence of the vintage.

Porter hesitated before looking off the starboard bow. The sound of chopping reached them through the night. He retrieved his speaking trumpet and called to the tugboat just ahead.

"Mr. Murphy, I fear the rebs are planning us some deviltry! Load your howitzer and have a look!" There was a quick reply, and the tugboat puffed off into the night. "We will get the army where they need to be yet, captain. Now see to your ship for the night."

Richards finished the glass of wine and left. Woodard was at the pilothouse on his return, propped against one side, supporting himself with one hand and holding a cup of coffee in the other.

"Evening, captain."

"Good evening, Mr. Woodard. Are you feeling better?"

The pilot contained a belch, then sipped at the coffee. "No, captain, I ain't. And further, that young whippersnapper of yours has hidden me whiskey!"

"He hasn't hidden it," replied Richards. "He poured it over the side at my order."

"How dare you..."

"I know about your son, Mr. Woodard." It was as if he had struck the man, watching the pain cross his features. "I am sorry for your loss, but I still have a ship to think of."

"Damn you and damn your ship, captain."

"Undoubtedly, Mr. Woodard." Words were never right for such a moment, and Richards was poor at consoling people. Yet he had to make the effort for Woodard's sake. "I understand how you must feel, but there is nothing for it. I can say I need your help. I have a whole shipload of sons aboard, and I would like to return them to their parents and families."

They paused, stirred by the sound of a cannon in the distance. It was the army howitzer aboard the tug. The sound revived the pilot a bit. He straightened slightly, the effort obvious. But his voice was level and his manner calm.

"I will do my best."

"I expected you would. If there's anything I can do on this other matter, please do not hesitate to ask."

"Thank you, captain."

They pushed on while the canal narrowed about them. It was built along the course of an old bayou, so it twisted and turned like a serpent as it wove through the countryside. The rebels had tried felling trees across their path the previous night: *CINCINNATI* and the tug had been forced to pull a large one out of the canal. The rebel efforts had created no delay, but mother nature was not so kind.

Limbs of trees overhung the bayou, reaching and grabbing the ships as they passed. Soon, they all looked like *CINCINNATI*, with their boats and pilothouses smashed, stacks awry, everything on the outside of the vessels swept clean. Further, all manner of animals and vermin were in those trees, escaping the waters of the floods. When struck, they fell onto the decks. Crewmen stood by with brooms, sweeping coons and snakes, squirrels and mice from the upper deck into the waters around them. But the bugs were faster, many finding their way into the ship before they could be knocked overboard. Richards watched it in disgust, for it would take months to clear the insects from the vessel, if they ever succeeded.

The natural hazards were more than those above the ships. At some points, the width of the canal was squeezed in by large oaks, and the crew of the forward ironclad was forced to chop the sides of the trees away to make a clear passage. Rafts of sticks and reeds rose from the bottom of the bayou, whose course usually contained barely enough water to float a canoe. They blocked the path or became entangled in the armor beneath ironclads or in their wheels. All forced the entire column to stop while the blockage was cleared. The second day, they only proceed about twenty of the sixty miles they needed. And the army, along to provide support on the road next to the canal, was left somewhere astern.

For five days they progressed, each day making less than the one before. From his vantage point astern, Richards watched the line of ships before them, strung out along the canal, roughly a quarter mile separating each of them. At any given time, they appeared spread across half the countryside, running every which way as they maneuvered the tight confines of the twisting pathway. And each day, evidence grew the rebels were aware of their presence and were preparing to stop them in any way they could.

"Anchor!"

The word came back from the ship in front of them, but the phrase was truly a joke. They had less than three feet beneath their bottoms, and there was nowhere to drift. But the end was in sight, for the Rolling Fork was just a few hundred feet in front of the leading tug. The entrance to the river was flooded, and it would take them a while to find a breaching point, but their objective was almost met.

"Better have a look, captain," said Woodard, handing the telescope and pointing down the length of the river.

A steamboat lay on the shore further down, men moving about it. The long, black shape of a cannon swayed above her deck.

"Rebels?" questioned Richards.

"Who else?" returned Woodard.

Word came back down the line. A tug had gone forward towards the Rolling Fork and was stuck fast in a mass of young willows just fifty yards from the river. *CINCINNATI* followed, trying to use her weight to press by and was held just as tightly. Another steamboat appeared, and Richards sent Keeler to the top of the pilothouse to investigate. The word was not good, for rebel troops were disembarking, fanning out and heading for the gunboats.

Gunboats in Steele's Bayou

CHAPTER EIGHTEEN

"It's not good, is it?" asked Keeler, watching the gray lines of troops move from the boat.

"That is an accurate assessment, Colburn," returned Richards.

The canal twisted away astern, its narrow length disappearing behind a bend a half mile distant. The ships would make little speed stern first if that were their only course. Rifles crackled from the front of the line, followed quickly by cheering. The CINCINNATI was backing, retiring to the safety of the ditch. It was not so much safety, but the walls of their dike did offer some protection from the rebel sharp shooters. Stuck in the willows, the rebels would have taken her at their leisure.

A cannon roared from one side, the shell whistling down to explode near the still stranded tug. It was the sound of an English rifled gun, which they knew to be Whitworths. These were the weapons off loaded from the steamboat. They were more than sufficient to penetrate the sides of the ironclads. Meanwhile, sailors labored to pull cables to the tug so they could free her as well.

The four mortars towed by the gunboats fired in a ragged salvo. Lofting their shells up at a high angle, they were not concerned about the dike rising on either side. But they were not the most effective weapons for firing on troops. If the heavy guns aboard the gunboats could fire only once every two or three minutes, the mortars were even more severely handicapped. Shells left them at ten to fifteen minute intervals.

To one side, there was a large Indian mound. Porter dispatched some sailors with howitzers there point a couple hours before. Now those men came tumbling down its side, pulling the weapons after them. Rebels troops were advancing, far too many for them to hold off.

"What now, captain?" asked Woodard.

"We have got to get out of here," said Richards. Again, he examined the length of canal behind them. "Unship the rudder, Mr. Woodard. If we go stern first, it will be an encumbrance."

"And if we advance?"

"We shall steer with the bloody wheels! Move it!"

"What about the guns, captain?" inquired Keeler as Woodard called for men to perform the indicated work.

Richards laughed and even he did not like the sound of it. The banks rose on either side of the ship to the level of the middle deck, masking the advancing troops from the guns. For all their weight of artillery, they might as well have been unarmed.

"Not much we can do with them at the moment, Mr. Keeler. " A stray musket shot rang off the side of the vessel, and Richards looked at it idly.

"That makes me feel better, sir," observed Keeler, his face breaking into a grin.

"What?"

"You. I have never seen a man so unimpressed by danger in my life. Porter himself would have flinched at that one."

"I guess I have never thought of it in quite that fashion, Mr. Keeler." He spared little for the conversation. He concentrated on what they would do to extricate their vessels. *Where was the damned army?*

"Aye, sir. Always so cool under fire, always so sure you'll never be hit. That's why I try to follow your example."

The words struck a cord in his thoughts. "Sure I will never get hit? Why would you think that?"

Keeler was perplexed at the reply. "Why, from watching you, captain. The shells are flying and there you are, more like you are standing in a rainstorm than under enemy bullets. Always pushing the ship into the most dangerous position: surely you must believe you cannot be hit. And it works, that's what so amazing!" Richards snorted at the comment, but Keeler continued. "And the glory, captain. Your name in the dispatches, medals and promotions. They'll be talking about *MACHINEEL* in the navy for a long time, just because of you!"

"Glory? You think that is why I do this?"

"Of course, sir." Keeler was really warming to the conversation, holding himself upright when another round glanced from the vessel. "You see, captain. I am learning from you!"

A group of rifles fired, and this time their target was the *MACHINEEL*. The minne balls whined about them, and Richards turned to his left at a tug on his sleeve. The material was torn by the passage of a bullet. At the same moment, something fell against him, and he came about just in time to catch Keeler as the lieutenant slumped to the deck, his head covered in blood. Richards knelt next to him, hearing the labored breathing.

"Get the surgeon up here!" he yelled at Levenson. The other man left at a run, and Richards grabbed a handkerchief from his pocket to press against the wound. Woodard's head appeared up the stairs, the officer talking nonchalantly.

"Rudder's on the fantail, cap'n." His eyes came to rest on Keeler, and the man let out a wail of anguish. "My God! Not Col too!"

"Get a grip, Woodard!" snapped Richards. There was the pinging of more musket rounds on the side of the ship. "Damn them rebels, if only we could fire back!"

Woodard came up and sat down next to Keeler, cradling the boy's head in his lap. "You have got the bloody field piece, cap'n! It's above the level of this damned ditch!"

"Right you are, Mr. Woodard." The surgeon's mate appeared, pulling the makeshift bandage from the side of his head.

"Not too bad, captain," he said after a moment's examination. "Just a scalp wound, no damage to the skull. Rebels must be usin' lousy powder." He continued in a more professional vein. "See how the ball travelled 'round the bone?"

"Just get him below and tend to 'im!" yelled Woodard, the concern still heavy. "And if he dies, I will show you lousy powder!"

Levenson and the surgeon removed Keeler. Richards remained sitting behind the wall of the pilothouse. "You are quite right about the six pounder, Mr. Woodard. Have the men bring up cotton bales to place around it for protection, then see what they can do against this army!"

"Aye, cap'n. And I have an idea about the big guns, too."

"Let's hear it." Another Whitworth shell screamed over.

Richards realized their position at the end of the line was critical. If they were sunk, the rest of the squadron would be boxed in.

"Crank the guns up, and do not use as much powder. Aim like them mortars."

Richards took little time to ponder the idea. "I do believe you have earned your keep on this expedition, Mr. Woodard." He touched the man's arm. "See to the cotton bales, and send Lewis up to see me."

"Aye, sir." Woodard crawled to the stairs, keeping below the rail of the pilothouse.

"And, Morgan..." started Richards.

Woodard's head snapped back up, and he smiled at Richards. "You must be loosin' your grip, cap'n. You used me Christian name!"

Richards returned the smile. "Be careful, Morgan."

"Aye, sir."

It was an interminable wait for the gunner, but the howitzer began firing from forward even as sailors try to pile a bulwark of cotton around it. Lewis came into the pilothouse as Richards drew himself upright, then ducked back under a volley of fire.

"You wanted me, cap'n?"

"Aye, Mr. Lewis. Mr. Woodard believes we can crank the guns up to fire over the level of the dike."

"Aye, I could knock the stops from 'em to do it. But what of it, sir? The rounds would go three or four miles before comin' down."

"True only with a full charge of powder, Mr. Lewis. If we used only a quarter the charge..."

The chief gunner's mate caught on quickly enough. "Aye, that would do it. We'd have to sight 'em like mortars, and cut the fuses a might longer."

"Get to it then."

"Yes, captain. Oh, the surgeon says the lieutenant's awake, sir."

"Thank you, Mr. Lewis."

The gunner left to get at his work. In the meantime, there was little to be accomplished by hiding in the pilothouse. He ducked down the stairs quickly to check on Keeler.

"His head hurts a might," whispered Harlan, taking away a bowl of blood soaked bandages, "And I had to give 'im a line of stitches, but he'll be around to tell his grandchildren about it."

Richards stepped into the small cabin. Keeler lay on the bed, his head heavily bandaged. "Mr. Keeler?" he said, softly. "Col?" he continued, raising his voice slightly.

"I guess believin' you won't get hit don't work as well as I thought, captain," managed Keeler, smiling weakly.

"I have done you a disservice, Colburn," confessed Richards. "I was no example to follow. I have been like you, since boarding that damned gunboat."

"What do you mean?"

"It is been rough. Several men get killed, and I tell you it is your fault. I have been going through the same thing since I lost *COHOCTON*. It is difficult telling men to die."

"No, sir, it's not like that..."

"Easy, lieutenant." He laid a hand on the young man's shoulder to steady him. "It is like that. But the truth is, getting myself killed will not bring them back. And that is what I have been trying to do, not get any sort of glory from all this!"

Keeler's eyes widened slightly at the confession. But he was too weak from his injury to do more than offer a faint protest. "Not true, sir."

"It is true, Colburn. I am going to be very busy, and I am

not sure how this will all turn out." There was a rush of water around the outside of the ship and he wondered what was happening now. But this needed to be concluded first. "I want you to know that. I think Mr. Woodard told you best. Be brave enough to face up to your responsibilities. Do not be stupid enough to get yourself killed."

"Aye, sir."

He stepped from the room back into the corridor. Woodard stood there facing him.

"Fine words, John."

"Yes, Mr. Woodard. Too bad it has taken me so long to find them."

"Admiral's signaling. Wants us to start reversin' down the creek."

"What's that damned water?"

"Rebels have cut the levee in front of us, sir."

Richards snorted as he headed up for the pilothouse. "Lucky for us. If they'd dumped cotton into the damned thing, this whole blasted bayou may just dry up!"

There was a welcome roar of one of the big guns. Lewis was in the pilothouse, yelling corrections down to his gunners after watching where the shells fell.

"A half pound less, then fire all the thirty-two's," he ordered.

"Make it quick, Mr. Lewis," announced Richards. "We will be underway momentarily!"

There was an explosion nearby as a shell crashed into the dike. Dirt and mud rained upon them, rattling on the top and sides of the ship. The three broadside thirty-two's fired, and there was a gratifying cheer from the ship as all the shells exploded in the line of trees harboring the rebel sharpshooters.

"Very good, Mr. Lewis," commented Richards drily.

"Keep it up." He rang slow astern on the repeater, and the ship drifted backwards.

"Me guess is the flow's runnin' about four knots, cap'n," observed Woodard. "She's goin' to be difficult to control like this."

"Just keep us moving, Mr. Woodard. If need be, we can put men at the sides with poles to help keep her I the middle."

The *MACHINEEL* moved with the current, banging along the sides of the canal. The stern swung back and forth as it struck first one side, and then the other. The firing dropped off as they moved away from the scene of the action. The rest of the squadron followed, drawing out of range of the Whitworth's which had replaced the yankee guns atop the Indian mound. But progress was slow because of the winding nature of their path.

"I can say I am breathin' a might easier, sir." Woodard mopped his forehead with a handkerchief and it was not that warm.

"They can march faster cross country than we are moving, Mr. Woodard," observed the captain. "They will catch up when they get their guns resighted!"

Woodard made no reply. The truth of the comment was evident. Then their eyes were drawn across the bow by the sound of splintering wood. What they saw was not encouraging.

The tug immediately ahead of them was towing a barge of coal. Drifting back as they were, the barge preceded the vessel, but caught a corner as they rounded a particularly sharp bend. The tug ran into the barge, jamming it across the bayou and cutting deeply into it. As they watched, the barge sank, the upper reaches of its load of coal still above the level of the waters.

"God damn it!" cursed Richards. "That's got 'em blocked for sure!"

"Shall we stop and help them?" asked Woodard.

They were still moving away from the squadron at half the rate of the current. It was not too quick, but they would have to do something to stop their progress if they were to await the rest of the ships. It was a hard decision but Richards did not pause to consider what the other ship captains would think. All their yards and poles were carried away by the tree branches. There was no way of signaling Porter his intentions.

"No, Mr. Woodard. We will continue." The two men in the pilothouse looked to him in surprise. "We have got to find the army to get us out of this mess. We shall do that!" He turned and went below, pulling out the chart of their strange course through the land.

"Where are we?" he asked. "Here?"

"No," said the first officer, "more like here." He touched the map a bit further up the course.

Richards shook his head, changing his mind. "Here!" He drew a mark on the chart between the two. "Here or nowhere!" Woodard nodded in agreement.

"The army was off-loading here." He judged the distance between them, trying to account for the troop movements through the flooded landscape. "My guess is they have advanced to about here."

"Ten miles, give or take," concluded Woodard. "Two to three hours backing down this blasted canal."

"We shall keep on until we find the army, Morgan. Dark or not, we must press through."

"If we do not find them, they'll say we ran, sir."

"I will take that chance, Mr. Woodard, if it gives us the opportunity to save the squadron."

The firing off their bow died away somewhat. Richards did not think it was merely the distance which masked the

270

noise. But their quest seemed in vain as the afternoon wore on. Still, Sherman had ten thousand troops in the vicinity, and they had but to find them.

He spent little time worrying about what Porter would think of his leaving. If events proved out, he would have the opportunity to explain. If not, Woodard's view would be more widely taken.

Daylight faded as the sound of massed rifle fire was heard before them. It could only mean the rebels had also found the union troops.

"See to your guns again, Mr. Lewis." Richards directed.

Gun smoke filled the woods to the east, along with the sound of rifles and a few cannon. Forms moved there but whether rebel or yankee, they could not tell. Then *MACHINEEL* was on a straighter stretch and a campsite was visible, the flagstaff carrying the stars and stripes.

"Full stop!" ordered Richards as they drifted down to it. He did not even wait for the vessel to halt completely before moving down to the mid-deck and jumping across to the dike. A soldier watched him in surprise.

"Quick, man!" shouted the officer. "Which way to Sherman?"

The soldier stared dully and pointed a finger over his shoulder. Richards took off at a trot towards a nondescript stand of tents. Sherman and his staff stood over a map, studying the lay of the land.

"General," said Richards, sweeping past the guards. "I am Commander Richards from the squadron!"

William Sherman looked at him, regarding the disheveled appearance. "We were wondering where you all had gotten off to."

"The squadron is in trouble. Admiral Porter needs your troops. Now!"

Sherman leaned forward, his voice intense. "Where at,

captain?"

"Right in here," said Richards, circling the spot where they had left the gunboats. "With the banks the way they are, it is difficult to use our artillery, and the rebels have a large body of men closing in from this direction." He made another mark on the map.

Sherman nodded, scratching his beard. "We could push up through here," explained Sherman, his finger tracing the course. "I would say it is about a four hour march. But these woods are full of sharpshooters. Every time we advance, the attack falters!"

"I will see to that, general. I will take *MACHINEEL* up on the rebel flank and pour it into them!"

Sherman grinned. "They might have a go at overrunning your one little boat, captain!"

"Better than losing the whole squadron, sir! Give me thirty minutes!"

Richards left without further. Sherman was a man who supported the odd combined operations with the navy ran on the river. The navy had never failed him, nor he it. He would do what it took to maintain the record.

"Move us back up past that last bend, Morgan," shouted Richards as he jumped back aboard the vessel. "Stand by the guns. Anybody in those woods is a rebel and we must move them out of there!"

There was a cheer from the gun crews as they moved back to their stations. Even as they advanced, Lewis fired the sixty-fours. Whole trees were blasted from the ground by the fall of those shells, and the rebels around them were thrown through the air by the explosions. *MACHINEEL* turned the bend, and all the broadside guns commenced to work, the load of powder varied constantly at each weapon to throw the shells throughout the entire stand of trees.

Light was fading, but the *MACHINEEL* kept at it. Richards ignored the musket fire returned by the rebel force.

At one point, they formed to make a rush on the ship, but a company of soldiers moved forward and drove them back. At last, the rebel troops withdrew from the woods, carrying their wounded and fighting a rear guard action as the blue uniforms pressed forward. Richards ordered a cease fire as Sherman rode up next to the ship.

"Good shooting, captain!" he shouted. "Get back to Porter, if you think you can beat us! We will be there by midnight!"

"Thank you, general!" Richards looked to Woodard. "You heard the man, lieutenant!"

"You want to navigate this in the dark?"

"We have little choice. Make the best speed you can!"

If the trip down the stream was bumpy, the one up was even worse. They banged into the sides and into trees. One stack was swept completely off the boat by a collision, a makeshift replacement being hurriedly erected. Other sailors were busy with buckets of grease, spreading it across the smooth sides of their vessel. If they were boarded, the rebels would find no foothold there.

Richards paced the wardroom, waving away the cold supper brought by the cook. Events were at a crisis and there was no thought of eating. The tinclad was getting knocked apart in the effort to rejoin the squadron, to pass the word to hold on the army arrived.

They rounded the last bend and almost rushed upon the men laboring to clear the coal from the canal. It was three hours of solid work, but they were still an hour in advance of Sherman.

"I will go up to the admiral, Mr. Woodard. Spread the boarding nets and stand by the guns!"

All the vessels were arranged much as he left MACHINEEL, boarding nets rigged and sides covered with grease. Most of the crewmen were inside, out of sight of any possible sharpshooter. Shots still rang from the woods about them, but they were widely scattered. The rebels were maneuvering their forces, gathering for a final rush on the trapped gunboats. Sherman could not get there soon enough.

"Commander Richards," hailed Porter as he stepped to the deck of the ironclad. "Glad to see you back!"

"I have been down to Sherman, admiral," announced Richards, not bothering with amenities. "He should be here within the next hour or two."

"I was wondering. How far off is his camp?" The admiral was calm and collected, showing no strain at the difficulty of their position.

"About four hours, sir."

Porter nodded in acceptance. "I questioned where you'd gone off to," he said finally. "I would have thought you better placed helping remove the barge."

Richards took a deep breath. It was not easy facing a difference of opinion with a senior officer. He felt a better appreciation of Keeler's trial.

"It seemed best to get the army, sir. I did not see us moving that coal in less than eight or ten hours."

"Probably right, captain," replied Porter. "I heard some grumbling at your departure, but I had a fair idea what you were about."

"I decided the risk of those comments was worth it if I got to Sherman, admiral."

"Well done, my boy," answered Porter. He extended a hand to shake Richard's, patting him on the shoulder as he did. "I had no doubts as to you intentions."

The admiral chuckled to a private joke, smoothing some of the whiskers away from his lips. "I would ask you down for some wine, but my cabin is full of prisoners at the moment. A couple of rebel officers who are telling me how they will take my gunboats." He laughed out loud. "It is amazing how much they will talk, after a glass or two!"

"Yes, admiral," retuned the youthful captain. Flag officers may have time to entertain rebel officers, but he had a gunboat and crew to worry about. "I best see to my ship!"

Richards withdrew, exchanging quick comments with the other vessels as he made his way down the line. All were heartened at the prospect of the army coming to their rescue. Aboard *MACHINEEL*, they settled down to await events.

"You know," reflected Woodard, as he paced the pilothouse, "I swore I would never tell the story of the *TERROR*."

"And we appreciate the promise, Mr. Woodard," quipped Richards, trying to relieve some of his tension. He was not successful.

"But I cannot tell the story of this one either!" protested the other man. "Who'd ever believe a squadron of gunboats stuck in a mud ditch a hundred miles from the river."

"I am here, Mr. Woodard," Richards retorted, "and I do not believe it!"

Shortly after midnight, they were stirred by an exchange of rifle fire to their starboard. It waivered and grew, then moved off to the east. A large column of men marched along the upper dike, a group of men on horseback leading them from the road. Sherman stopped when he reached the *MACHINEEL*.

"Are we in time, Richards?" he called out.

The young commander stood and saluted the army officer. "Aye, sir, you are."

The general looked down at the batter and town upper works of the gunboat. "Looks like your ship needs a might bit of work after the trip!"

"Yes, general. At least with you here, it will be us doing the work instead of rebs!"

Sherman laughed at the joke. "Good for you, commander. Where is my friend David?"

"At the front, sir. He is waiting to greet you with a glass of whiskey, I am sure."

Sherman laughed again. "You should have mentioned that before, Richards!" He pulled his horse back into the road. "I'd have gotten here sooner!" He galloped off, the soldiers cheering as he raced by.

ADMIRAL PORTER'S FLEET RUNNING THE REBEL BLOCKADE OF THE MISSISSIPPI AT VICKSBURG. APRIL 16TH 1863

The Mississippi Squadron runs the guns of Vicksburg

EPILOGUE

It was another week before all the gunboats were out of the bayou and back on the Mississippi. For a week after that, the crew labored to repair the damages sustained by the fruitless expedition. When finished, *MACHINEEL* appeared just as she had in Cairo, fresh from the yard's hands. Neat and clean, she was ready to go back into battle.

But as always, things were shifting on the river front. Grant was in charge and he was marching his army across the Louisiana point to get at Vicksburg from below. And Porter, ever willing to place his gunboats where they could provide the most support, prepared to run the batteries to do just that. While Richards was readying the gunboat for the run, he received new orders from Washington.

Whether his exile on the river was the result of the loss of *COHOCTON* or simply Rebecca twisting her father's arm, he might never know. And whether his western service was responsible for the change, he would not know either. But the orders were there.

Commander John Richards to report to the Brooklyn Navy Yard forthwith and assume command of the USS SHILOH, to be commissioned at the earliest convenience.

It was simple parting with Porter. The admiral was sorry to lose him, but happy for the other man's promotion. On *MACHINEEL*, it was different. For all their tribulations together, the miserable little gunboat was his ship. He would miss her.

"Make sure the lashing are tight, Mr. Woodard," he said, stepping to the fantail with his bag.

The tinclad lay alongside the *MOUND CITY*, the hard luck vessel that had been near them so much this past twelve months. The tinclad was lashed to the starboard side, to use the ironclad as a shield during the run past the batteries and to provide engine power to the other vessel should she be disabled. Farragut's example had shown it to be a wise precaution.

"Not your concern anymore, cap'n," replied Woodard. He extended his hand and Richards took it. Woodard shrugged a shoulder in the direction of *MOUND CITY*. "Of all the ships for us to be matched with!"

Richards grinned. "Perhaps some of *MACHINEEL*'s luck will rub off on her."

The Irishman shook his head. ""I'll be keepin' all me own luck, cap'n." Woodard smiled, giving Richards a wink. "But Godspeed to you, sir."

"And to you, Morgan. My best to your wife when you see her next."

Woodard chuckled. "Goin' to the wrong side of this blasted town again, I'm thinkin'. But we'll make it."

"I have no doubt." He glanced up and saw Keeler at the rail, his head still bandaged but starting to get around. "And good luck to you, Cole. Though with a skull so thick, you should be safe for the rest of the war!"

Keeler smiled. "Aye, sir. And thank you. For everything."

Richards stepped over to the side. He had taken the ensign *MACHINEEL* flew during the Steele Bayou trip as a keepsake of this command. He wondered how he would explain the grease stains on it to some child or grandchild? He would just remember Woodard's stories and a way would come. He saluted the stern and stepped to the entry port. He took one last look around before going into the boat. He heard Woodard, the new captain, calling out as he left.

"Let's move it there, lads," he yelled. "And you, Cole! You belong in bed!"

"The surgeon suggested I get out for a while!" protested the younger officer.

"Nuts!" returned Woodard. "Then have the steward set you out a chair by the forward gun. And you will get below before we start south! Now move it, laddie!"

Richards smiled. It was Woodard's ship now and she would be run differently. He held no doubts, however: he would continue to hear of the *MACHINEEL* on the river. She was in good hands.

It was after dark when his transport started north. There was a rubble of guns astern as the Vicksburg batteries fired. Porter's fleet was moving south. Richards stood at the stern, watching the flashes on the horizon, so much like the distant thunderstorms of the previous summer.

There was a feeling of a job left unfinished. Vicksburg still dominated the river, but it would not last long. If Porter passed the city, and there was no questioning he would, Grant would get across and behind the town. It was nearing the end of the town's prominence.

He brought his thoughts to New York. A new ship, one of the Monitors, and that meant service along the east coast. New York also meant Becky and a chance to continue their lives together. He left the deck and went below to his cabin, to reread her last letter and get some sleep. It did not occur to him it was the first time he had ever walked away from the sound of gunfire. Behind him, the horizon was lit by the defenders of Vicksburg.

THE END

ABOUT THE AUTHOR

D A Joy is a graduate of the University of Nebraska at Omaha Writer's Workshop with a Bachelor of Fine Arts in Creative Writing. Don has written stories since he was a child and started writing his first book in high school. He has worked as a business analyst and project manager across the country while still living in Nebraska. Outside of work, he maintains a range of interests including history, reading, films, and hobbies such as building models from ships to planes to starships, and participating in local and national competitions. Other interests include science, astronomy and the investigation of unexplained phenomenon.

"A Sudden Thunder" and "The Narrow Fury" are the first in *The Richards Line* of novels dealing with the naval history of the Civil War – or the War Between the States. They combine a deep knowledge of the naval aspects of the Civil War to paint the first years of the war through a combination of actual historical events combined with typical actions to present a personal view. Beyond the war, these are also the stories of men's service to their countries and the impact on their lives, friends, family and loved ones. Future novels will show the progression of the war, presenting the views of both northern and southern participants, and how life continues even under those harrowing circumstances.

"Murder in Whitechapel", his first published novel, combines a life-long love of Sherlock Holmes stories with an interest in the darker side of humanity displayed by Jack the Ripper. It provides Holmes' view of the pursuit of the serial killer in London using only his keen intellect and without the aid of modern forensics. And while Holmes is a fictional detective, the case surrounding Jack the Ripper and the murders is dealt with using the actual facts and suspects known to Scotland Yard in 1888.